Tracking Tilly

The Little Red Truck Mysteries
Book One

Tracking Tilly

JANICE THOMPSON

BARBOUR
PUBLISHING

Cover Illustration by Victor McLindon

Published by Barbour Publishing, Inc., 1810 Barbour Drive, Uhrichsville, Ohio 44683, www.barbourbooks.com

Our mission is to inspire the world with the life-changing message of the Bible.

ecpa Member of the Evangelical Christian Publishers Association

Printed in the United States of America.

DEDICATION

In memory of my mother, Shirley Moseley, who spent many of her happiest years in the Mabank area. And to the fine people who live in that neck of the woods, this one's for you.

CHAPTER ONE

"Three thousand nine hundred dollars!" The bidding paddle slipped out of my trembling hand and landed with a thud on the concrete floor below. I reached down to pick it up and could feel the heat in my cheeks at the embarrassment this clumsy move had caused.

Or maybe it was the heat inside of the auction house. It had to be in the nineties. A trickle of sweat dribbled down my back, as if to prove my point as I sat back up.

"Three thousand nine hundred and *fifty* dollars!" A strong male voice rang out from across the aisle.

I turned to see who had outbid me. Ugh! Mason Fredericks. Really?

My cheeks warmed, and I avoided his eyes.

I'd never been one to let a fella get the better of me, especially not a guy who had busted my heart into a thousand pieces back in high school. I would show Mason a thing or two. RaeLyn Hadley didn't play. Not when it came to something this serious.

"Okay," I muttered under my breath. "This. Is. War."

Mason's brows elevated mischievously, and I wondered if he might be bidding against me just to aggravate me. Wouldn't be the first time he'd tried to steal something from me. This time, though? I wouldn't let him get away with it. There was too much at stake.

"Four thousand!" I called out, my words sounding a little too shrill for my own liking. I swiped the perspiration off the back of my neck and tried to ease the pain in my backside as I shuffled my position on the wooden slat.

"Forty-two hundred!" Mason countered.

Why don't they put in real chairs?" Mom groaned and shifted her position on the slat to the right of me.

"Because this auction house is fifty years old," I responded, followed by a raucous, "Four thousand *three* hundred!" There. That would show him. I wasn't messing around.

"RaeLyn, you've got to slow down. That's too much money." These words came from my dad, who sat on the other side of my mom, his brow wrinkled in concern at my enthusiastic bids.

I wasn't one to defy my parents. Even at twenty-six I knew better than to sass them, especially in a public forum like the Big Red Bid, Mabank's most famous auction house. But after years of Papaw's beloved truck, Tilly, being separated from the family, we finally had a chance to win her back. And I wouldn't stop until she was parked under our carport where she belonged.

"Four thousand *four* hundred!" Mason called out. I could almost hear a tinge of laughter in his voice. Was he trying to prove some kind of point just to get at me?

Frustration wriggled its way up my spine and settled into my tightened shoulders. Suddenly I was a high school senior once again, battling with my best friend Stephanie Ingram over who would win Mason's heart.

She'd won that battle back then. He had not only taken my best friend to the prom, Mason had proven to be the force that would eventually drive her from my life altogether.

That thief.

Today, the victory would be mine. Papaw's truck would belong to the Hadley family once more, a piece of his legacy home to roost, and Mason could go back to doing whatever it was he did these days. I couldn't care less.

Mason winked at me in playful fashion.

Oh. No. You. Didn't. I gave him my best *Stop it or else* stare, but he responded with a crooked smile, which revealed that adorable little dimple in his left cheek. It captivated me now, just like it had done all those years ago at the Mabank senior prom when he and Stephanie had sashayed in dolled up for the night, the king and queen of Mabank High.

"Shake it off," I muttered to no one but myself.

"Shake *what* off?" Mom swatted at herself, as if sending a fly on its way.

A quick glance back at Mason clued me in to the fact that he planned to keep this nonsense going. His quirked brow left nothing to the imagination as he flashed another playful smile my way. Fine. I would show him.

"Four thousand *five* hundred," I hollered out.

My dad dropped his head into his hands and muttered something under his breath.

I understood his concerns. With the economy in such a state and our family ranch struggling to stay afloat, he seemed hyperfocused on finances these days. Waste not, want not, and all that.

Still, I'd been prepping for this day for some time, even sacrificing so that I could make this purchase. Papaw's truck would be a solid investment—both financially and emotionally. And I could almost envision how amazing that truck would look, all fixed up and taking her place of honor in front of our family's new antique store, a reminder to our customers that the Hadley family believed in legacy.

"Stay focused, honey." Mom patted my knee and shifted her attention to the auctioneer.

"Oh, I am." Mason held no spell over me these days. I did my best to keep my eyes riveted on the auctioneer, a middle-aged man with a rapid-fire voice and slicked-back toupee. At least, I thought it was a toupee. He had that suspicious comb-over hair that made one doubt its authenticity. I shifted my gaze to his lips. They moved at the speed of light. I could barely keep up.

A female voice sounded from Mason's right, offering a bid of forty-six hundred. Ugh. I squinted to get a better look at the voluptuous blond sitting next to my archnemesis. The woman looked vaguely familiar. Not that you heard the words "vaguely familiar" here in Mabank very often. Everyone knew everyone around these parts. Only, I didn't know that particular gal.

I nudged Mom with my elbow and gestured with my head to the blond. "Who's that?"

Mom gave her a quick glance then looked back my way. "The auctioneer's ex-wife, Meredith. You've met her before."

"Have I?" I strained to see past the crowd.

Mom quirked a brow. "She showed up at the Pioneer Days event dressed up like the Statue of Liberty."

"Oh, *that* blond." I gave her another glance. No one in town would ever forget that costume. Still, she looked different without the headpiece and the low-cut sequined top.

The vivacious blond leaned Mason's way and whispered something in his ear. He smiled at whatever she said.

Why that bothered me, I could not say. I hadn't given Mason Fredericks a thought since college.

Okay, there was that one time I'd run into his mama at Brookshire Brothers in the baking aisle. She'd casually mentioned him, and I'd dropped a five-pound bag of all-purpose flour on the floor, covering the ceramic tiles and creating a mess for the manager to clean up. But that was years ago. These days, I never gave him a thought.

Well, almost never.

Watching Mason casually flirt with the blond made those familiar feelings pop up once again, so I shifted my attention back to Harlan Reed, the auctioneer. The man had a bit too much swagger, which showed up every time he took his place behind the podium. But I would rather look at him and that ridiculous toupee than focus on Lady Liberty and the guy who'd broken my heart.

"Four thousand six hundred and fifty!" a shaky male voice called out from the far side of the room.

My parents and I turned in unison, and my breath caught in my throat when I saw a familiar elderly man with his bidding paddle raised in his shaky hand.

"Well, butter my backside and call me a biscuit." Mom's mouth fell open as she stared at the man. "Is that Wyatt Jackson?"

"What's left of 'im." My dad shot daggers from his eyes at the older fella. "He's got some nerve, showing up here to bid on Tilly. That old cuss has caused enough trouble for our family without stealing Pop's truck out from under us. If he had any kindness in his heart at all, he would honor my father's memory by backing down."

Dad raised my paddle and waved it with great vigor as he called out, "Four thousand *seven* hundred!"

So much for showing restraint.

I gave the elderly Wyatt Jackson another quick glance and noticed how frail he looked. I'd never fully understood why my parents disliked the man so much. Though, it did seem strange that he, of all people, was here, bidding against me. Was this just a coincidence or something more?

With my dad in the game, the numbers continued to climb, but I found myself a little distracted by Wyatt, who seemed weak and shaky as he barely held on to the paddle. I hadn't seen him in ages, but the stories about him were notorious, especially in my family.

I gave him a closer look. Wyatt had that weathered look that so many of the ranchers in the area had, from spending too many years in the sun. What really stood out was the bald head with age spots. I'd never considered the possibility that people would age on their heads. I ran my fingers through my hair as I pondered the possibilities.

"Pay attention, RaeLyn!" My dad jabbed me with his elbow. "Clayton Henderson just bid five thousand dollars!"

Dad gestured to the man seated directly in front of us, and I groaned aloud. That's all we needed. Clayton Henderson was the richest man in Mabank, and the rest of the surrounding areas too, for that matter. He already had everything a fella could ask for—the biggest house in the county, a new bed-and-breakfast on the lake, and several businesses in town. Why did he need Papaw's truck?

Was everyone in Henderson County going to bid against me? I'd counted on an easy win, not a fight to the finish with people who had no emotional ties to this vehicle like I did.

"Fifty-one hundred!" I hollered, doing my best to steady my trembling voice.

Mom looked like she might be ill. I was feeling a little nauseous myself. Hopefully it was just the heat. Still, if I spent much more, I wouldn't have enough left to do the renovations on Tilly. My goal to restore her to her former glory was key.

Clayton swung around to give me a pensive look. He had an imposing stature even when seated. And those sharp, angular facial features only contributed to his commanding presence as he glared at me. The man was always meticulously groomed, every salt-and-pepper hair in perfect place.

He exuded authority—and never more than right now, when bidding against me. The daggers shooting from his dark brown eyes spoke his message loud and clear: *Stop it. Right now.*

Only, I wouldn't stop it. Tilly meant too much to me to let her go on purpose, especially to the man who already owned everything.

I offered a weak smile, which I hoped would cause Clayton to have sympathy for me. Everyone in town knew Tilly belonged at home with our family. Surely my fellow competitors would back down. I hoped.

Clayton turned back around and bid fifty-two fifty, his voice anything but empathetic.

Wyatt tapped out at fifty-six hundred, Meredith stopped at fifty-seven, and I finally bested Mason when I bid six thousand dollars.

After I swallowed the giant lump in my throat anyway. At that point, the room grew silent. Clayton muttered something as he set his paddle down. So did Wyatt, who looked as if he might be ill. And in that moment, I felt like throwing myself a party.

Was Tilly really going to be mine?

CHAPTER TWO

"Going once!" The auctioneer's voice rang out at Indy 500 speed. "Going twice!"

I felt a wave of relief wash over me, followed by an immediate gripping of nausea. Had I really just bid six thousand dollars on a seventy-year-old truck that was in rough condition?

Yes. Yes, I had. And I wasn't the tiniest bit sorry. In fact, the only emotions wrapping me in their embrace right now were joy and excitement at the possibilities of restoring Papaw's old truck and making her my own. She would return to her former glory, then sit in front of our new antique shop, a symbol to everyone in Henderson County that the Hadley family cared about the past as well as the future.

"Sold to the lady for six thousand dollars!" The auctioneer gave me a polite nod then turned his attention to the next item up for bid, a tractor trailer. As a picture of the tractor came up on the screen at the front of the room, everyone seemed to shift gears. A couple of people kicked off the bidding, and the room was soon buzzing with excitement again.

My heart leaped to my throat as memories of Papaw swept over me, and for a moment I thought I might cry. Until I noticed Mason giving me a curt nod from across the aisle. His way of conceding, I supposed. Suddenly my need to win was superseded by my desire to get Tilly home where she belonged. But with a seventy-year-old truck to haul, I needed a plan.

Dad nudged me with his elbow. "Let's get out of here. Wyatt keeps glaring at us, and I don't trust him as far as I can throw him. The sooner we get Tilly home, the better."

"Okay." I rose and led the way, my gaze shifting only momentarily at Mason, who offered me a little shrug.

Off in the distance, Lady Liberty bounded from her seat and headed to a side door. She disappeared from view moments later.

My parents tagged along behind me as I eased my way down the center aisle of the auction house toward the back door. Out of the corner of my eye, I got a closer look at Wyatt Jackson. My dad definitely wasn't exaggerating. The older man was far from happy. But why would he care so much about my grandfather's truck? The two men had been at odds for as long as any of us could remember. He had no sentimental attachment to Tilly. Not that I knew of anyway.

From behind me, my dad muttered something I couldn't quite make out. No doubt I would get an earful when we got home. Maybe one day I would fully understand the falling-out between Wyatt and my family members. For now, though? I just needed to get out of here.

We made our way outside to the parking lot, where I turned to the left to reach the lineup of vehicles up for auction.

There, parked between a '57 Chevy and a '73 Ford Pinto. . .Papaw's Tilly. *My* Tilly.

I stared at the rusty old truck, and tears filled my eyes. A rush of memories flooded over me, and I was a little girl once again, riding alongside Papaw as he headed to Tractor Supply to pick up feed for the horses on our family's ranch. I remembered the smell of his clove chewing gum, which he always kept in the glove box. And the chewing tobacco, tucked under the seat so that my parents wouldn't fuss at him.

Those memories, along with images I held so dear of my grandfather, settled over me, bringing such joy, I could hardly contain myself.

I ran my hand along the driver's door handle, and another vivid memory rushed over me. Oh, how I'd loved riding in the back of this truck across the field, bales of hay stacked all around me. Papaw played country music on the radio, something by Willie Nelson, no doubt.

I was half tempted to jump into the bed of the truck right now, just to relive those old days.

Instead, I found myself distracted by the rough condition the old truck was in. The once-pristine red paint was faded and chipped. And I'd never seen so much rust on a vehicle. It was going to take a lot of work to turn her around. And who knew if she still ran?

"Sweet old Tilly." Tears filled Mom's eyes as she ran her palm along the side of the driver's door. "Looking pretty dilapidated."

"Kind of like me." Dad opened the driver's side door and popped the hood. Minutes later, we all stared down at the engine. It didn't look too bad. But, without the keys, we couldn't be sure if Tilly still had any get-up-and-go left in her.

Just as we popped the hood back down, a familiar blond woman approached, clipboard in hand. Lady Liberty. But today Meredith was decked out in more professional attire. Still, her perfect hourglass silhouette was accentuated by a fitted suit that hugged her body. I didn't have long to think about it because she seemed to be in a rush. She took several rapid steps in our direction, her gaze shifting to the auction house, then back to us.

"You folks here for the truck?" The pen slipped out of her hand as she glanced down at her clipboard.

Dad reached down to pick it up.

"Yep." Still, I couldn't figure out why she was asking these questions. Was she an employee or a bidder?

Mom seemed confused too. She reached for her phone and started texting someone. Weird.

I found myself distracted by Meredith's striking blond hair with its hints of honey-colored strands. She wore it styled in loose waves, and it framed her face beautifully. She must've paid top dollar for that hairdo. You didn't get that look at Curl Up & Dye, my usual spot for a trim.

My long, somewhat stringy brunette strands were boring in comparison. Should I do something about that? Have a few highlights put in, maybe? Go with a layered look?

"You folks planning to pay with cash or card?" The blond cast another glance at the auction house, then back at me.

Did this woman really think I had six thousand dollars cash in my pocket?

"Actually, I was planning to write a check," I countered.

"Perfect. A check is always welcome." She offered me a bright smile just as Dad passed the pen my way.

I reached to open my purse and came out with my checkbook. "Do I make it out to the auction house?"

She shook her head. "No, we have a stamp for that. Just fill in the amount and sign it."

Those instructions gave me reason to pause. I didn't like the idea of passing off a check made out to no one in particular.

As if to reassure me, she offered a confident smile. "It's okay, I promise. After you give me the check, I'll go fetch the keys and you can take her right home."

"Are you saying the truck runs?" Dad asked. "We were told otherwise. Best news I've heard all day."

She chewed her lip and then shrugged. "Oh, I don't honestly know. I just assumed."

At this point, a young man wearing a BIG RED BID shirt came out of the office, about twenty yards to our right. He was engaged in a lively conversation with someone on the other end of his cell phone but gave us a wave, as if to signal us to stay put.

Meredith gave him one look and excused herself. She took off across the parking lot and climbed into a white SUV.

The man continued our way, all smiles as he tucked his phone into his pocket. "You guys won the bid on the truck?"

I nodded and responded with a quick "Yes," while keeping a watchful eye on Meredith, who was now backing out of her parking spot.

"I'm Ben." He extended his hand, and I noticed his sparkling blue eyes and youthful countenance.

I offered him my hand for a quick shake, along with an introduction: "RaeLyn Hadley."

"RaeLyn." His hand lingered in mine for a second, and he seemed to be looking me over. All righty then. "I'll need your bidding number and

ID, and then I'll get you started on the paperwork. I've got the title ready to transfer along with the details on the make and model. You've got quite a bargain. These old Chevys are worth a lot more than six thousand dollars."

"Happy to have her back," I said.

"Back?" The young man gave us an inquisitive look.

"Tilly was my dad's truck," Dad explained. "He passed away ten years back. She was like a member of the family."

"Well, I'm doubly happy for you, then." Ben flashed a warm and genuine smile. "To be honest, I'm kind of surprised you won this one."

"Why is that?" I asked.

"There was an older man out here before the bidding started, going through every square inch of this old truck. I felt sure he would outbid everyone."

"Wyatt Jackson?" Dad asked.

"Yep. I held on to his license while he looked her over, top to bottom. I think maybe he used to have a truck like this when he was younger. Or maybe he always wanted one but never got it? Something like that. It's funny how an antique vehicle can bring back so many memories. He seemed infatuated with her. Said he would give everything he had to get her back."

Well, that was troubling.

Ben rested his hand on the hood of the truck. "Well, I'm just happy to see this great old truck's going to someone who will give her a new life. There's nothing like being reborn."

"Amen," Mom said. "But can we get out of this heat? My hair's frizzing like a crow's nest in this humidity."

Ben offered a nod. "Sure. Follow me inside, and we'll get you all taken care of."

I followed behind him into the office area, where he invited us to take the seats across from his desk. Well, Mom and I sat. There were only two chairs.

I filled out the paperwork, then reached back into my purse for my checkbook once more. "So, do I make it out to you, then?"

He glanced up from his computer, confusion etched on his face. "Make what out?"

"The check? That lady told me I could make out a check for the truck."

His smile faded right away. "Who told you that?"

I said, "The Blond," as Mom chimed in with "Meredith."

Ben looked legitimately stunned. "Are you saying *Meredith* tried to take a payment from you?"

"Yes." We all spoke in unison.

His eyes widened. "Meredith hasn't worked for Harlan since their divorce four months ago. I can't believe she would do that. Wow." He paused and leaned back in his chair. "Wait till Harlan hears this."

I gripped my checkbook. "I told her I was writing a check, and she said that was fine."

Ben shook his head and set his pen down. "I wouldn't trust her within ten miles of a check. I'm really glad you didn't give it to her."

I was suddenly pretty glad too.

He released an exaggerated breath. And we don't take checks, sorry. Well, not unless you've got a cashier's check. But we can take a card."

Fine. I reached into my purse to grab my credit card, the one I only used for emergencies. He took it and passed a stack of papers my way. Ben also gave me the spare set of keys, reserving one for the tow truck driver. As I took them in hand, I fought the temptation to squeal. I settled for a joyous, "I can't wait to drive her home."

"Drive her home?" Ben's eyes narrowed. "That truck doesn't run. I thought you knew that."

"Oh." My enthusiasm waned. "Meredith said it did."

He leaned back in his chair and cupped his hands behind his head. "I have no idea why she would say that or why she tried to take your money. But, no. The truck doesn't run. We can tow it out to your place tomorrow, but it's going to cost you an extra hundred and fifty dollars. Just pay the tow truck driver when he arrives."

"Oh. Okay." I had a feeling I'd be pouring a lot of money into Tilly, but I had to get her home first.

I paid the man, and he handed me a receipt. Then my parents followed me out to the parking lot, where we headed back to Tilly for a closer look.

I used the keys to open the passenger side door. The glove box was standing wide open. I was bummed to see that the lock mechanism appeared to be damaged, as if someone had tried to forcefully enter it. There were scratches and dents on the surface and pry marks along the edges of the box.

Yes, someone had surely tried to gain access to it. But why? And when? I gave the hinges a closer look and saw that they were broken as well. Ugh. Just one more thing to fix. But at least Tilly was mine now. I could do with her as I pleased. And I would, as soon as I got her home.

Mom glanced at her watch and grimaced. "Bessie Mae's gonna have a fit."

"Why? Because Wyatt tried to steal Tilly right out from under our noses?"

"No." Mom shook her head. "Because she's making homemade chicken and dumplings for dinner, and we're late. You know how she is on dumpling night. Everything is timed down to the minute."

I knew how my aunt was, all right. Even at eighty-two, she still had a feisty edge that put the fear of God in me when she got riled up.

No doubt she'd be riled up over the news about Wyatt too.

"Better lock her up." I walked around to the driver's side door and grabbed the handle but had to fight to get it open.

"You're gonna wanna get that looked at."

I turned as I heard the familiar voice and discovered Mason Fredericks walking straight toward me, that shock of honey-colored hair swooping down over his left eye in the late-afternoon springtime breeze.

I offered a little shrug. "I will. She's gonna get renovated, top to bottom."

A hint of a smile turned up the edges of his lips as he rested his hand on Tilly's hood. "Exactly why I was bidding on her myself. I never turn away a classic like this. I can flip them and get top dollar."

No doubt he could. I'd heard all about his new antique-car business in nearby Gun Barrel City.

"Well, Tilly's not for sale," I countered. "Not anymore anyway. She's mine—lock, stock, and barrel. And she's coming home where she belongs. Finally. After all these years."

"Tilly?" He gave me an inquisitive look.

"She was my papaw's truck. Don't you remember?"

He paused, and a contemplative look came over him. Then Mason's face lit up with obvious recognition. "Oh, right. No wonder she looked familiar. But so many people round these parts owned this same model back in the day, I honestly didn't make the connection."

"Back in the day." Dad smiled. "Haven't heard that expression in a while."

"You driving her home?" Mason asked me.

At that very moment, Wyatt shuffled by and called out something unintelligible. He kept walking. My dad didn't handle this exchange very well. For a minute, I thought he might bolt after Wyatt Jackson. I sure hoped he wouldn't. We'd seen enough action today already.

"It's not worth it, Chuck." Mom reached to rest her palm on Dad's arm. "We took the prize."

"We sure did." Still, Dad didn't look content in that knowledge.

Wyatt hovered nearby, engaging Ben in conversation about something. He didn't appear happy.

I returned my attention to Mason. "She doesn't run. They gave me the name of a tow truck driver. I'm supposed to call him tomorrow sometime."

Wyatt paused from his conversation with Ben to give me a pensive look as I shared Tilly's current condition. Talk about awkward.

"Tell you what, let me get one of my tow trucks to haul her out to your place." Mason pulled out his wallet. "I can send one of my drivers in the morning. No cost."

I turned his way. "You would do that?"

"Well, sure. My guys have already gone home for the day, but we can get it midmorning, if that works for all of you."

"Works for me." I offered what I hoped looked like a grateful smile. "Just call when you're on the way."

"Will do. Just leave the keys on the dash, and we'll take it from there." Mason opened his wallet and came out with a couple of business cards. He passed one to me and another to my dad. "Let me give you my card, just in case you need to get in touch."

I glanced down at the logo on the business card and had to smile when I saw the name of his business. *Rearview Mirror.* Interesting.

Before I knew what was happening, Mom was inviting Mason to dinner. At the words "chicken and dumplings" his eyes widened.

"Bessie Mae's chicken and dumplings?" he asked.

We all nodded in unison.

"A fella forgets a lot of things when he moves away from his hometown, but he never forgets Bessie Mae Hadley's chicken and dumplings. I've been away for so long I hardly remember what a good meal tastes like."

"But you're back home now?" Dad asked.

"Yes, sir." The edges of his lips tipped up in a playful fashion. "Opened a car lot in Gun Barrel City. We sell refurbished antiques.

"I'm a refurbished antique." Mom laughed. "But I don't think you'd get much for me. She paused and looked back and forth between Mason and me. "You two young'uns should probably ride together. I've got something I need to talk to your father about on the ride home."

Okay, was it my imagination, or was my mom trying to set me up with Mason Fredericks? And what in the world did she need to talk to my dad about, unless it had something to do with our current financial state, something we definitely didn't need to be talking about in front of Mason, or anyone else, for that matter.

I didn't argue with her, especially when Mason gave her a bright smile and a chipper "Sure. Sounds good."

I placed the keys on Tilly's dash, and next thing you knew I was tagging along behind him on the way to his truck, a gorgeous '90s Ford F150 Lariat. After eight years of putting this fella behind me, I suddenly found myself looking in the rearview mirror.

CHAPTER THREE

Mason opened the passenger door of his truck for me, and I slipped inside onto the bench seat. He walked around to the driver's side and climbed in across from me.

I ran my hand across the leather of the seat, a flood of memories washing over me. "I haven't been in a Lariat since I was a kid, Mason. I think my dad owned this model once upon a time."

"Probably. Most of the men around here did." He slipped a key into the ignition, and a few seconds later the steady hum of the engine sounded. "The Lariat was pretty popular in the '90s. My dad had this one even before I was born. I have a lot of great memories of hauling car parts with my dad in this truck."

"So, this was your father's truck?"

"Yeah." He grew silent, and I knew why. Everyone in town knew about the accident that had taken his father's life last spring out on Highway 75. Must've been in a different vehicle. Either that, or Mason had already restored this one.

Before I could say, "I was so sorry to hear about your dad," he had changed the subject to the weather, a common topic of conversation in Mabank when you didn't know what else to say. I had a feeling we'd be talking about the weather a lot.

Minutes later we were on the road, headed to my family's acreage, about five miles away, just on the other side of the lake. I didn't even have to instruct Mason. He seemed to remember just how to get there. Though, he seemed to be taking the long way. If I didn't know any better, I'd say the guy was stalling.

"You almost outbid me on Tilly," I said after a moment's reflection.

"Yeah, sorry about that. It took me a while to figure out why you were bidding on that old truck." He offered a quick glance then turned his attention back to the road. "I finally realized it must mean something special to you."

"Yeah. And I'm so happy to have her back. You have no idea." I didn't mean for my voice to crack, but there it was.

"I wouldn't have bid on her if I'd known what she meant to you." He looked my way, and I could read the genuineness in his expression. "I promise. I just love to flip those old '50s models. That one has a stove-bolt six engine, and I love to work on those. It's a really roust inline-six cylinder. You know?"

I didn't. . .but didn't say so.

"That engine is known for its durability, so that truck will be around forever if she's well cared for."

"True."

"And let's face it: it's going to be a blast for whoever does the work on her. The collectors will be beating down your door to buy her from you."

"I won't sell." And I meant it. Still, an idea hit in that moment, and I voiced it aloud. "Mason, I'm going to need someone to fix her up. So, maybe I could hire you to do the work on her?"

"Really?" His eyes lit up as he spoke the word. "You would do that?"

"Sure. I mean, that was the plan all along, to hire someone else to do the things I can't. And that way we both win. I get Tilly back, and you get to work on a classic with all of those details you just spouted off that I can't seem to remember."

His smile lit up the space between us. "Sounds amazing. You've got my card."

"I do. And I love the name. Rearview Mirror?"

"Yeah." He chuckled. "It was something my dad always said. He said there's no point in looking in the rearview mirror. You need to keep your focus on the road."

Which was ironic, since he crossed over the line onto the shoulder at that very moment.

Mason laughed and pulled his truck back into the lane. "Sorry about that. Just thought I'd give you a living example."

"Very funny." I paused to think through my next question. "So, does the new business mean you're back in Mabank for good?"

Mason ran a hand through his hair. "Yeah, I figured it was time to come back, reconnect with where I came from. And Pop left me the shop and the apartment above it, so. . ."

"Oh, right. It was always a used-car lot, right?"

"Since I was a kid."

"So, do we just have the tow truck driver take Tilly straight to your place in the morning, then?" I asked.

He nodded. "Sure. I'll get started on her right away. This is a win-win for both of us."

We crossed over the lake, and my gaze shifted. I remembered another time I'd crossed this bridge with Mason Fredericks. I was seventeen, and we were on our way to the lake for a swim. With Stephanie.

I turned my gaze back to the road. We were just a couple miles from my family's place now, and I needed to stay focused.

All around me, Mabank was showing full signs of spring. A magnificent transformation had taken place as the always-beautiful scenery took on an even lovelier glow. The fields, the flowers, the lake—it was all a living canvas, painted with the hues of springtime I loved so much.

"Why was your dad so riled up over Wyatt Jackson bidding on Tilly?" Mason asked, interrupting my reverie. "I couldn't help but notice the look on his face when Wyatt called out that first bid."

"Ah. Well, apparently Wyatt was Papaw's archnemesis."

Mason glanced my way, creases forming around his eyes as he asked, "How so?"

"I don't know the whole story, but I do remember there was some sort of lawsuit. He tried to claim that he owned a portion of our sixty-three acres."

"Land dispute?" Mason's brow furrowed, and he appeared to be thinking. "When was this?"

"When I was little. The courts sided with Papaw, of course. This land has been in our family for multiple generations, and no one has ever questioned it before or since. But Wyatt Jackson saw that my grandfather was bringing in some serious cash and decided it should be his. For whatever reason."

"Mineral rights?"

I nodded. "Yep. Good money at one time."

Should I mention that those monthly checks had dwindled down to practically nothing and that we needed every penny to keep the place running? Nah, that would be a story for another day.

Mason appeared lost in his thoughts. "I still don't understand why he would bother to claim any of the land was his, do you?"

"No, but seeing him today really upset my parents. My dad was fit to be tied."

"There's got to be more to the story." Mason tapped on the brake and flipped on his signal to turn onto my street.

"Clearly." I paused to think it through. "But that's one subject we just don't mention around our place. I do have the sense that Wyatt and my grandfather had a falling-out and never got past it, but I don't know the specifics."

"I hate it when stuff like that happens." Mason took the left-hand turn onto the narrow rural road, which was just as bumpy as it had been the last time he'd driven me home all those years ago.

"Yeah. Me too."

He rounded the turn as we approached my driveway, and he slowed. "So, question." Mason paused, and I wondered what he might say. "Why did you and I lose touch with each other?"

I gave him a pensive look. "Really?"

"Yeah. What happened to cause you to drift away?"

Was he kidding? "Me? Drift away? I didn't go anywhere. I'm right here in Mabank, where I always was. You're the one who drifted. . .after you stole my best friend away from me."

"Whoa." He glanced my way. "Stole your best friend?"

"Stephanie? She hasn't spoken to me since the two of you started dating, remember?"

"Well now, your recollection and mine are a mite different."

"How so?"

"First of all, I didn't steal your best friend away from you."

"Did you, or did you not, move her away to Waco to go to Baylor?"

"Um, she got accepted at Baylor, and so did I."

"Stephanie wasn't even interested in Baylor until she heard you were going. Then she up and left me, high and dry." Well, not high and dry, exactly. I'd journeyed off to A&M, thanks to a scholarship, and had enjoyed four amazing years there while Stephanie and Mason did their thing in Waco. Whatever that was.

"We dated a year and a half, and then she found someone else." Mason paused and gazed so intently at me that I felt a little perspiration on the back of my neck. "Star quarterback for the Bears. A guy named Anderson."

"First name?"

"Last. Anyway, she left school halfway into her junior year and married, the guy. They moved to Omaha. Or maybe it was Idaho? I can't remember."

Okay, I'd heard something to that effect, but it hadn't eased the pain of her not speaking to me for so long.

"Last I heard, they had a baby, so. . ." He paused. "It's all water under the bridge now."

"People always say that."

"Say what?" He gave me an inquisitive look.

"'It's water under the bridge.' When there's something in the past they don't want to deal with, they just wave a hand and say, 'It's all water under the bridge.'"

"But it is. And we can't change the past anyway. So, we need to let bygones be bygones."

Another phrase that was woefully overused.

Mason turned and headed down the long driveway, stopping just short of the three-car carport, where Dad's truck was parked alongside Mom's SUV and Aunt Bessie Mae's 2002 Pontiac, an oversize vehicle in a soft baby blue.

He parked behind the SUV and shut off the engine before looking my way with an inquisitive look. "Where's your Bug?"

"I sold it. I've been sharing the SUV with Mom. Looks like they beat us home, by the way."

"Sold your VW Bug? I thought you'd keep that thing forever."

"Nope." I reached for the door handle. "When I heard that Papaw's truck was up for auction, I sold it so I'd have the money to bid."

"Whoa." He reached over and grabbed my hand. "I wish I'd known all of that before I bid against you. I never would have. I hope you know that."

I shrugged. "Still would've had Wyatt and Clayton to contend with. And that blond."

"Meredith Reed."

"You know her?"

He shrugged. "Only a little. She came to my workplace a few days back, asking me a bunch of questions about the value of some of the trucks up for bid today. I didn't think much about it. Just figured she was a collector."

"She's Harlan's ex-wife."

"Number Four." He opened his door. "I heard all about it from Dot."

"You've been hanging out with Dot?" This was surprising. My mom's best friend didn't exactly run in the same circles with us twentysomethings.

"She came by the shop to ask if I would consider joining the chamber of commerce. Apparently she's the head of it?"

"Right."

"And she filled me in on Harlan and his ex-wife after she saw Meredith leaving my place."

"Gotcha." That made sense.

I started to open my door, but Mason had gotten out and beat me to it. He eased it open with the words, "I don't really know Meredith Reed. She just plopped herself down next to me today and acted like we were old friends. Felt like she was trying to get to know me."

"Don't *all* the girls want to know you, Mason?" I swung my legs and stepped out onto the driveway.

"Very funny." Still, he didn't smile as those words were spoken.

He pointed at the fifth wheel under the second, taller carport. "Hey, your mom finally got her fifth wheel!"

"Yeah, they travel a lot. They're part of a camping club that goes all sorts of places." Still, I couldn't believe he'd actually remembered that my mom always dreamed of traveling.

At that moment, my dog came running up to greet me. I patted Riley on the head, and she relaxed under my touch. Afterward, she took several tentative steps in Mason's direction and sniffed at his shoes.

Mason leaned down and patted her on the head, then scratched behind her ears. "Who do we have here?"

"Riley. She's a cattle dog." I paused. "Well, kind of a Heinz 57 version of a cattle dog. I have yet to actually see her round up any cattle. But I told you all the girls wanted to get to know you, and here's the proof. She's usually more skittish around strangers."

"I see." Mason knelt down and gave my beautiful black-and-tan pup a closer look. "Reminds me of a dog I had as a kid."

I led the way to the back porch, our usual point of entrance for the Hadley home.

Mason stopped to stare out onto the vast expanse of property off in the distance. "It's just like I remember it—the white fence, the gate, the horses." He turned his gaze to the huge pecan tree just beyond the back porch. "I remember bagging up a lot of pecans."

"And you ate a few of Bessie Mae's pecan pies too, as I recall."

"I did." He quirked a brow as he pointed to the porch swing on the far side of the pecan tree. "I seem to recall the two of us sitting there, whiling away the hours."

"B.S."

His brow wrinkled. "I'm sorry?"

"B.S. Before Stephanie. You and I had a lot of time together B.S."

"Oh, I see." He laughed. "So, that's how this is going to be. You won't even let me have my memories."

"Memories schmemories. It's all water under the bridge now. Remember?"

"Yeah." He paused, and a comfortable silence rose up between us. "We used to talk a lot about what we wanted to be—and do—when we grew up." He brushed a loose hair off my cheek. "You went to A&M to study communications?"

"And journalism."

"But you're back here, helping your parents out instead of working in the news biz?"

"I do some freelancing with *Mabank Happenings*."

"Yeah, I saw that you have a column in the paper now. That's pretty impressive."

"I'm not sure the *Mabank Happenings* column is going to rival a gig with the *Dallas Times*—my once-upon-a-time dream job—but it brings in a little extra money, and we could use that right about now. Things have been really tight."

"For all of the ranchers." He sighed. "I've heard. But that job at the paper probably gives you a lot of insight into Mabank. I'm really glad someone is working hard to keep the town's stories going."

"Kind of like this property." I gestured to the lush, rolling acreage. "I really want this piece of land to stay in the family for generations to come, which is why I hope the economy turns around. My papaw's parents bought it for next to nothing in the '30s, and then it passed to him, then to my dad. So, if we play our cards right, we'll keep it going a long time."

"I've always wanted property too." He sighed as he looked back toward the white railed fence where a couple of our horses approached, looking for some attention. "I mean, I love flipping cars, and the new shop is a dream come true for me. But living in the apartment above the business isn't my idea of the perfect home. It's hard to enjoy your frozen lasagna when it smells like motor oil."

I couldn't even imagine living like that. I cast my gaze to the field, where several of our mares stood nibbling on hay. "There's something to be said for wide-open spaces." I breathed in the air, feeling very content in this very moment.

He pointed to our huge red barn off the field. "Hey, I don't remember that barn. Is it new?"

"Yeah. We've still got the old one on the far end of the property. But this newer one—which my dad and the boys built a few years back—is in the process of being converted into an antique store. We've still got a lot of work to do on it."

He pointed to the sign. "Trinkets and Treasures?"

"You're very astute. And a good reader too." I laughed. "And yes, I know it's a hokey name, but Bessie Mae came up with it, and since most of the stuff in the store will be family items passed to her, she got the final say."

"Oh, I'm not questioning the name. I think it's a good fit. But what gave you the idea to open an antique store?"

"Actually, it was my papaw's idea." I paused as memories flooded over me. "He always said we should sell off some of the junk—as he called it—that my grandma and her family had passed down. When it reached the point where the barn was overflowing with stuff, he threatened a time or two."

"But he never did?"

"Nah, he was all talk. But now that we're a couple of generations removed from their belongings, it's easier to imagine selling some of them. The barn was the perfect size, and Dad and the boys put in that gravel parking lot just in front of it so folks will have plenty of room to park."

"Well, hopefully that parking lot will be full day in and day out."

"Thanks. I'll show you around some day. But right now we'd better get inside. Don't want to upset Bessie Mae." I turned to lead the way to the back door.

Mason turned abruptly and pointed to our right. "Hey, you guys renovated the little house next door. Wasn't that the original house on the property?"

"Yep, from the 1930s. It's the house Papaw and Bessie Mae grew up in." I paused to think it through. "Actually, I think Aunt Bessie was still living there when we graduated. My parents converted our three-car garage into a big suite for her, complete with a sitting area and bathroom. It's a lot nicer than what she had over there."

He flashed a smile. "That's great. So, who lives in the little house now?"

"Jake and his wife, Carrie," I explained. "She's about to have a baby any minute now, and they've been working on getting the place ready."

"I heard he'd married an out-of-stater."

"Three years ago. Carrie Boyen. They're a match made in heaven. Unless you get them talking about politics. On that topic, there's a vast divide." I leaned in to whisper, "She grew up in California."

"Oh boy." Mason paused. "I'm sure that's entertaining."

"Oh, it is, trust me." The stories I could tell.

"I heard Jake is coaching at Mabank High."

"Yep. They're hot and heavy into baseball season now, but it's been a good way to bring in some extra money."

And that was enough about that. I didn't need to share our financial woes with Mason.

"Anyway, they'll be joining us for dinner. Dallas and Gage too," I added. "Not sure about Logan. He's kind of a loner these days. He works at the bank in Athens, and we rarely see him when he's home. He's living out in a trailer on the far end of the property."

"Any idea what he's doing out there all by his lonesome?" Mason asked.

"I have no idea, but my imagination works overtime. I mean, he comes out to help my dad with the books. And he's been helpful with the new antique store. But when he needs his space, he needs his space. To be honest, I think the family's just too much for him, especially my younger brothers. They're a hot mess. But he shows up every now and again for one of Bessie Mae's meals."

"She's a classic."

"You make her sound like one of your cars." Still, he wasn't far from the truth. My great-aunt was a bit of a classic, to be sure. And right now, as she waved to us from the other side of the screen door, he was about to find that out once more.

CHAPTER FOUR

Aunt Bessie opened the screen door and ushered us into the house, her soft blue eyes twinkling with merriment. "Get in here, you two." We stepped inside, and she turned to face Mason. "Well, as I live and breathe. I heard you were coming, but I didn't believe it. Had to see it with my own eyes." As she smiled, the fine lines formed around her mouth and eyes.

"I'm here," he responded with a lopsided grin. "Just moved back to the area."

"So I heard. We're so glad you're back home where you belong. It's been too long."

"It has. And I'm glad to be back."

Bessie Mae opened her arms wide, and Mason gave her a warm hug. Off in the distance the television blared one of her favorite movies, a John Wayne classic, *North to Northwest*. I grabbed the remote and lowered the volume as she continued to hug Mason.

When she finally released her hold on him, my aunt gave him a pensive look. "Well now, let me have a good look at you. It's been a spell since I saw you last."

"Eight years."

"I remember when you were no bigger'n a minnow in a fishin' pond. Now you're all grown up."

"I am. But you haven't changed one bit."

"I'll bet you say that to all the girls."

"Nope." He laughed. "Just you." Mason pointed at the television. "And I see your taste in movies hasn't changed. Is that a John Wayne movie I spy?"

"She found some channel on satellite TV that plays John Wayne movies all day long," I explained. "We're all at the point where we can quote them verbatim."

"*True Grit?*" he asked. When I nodded, he came back with: "I never shot nobody I didn't have to."

To which I responded: "You must pay for everything in this world one way or another. There is nothing free except the grace of God."

And then we both laughed. Just like we did all those years ago when we quoted those very same lines in this very same room. In that moment, it felt as if nothing had changed between us.

"I do love a good movie quote," Bessie Mae said. "And you two do it up right."

"Thank you, ma'am." Mason offered a little nod.

"There's just something about the Duke in this role as Rooster Cogburn." Bessie's eyes took on a faraway look as she gestured in the general direction of the muted TV. "Gets me every time. The tough, gritty marshal, loaded with determination and resilience. Now there's a real man for you." She paused and then turned her attention to Mason. "Well, speaking of good men... We were all so sad to hear about your daddy."

"Thank you." He offered a little shrug. "It's still so hard to wrap my head around."

"I'm sure," I added, feeling the weight of those two little words.

Bessie Mae brushed her palms on her apron. "It's never easy to lose someone you love, especially in such a tragic way. I'm sure it was a terrible shock."

"It was. But I'm doing my best to live up to his legacy. He was one of the best men I ever knew."

"And did such a fine job of raising his son all on his own after your sweet mama..." Bessie Mae paused and shook her head. "Well, anyway, you've overcome a lot, young man, and you certainly deserve a good meal. And you know what the Duke always says."

"What's that, Bessie Mae?"

"Courage is being scared to death but saddling up anyway." She gave him an empathetic look. "You've had to do that a lot in this life, but you've faced it all with great bravery, and I'm really proud of you."

"Well, thank you. That means a lot."

Bessie Mae's nose wrinkled, and she turned her attention to the pot on the stove.

As she lifted the lid, the most delicious aroma wafted over us. I stifled a laugh as Mason sniffed the air.

Bessie chattered on and on with a twinkle in her eye as she stirred the pot of dumplings. "Almost done. Just another minute or two. You've gotta get 'em when they're just right. Now, RaeLyn, you go and fetch those brothers of yours. It takes them all day to get in here when I call."

I left Mason to visit with my aunt while I made my way to the bedroom my twin brothers shared. I rapped on the door, but the sound of an argument on the other side convinced me they probably didn't hear me, so I knocked a little louder and hollered out, "Supper's ready! Dumplings!"

Seconds later they emerged with mirrored scowls on their faces. Nothing new there.

My twin brothers had a love-hate relationship with each other. I knew they secretly couldn't live without each other, but there were times when their squabbling almost convinced me otherwise.

Dallas, older by six minutes, liked to use that older brother thing to his benefit. Gage was often chided as being the baby, the mama's boy. But, truth be told, they were both childish and immature, preferring their video games and TV shows to real-life responsibilities like everyday chores on the ranch.

They breezed by me in the hallway and almost knocked me down.

By the time I arrived back in the kitchen, the whole family had gathered and were making friendly with Mason, who seemed a little overwhelmed but otherwise happy. They peppered him with questions, which he graciously answered, and then the conversation shifted to how good the dumplings smelled. I couldn't argue that point.

"Where's Logan?" Mom asked. "Is he joining us tonight?"

"Something's wrong with that boy." Bessie Mae clucked her tongue. "Ain't natural to be alone so much out there in that trailer."

Gage rolled his eyes. "I'll trade places with him. I'd give my eyeteeth to have some peace and quiet for a change."

"Feel free to move on out anytime you like," Dallas quipped. "I'll help you pack." This led straight back into an argument between the two of them. Nothing new there. These two weren't happy unless there was a fight going on.

I couldn't help but wonder what Mason thought of us now. No doubt he was happy for his current quiet living situation in comparison to this chaos.

No, he actually looked downright entertained by all of this, if such a thing could be judged from the comical expression on his face.

The back door swung open, and my oldest brother stepped inside holding a plastic grocery bag in hand. "What'd I miss?" Jake asked as he set the bag on the countertop.

"RaeLyn brought a date for dinner," Gage said, then gestured with his head to Mason, whose eyes widened.

"Oh, it's not a date. I—" My words fell off midsentence as my gaze shifted to the handsome fella standing to my right.

"Mason." Jake stiffened a bit as he clamped eyes on my brother but then extended his hand. "Long time no see. Heard you were back."

"Yeah, I've been back a month or so."

"What brings you out this way?" Jake gave him a pensive look, as if he didn't quite trust him. Then again, Jake had always been my protector.

"I ran into your family at the auction, and next thing I knew, I was being invited over for Bessie Mae's chicken and dumplings."

"I brought dessert." Jake held up the bag, and I could make out the containers of ice cream inside.

"We're trying to figure out if Logan is going to be joining us," I said in an attempt to change the direction of the conversation.

"He's on a date tonight." Jake opened the freezer and pulled two half gallons of ice cream out of the bag. "That's about all I could get out of him. No details."

We all paused at once. Logan was such a loner. Other than his job at the bank and occasionally helping Dad out with purchases and other financial issues, he pretty much stayed put in that trailer of his at the back of the property.

"Well, I'll be." Mom paused and then lifted her hands in the air. "If that boy finds himself a good wife, my life will be complete."

"Does that mean you'll stop trying to match up the rest of us with every girl in town?" Gage asked.

Mom flashed him a look that read, "Don't be silly."

The back door swung open again, and my very pregnant sister-in-law stepped inside. Poor Carrie looked like she was ready to pop. Eight months of pregnancy appeared more like ten or twelve on her tiny frame.

Carrie's brow wrinkled as she said, "Jake, did you bring the Blue Bell? It went missing from our freezer."

"Got it!" He held up both of the half gallons and then shoved them into the freezer.

We all paused for a moment of reverent silence for our favorite ice cream brand. I knew without even asking that those two half gallons would be homemade vanilla and cookies 'n cream. No matter what Bessie Mae had cooked up for dessert, there would be ice cream on top. We took our Blue Bell very seriously here in Texas. Even during difficult economic times, there would always be ice cream in the freezer. That's just the way it was. Some things were worth sacrificing for.

"If we wait another minute longer, these dumplings won't be worth eating," Bessie Mae said, her words more a call to action than anything. "Now, who's gonna say the blessing?"

We all found places to sit—some of us at the table and others at the nearby island. I found myself next to Mason, who took my hand as my dad prayed over the meal with his usual dramatic flair.

Moments later Bessie Mae ladled chunks of steaming chicken and dumplings into our bowls, and the room filled with love, laughter. . .and the clinking of spoons bumping up against bowls as we gobbled down those thick, hot dumplings.

Seated here, in my cozy family kitchen, the aroma of simmering chicken and dumplings wafting through the air, I felt completely at home. And yet my nerves were still a bit frazzled that Mason was seated next to me, oohing and aahing with every bite. Not that I blamed him for the animation. If I'd gone without my aunt's cooking for eight years, I would be over the moon too.

Still, I wondered what Mason thought of us after all these years, still gathered around the family table with our mismatched soup bowls and worn embroidered tablecloth passed down through multiple generations. Did he think we were hokey? East Texas hicks?

No, from the look on his face, he was nothing but happy to be there and perfectly at ease seated at our table.

And I was happy too. In fact, I was feeling a sense of nostalgia and warmth I hadn't felt in ages.

Or maybe that was just the heat in the room. It was pretty warm, even for March. And Mom wasn't one to turn on the AC until we absolutely had to.

The conversation bounced around for a while but finally landed on the auction.

"So, you won 'er back?" Jake asked, as he gave me an admiring look.

"Yep." I took a swig of my sweet tea and rested against the back of my seat. "Tilly's coming home where she belongs. Mason's arranged to have her delivered to us midmorning."

"That's great." My brothers lit into a conversation about Papaw's 1952 truck, which got Mason fully engaged in the conversation. He had a lot to say about it, in fact.

"That truck's got one of the most iconic designs out there." His animation level rose more with each word. "Rounded fenders, horizontal-bar grille...timeless. She'll be a real beauty when she's fixed up. You don't see trucks like that every day, at least not these days."

"I told Mason he could help work on her," I explained. "Since that's his area of expertise and all."

This led them back into a discussion about that particular make and model, and how fun it was going to be. Before long they were talking about shades of red paint, giving suggestions for which one I should choose.

"Boys and their toys." Mom laughed. "That never changes. Trucks and football. The two topics of conversation that rule the day in the Hadley household."

She wasn't kidding. The topic rarely jumped from those two things.

Well, unless my dad broached the subject of our finances, which had him a little unnerved this past year.

And the weather. Always the weather.

As we wrapped up the second round of dumplings, Bessie Mae pushed back her chair and attempted to stand. Poor dear was having a harder time lately getting around. Mason must've noticed. He sprang from his seat and helped her up.

"Well, thank you kindly." She flashed him a warm smile. "And for that you'll get a double portion of my dewberry cobbler once I get it whipped up."

"Dewberry cobbler?" He rested his hand on his stomach. "Are you serious?"

"Well, sure. It's dewberry season, and RaeLyn picked buckets of 'em last week. Our freezers are about to pop with berries. It won't take me more than a few minutes to fashion up a cobbler, so I hope you're not in a hurry. Would've done it sooner, but my back was giving me fits today." She rested her hand on her side. "I'm at the age where my back goes out more than I do." A little chuckle followed. "Now, am I gonna have to wash these berries all by myself, or are you two gonna get over here and help me?"

I guess that was an order to help. I rose and made my way toward them.

"Would you pass me that bowl of dewberries from the fridge, RaeLyn?" My aunt's eyes twinkled as she offered instruction. "Let's get this show on the road."

I reached into the refrigerator for the huge bowl of fresh dewberries and set it on the counter next to her, then watched as she transferred them into a colander, which she placed in the sink. Moments later, the water was running over them.

Mason stuck his hand in the bowl and popped a juicy berry into his mouth. A look of delirium came over him. "How many times did we go dewberry picking together when we were kids, RaeLyn? A thousand?"

"At least."

"Remember how we used to sneak onto the Jackson property to pick berries in the far back corner, just past that dilapidated old shed? They were the best in the county."

"You stole berries from Wyatt Jackson?" Mom's brows arched. "Don't tell me that's where you got these."

"Nope. These are all from our own property. Haven't been to Wyatt's place in years. And even then, it was on the far edge of his property, right alongside the field next to him."

"Sure wouldn't recommend trespassing over there these days," Bessie Mae said. "He'd probably come after you with a shotgun."

"No one ever picked his dewberries but us, so they would've just rotted on the vine." I shrugged. "But they're not worth dying over, so I won't be going back. No need to worry."

"They were some good memories, though." Mason flashed a playful smile. "Sneaking around was always fun."

I nodded but didn't say anything else. To be honest, these endless treks down memory lane were wearing me down. I couldn't go on being miffed at Mason if he kept parading me back to the good old days. And besides, I wasn't keen on my parents wondering how much sneaking around I'd done back in the day. Berry stealing was the height of my crime spree, and I didn't need my mom thinking otherwise.

At the table, my family carried on and on about Logan, trying to guess how his date was going. I wondered too but didn't add any comments. Logan was the topic of conversation way too much, to my way of thinking. Poor guy just needed to be left alone. I wouldn't want them dabbling in my love life, after all. If I had one anyway.

Mason and my aunt kept up their playful banter as they worked side by side. My heart twisted a bit as I remembered another time, years ago, when Mason had helped my aunt in the kitchen. They'd baked a chocolate pie together. She taught him how to roll out a homemade pie crust that day. Maybe the guy had some hidden talents that went beyond car renovation.

Bessie Mae got the berries going on the stove. It wasn't long before the sweet aroma of simmering dewberries enveloped the room, creating an enticing atmosphere that made my mouth water.

Mason watched over the large saucepan, which bubbled with the thickening concoction of dewberries, sugar, cornstarch, and a splash of lemon juice. As always, I was drawn to the delicious fruity scent rising from the pot.

I gave it a quick glimpse and practically swooned as I saw those deep purple berries glistening in their gooey syrup. Yum.

Off in the distance, Bessie Mae rolled out the buttery homemade pie dough using that well-worn rolling pin of hers, the same one I'd seen for years. And yet the time she took—as well as the love and attention she poured into each gentle roll—convinced me that my aunt baked with every fiber of love she had inside of her.

She'd done this thousands of times before and could probably make one in her sleep. I loved her rustic crust-making skills, which produced a flaky pie crust with speckles of butter throughout. Was there anything more comforting? She plopped the crust into a familiar chipped ceramic pie dish and set it aside to give the berries another stir.

My aunt hummed as she worked—her favorite hymn, "When the Roll Is Called Up Yonder." Before long, Mason was singing it with her. This got the whole family started, and within seconds we had three-part harmony going.

Bessie Mae paused long enough to dab the mist from her eyes with her apron hem, then dove right back into her work, now putting Mason to work transferring the berries to the baking dish. Then, with his help, she covered the top in rustic slices of dough, one overlapping the other.

Mom decided we all needed to play a game of cards while waiting on the cobbler to bake, and before I could say, "No thanks," Jake was dealing. Turned out Mason was as good at card playing as he'd ever been. Dallas and Gage joined us but ended up in an argument midgame. Mason didn't seem to notice. He looked my way more than once, a comfortable smile on his face.

Carrie gave me a "What do we have here?" look out of the corner of her eye, and I could almost read her thoughts as she looked back and forth between Mason and me. I shook my head and willed her to keep those thoughts to herself.

Though, to be honest, there was something rather comfortable about having Mason in our kitchen once again. He was a good fit. Always had been.

But I wasn't ready to admit that to anyone else yet. Maybe not even to myself.

CHAPTER FIVE

Bessie Mae added another squeeze of lemon juice to the dewberry filling, and the room was infused with the warm, comforting aroma of spices. I inhaled deeply, almost tasting the flavorful cobbler to come.

By the time my aunt dished up the sticky, sweet dessert, we were all starving once again. At least we acted like we were. And huge scoops of Bluebell were just the ticket. I opted for vanilla on mine. Mason took a scoop of each.

Just as I started to take a seat at the table, Mom nudged me with her elbow. "Y'all should sit out on the back porch to eat your cobbler, honey. It's warm in here, and besides, we need to clear this table. Can't do that with folks sitting around taking up space." As if to encourage me further, she opened the back door and glanced outside. "Sure is a pretty sunset out there tonight. Just gorgeous."

Good grief. Talk about laying it on thick. I needed to get out of here before she started measuring me for my wedding dress.

Still, Mason took the bait. He held the door open for me, and we both made our way to the porch swing, just a few yards from the back patio. Riley followed along behind us, sniffing at the bowls in our hands.

As we eased our way down onto the swing with the pup curling up at our feet, I was seventeen once again, sitting next to the boy who made my heart skip a beat.

B.S. Before Stephanie.

We sat, steaming bowls of cobbler in hand, in silence. For a while anyway. I couldn't help but comment on the red and orange hues in the sky above us as the sun slid behind the barn and disappeared from view.

The air was filled with that sweet fragrance of spring I loved so much, a true symphony of floral scents, mixed with the obvious smells one always found on the farm. Still, it all felt familiar and comfortable.

The soft creaking of the porch swing outside and the distant hum of crickets were the only sounds that permeated the Hadley family home as I leaned back against the swing.

Before long we were laughing and talking as though no time had passed between us at all. And I felt sure, in that moment, it hadn't.

Mason left sometime after eight thirty, and I helped Mom tidy up the kitchen. She was dying to hear how my time on the swing had gone.

"It was no big deal, Mom." I placed a stack of clean plates in the cupboard.

But she gave me a look that said, *I suspect otherwise.*

She might be right. Those old feelings had come rushing over me, and I could not deny them, no matter how hard I tried.

Okay, I wasn't trying to deny them at all.

Neither could I deny the loud squabble going on in my brothers' room as I made my way toward my bedroom. Nothing new there. The soft glow of the moon spilled through the window, revealing the silhouettes of Dallas and Gage as they bickered.

My eyes narrowed as I observed the scene. This wasn't their first squabble, and it certainly wouldn't be their last. I sighed, caught between exasperation and a hint of amusement.

"Guys, it's late. Can't you argue quietly?" I finally interjected, stepping into the room. My presence seemed to go unnoticed for a moment as they continued their verbal jousting.

As I turned to leave, the distant murmur of their voices lingered in the night air. Siblings, bound by blood and shared history, navigated the delicate balance between camaraderie and conflict, and tonight's dispute was just another chapter in the ongoing saga of the Hadley family dynamics.

I walked into my bedroom and closed the door behind me, lost in my thoughts about the day. I couldn't stop thinking about Tilly. And Mason. Somehow those two just seemed to merge into one now. How wonderful to know he would be the one in charge of fixing her up again.

I could almost envision Tilly in her completed state now—bright red paint, polished trim work, new leather bench seat. She would be a showcase, one I would be happy to drive.

Drive.

Hmm. One of the first things on my list was getting Tilly's engine up and running. I had big plans to do a "before" photo shoot in the field on the south end of our property, the one with all of the bluebonnets in bloom, so I had to get her running quickly.

Or maybe. . .I shot off a text to Mason: Hey, do you think your tow truck driver would make an extra stop along the way tomorrow? I want some pictures of Tilly in our sw corner field in her current condition. I thought Before and After pictures would be fun."

He wrote back, I don't see why not. I'll be in touch midmorning. And we ended it at that.

I spent the next few minutes showering and dressing for bed. Then I climbed under the covers shortly after ten. Riley jumped up onto the bed and took her usual spot beside me, burrowing under the quilt until she was content.

Once comfortable, I opened my iPad to do a little digging on social media. All this talk about Stephanie Ingram had made me curious. Whatever happened to her. . .really? Was she really in Omaha? Or Idaho?

I did some browsing on Facebook until I finally located a Stephanie Ingram Anderson. A quick peek at her face, and I knew it was the same girl. She had those gorgeous brown eyes and thick dark hair. And she had aged beautifully. Some girls just had really great genes.

Only she didn't live in Omaha. Or Idaho. This Stephanie lived in the state of Iowa. Ames, to be exact. And she was married to a Connor Anderson. Who happened to be incredibly handsome, based on his pictures on her page. He definitely looked like a football player, his broad shoulders showing themselves off in the photographs of the two of them. And their baby girl was an absolute doll. How could I be mad at an old friend with a baby that cute?

In that moment, the whole thing just seemed so silly. We had once been close. I should reach out to her again, for old time's sake. After all, any angst between us really was water under the bridge now. Right? Isn't that what Mason would say?

I shot off a quick friend request, my heart rate picking up as I pressed the SEND button. A rap sounded at my bedroom door, and I called out, "Come in."

Mom popped her head in the door. "You're in bed already?" she asked. "I figured you'd still be wide awake."

"Oh, I am. I'm just looking up an old friend on Facebook, that's all."

"Who's that?" She took a couple of steps into my room, then took a seat on the edge of the bed next to me.

"Stephanie Ingram."

"Oh, I see." My mom paused and gave me a curious look. "What prompted this? Spending time with Mason?"

"He mentioned that she was married and living in Idaho." I paused. "It's Iowa, by the way. Not Idaho."

"Oh, wow. She's a long way from home."

"Yeah. But she looks really happy. She's got an adorable baby girl." I turned the iPad around to show her a picture as proof.

"That's nice. Married with a baby." Mom smiled, and for a moment I thought she was expressing wishful thinking about me, her only daughter. My mother wouldn't be completely happy until all of her offspring were married and having babies.

"I sent her a friend request."

"And?" Mom gave me a pensive look.

I set the iPad down in my lap. "And I'm waiting to see if she responds."

"Hopefully she will. And by the way, I'm awfully glad you stayed put here in Mabank, honey." Mom flashed me a warm smile. "Don't even think about moving off, okay?"

"I have no plans to go anywhere."

"Thank you. I like things just as they are." She cleared her throat. "Now,

I'm not saying you need to stay single forever. You could get married to a good local boy and stay put and give me some grandchildren, and I'd be as happy as a lark."

And there it was.

"Good night, Mom." I pursed my lips and hoped she would take the hint. This was one conversation I didn't want to have. Not tonight anyway.

She laughed and then eased her way out of my room, muttering, "You can't blame a gal for trying!"

No, I couldn't.

I picked up my iPad and decided to watch a show, my usual winding-down activity each day.

I couldn't get interested in the true crime documentary, though it kept playing in the background. I stretched out across my bed, still deep in thought over how the day had gone. From the highs and lows of the auction to the bliss of dinner and hot, bubbly cobbler, this day had come packed full of surprises. Did Mason still find me the same? I still felt like a kid at heart, especially here, in our family home.

I rolled over and examined my pink-on-pink bedroom. Maybe I should fix this place up. Make it look like an adult lived in here. Once a nostalgic haven of my fond childhood memories, it now seemed a bit outdated and worn.

Yeah, I would do that. Soon. Tilly would get her transformation and so would this room. I'd paint the walls in a lovely soft gray and replace some of my colorful belongings with shades of white and cream, get rid of some of the Pepto-Bismol pink.

The gingham curtains would have to go. And I'd need some new throw pillows.

I could almost see it all now.

One thing that would never go: Papaw's rolltop desk. I used it to write my articles for *Mabank Happenings*. It would hold a place of honor in my tiny room as long as I lived here.

However long that might be.

Maybe forever, the way things looked right now.

A short while later, I dozed off, still thinking about how the day had gone. I must've slept like a stone because I didn't hear my alarm go off. I did, however, hear my phone buzzing as a call came through.

Still half-asleep, I answered it to a brusque male voice: "This is Harlan Reed from the Big Red Bid."

"Oh, yes." I kicked back the covers.

"You guys picked up the truck without letting me know. I said to call first."

"Oh, sorry." I sat up in the bed and stifled a yawn. "I didn't realize Mason already sent a tow truck to get it. What time is it anyway?"

"Seven fifteen."

"Man. I thought he said midmorning. Sorry." To my right, Riley stirred under the covers, finally popping her nose out.

"Well, someone came and got it. When I got here this morning, the truck was gone."

"*Gone* gone?"

"Yep. I left the keys on the dash for the tow truck driver, like you asked. But it would've been nice to have a heads-up. There's paperwork we still needed to sign, and I've got a copy of the title to pass off to you."

"So sorry."

"Can't figure out how he got past the gate, though." Harlan sounded troubled by this. "Found it locked, as usual."

"That's so strange." I hefted myself from the bed and took a few steps toward the bathroom. "Let me call you right back."

A couple of minutes later, I gave Mason a call.

He answered right away with a yawn. "You're up early."

"So are you. That's why I'm calling, actually. The auction house just called and said your guy picked up Tilly."

"Huh?" A definitive pause hung in the air between us. "I'm still in bed."

Alarm bells rang in my head. "Your guy didn't go get the truck?"

"How could he? I haven't called him yet. I planned to send him midmorning, like I said. Why?"

"Because Tilly is missing from the auction house parking lot, that's why."

"No way."

I could feel my pulse rate pick up as I spit out the words, "You told me to leave the keys on the dash, and I did. And now the truck is gone. Harlan seems to think your guy came and got her."

"I honestly don't know what happened to the truck, RaeLyn, but I had nothing to do with it, I promise."

My head was spinning as I thought through his impassioned words. "I'll call you back later when I know more."

"So, you don't need me to send one of my drivers over to get the truck. For real?"

"I guess not." I ended the call and slipped on a robe, then headed to the kitchen. I found Bessie Mae in her usual morning spot, seated at the table with her Bible open and a cup of coffee nearby.

Beams of early-morning sunlight peeked in through the windowed back door next to the breakfast table, showing off the fine lines on her face, which only deepened as her lips curled up in a smile.

She greeted me with a bright, "G'morning, sunshine!"

I grunted my response as I opened the back door to let Riley out. Then I reached for an empty coffee cup from the cupboard.

"RaeLyn? You okay, honey?"

"No." I walked to the coffeepot and grabbed a cup. "Tilly's gone missing."

"What?" She pushed her chair back and grabbed her empty cup. "Are you serious?"

"Yeah, Harlan Reed just called me. When he got to the auction house this morning, the truck was gone from the parking lot." I poured a generous amount of creamer into my coffee and gave it a stir.

"Mason said he was going to have her towed this morning, right?"

"Yes. And I left the keys on the dash so the tow truck driver could move her. I just talked to Mason, and he claims he didn't send his guy yet. And the gate was locked, so I don't know how he would've gotten past it."

"Oh my."

"But. . ." My words hung in the air between us. Had Mason set me up? My expression must've conveyed that possibility because Bessie Mae rested her hand on my arm.

"But?" She gave me a tentative look as she released her hand and poured herself another cup of coffee.

"But I'm suddenly not so sure I believe him. He was the number one person bidding against me, after all. I suppose it's possible he. . ." My words drifted off as I thought this through.

Bessie Mae stopped midpour and stared at me. "RaeLyn Hadley, are you telling me you actually think that wonderful young man who sat at our table last night had something to do with Tilly's disappearance?"

Right now, in the heat of the moment, it was the only thing that made sense. "Yes, ma'am." I nodded. "I think he wormed his way into our family dinner last night to get the scoop on Tilly and to work some sort of plan to have her for himself." I plopped down at the table and took a sip.

"And here I thought he came because of my chicken and dumplings." Bessie Mae's lips curled down in a pout.

"Oh, I'm sure that was just the icing on the cake. But I suspect he came for far more than that. I should've known better than to trust him. He stole my best friend in high school, remember?"

"You mean, he picked your best friend over you." My aunt stared intently at me. "Isn't that really what happened?"

Ouch.

"Yes, and Stephanie and I parted ways. We were never close after that. I lost my best friend, and it was all his fault."

My aunt did not look convinced. "Stephanie was a sweet girl, but I never cared for how insecure you were around her." Bessie took a seat next to me at the breakfast table. "Besides, God has given you an amazing best friend in her place, one who's better suited to you."

I couldn't help but smile as she mentioned Tasha, my BFF. Though she was a couple of years younger than me, we were as close as sisters. Feisty and full of warmth and sass, Tasha was far kinder to me than Stephanie had ever been. Still, that didn't negate what Mason might have done with my truck.

Judging from the expression on my aunt's face, she wasn't buying my explanation. "Gracious. I always thought he was such a sweet boy." Bessie Mae clucked her tongue. "Never would've guessed him to be a friend thief. Or a car thief."

"Who's a car thief?" Dad's voice sounded from behind us, and I turned to see he was standing inside the open doorway. He stamped his feet on the mat and mumbled something about needing to order more cattle feed, then headed to the sink to wash his hands. I knew Mom would scold him for not taking care of that task in the bathroom.

Sure enough, she turned up seconds later, clucking her tongue and reminding him that the kitchen sink should be used to wash dishes, not clean up his hands after he tended to his cattle.

Dad just shrugged and dried his hands on one of her pretty dish towels, then started grumbling because Dallas and Gage were still sleeping at this time of morning. We got an earful about how lazy those boys were, and how they weren't going to amount to a hill of beans if they didn't stop playing video games all night and sleeping all day.

I couldn't really argue the point.

"If they're not going to keep up with their chores around the property, then we'll have to boot 'em or insist they get real jobs," Dad said. "They're supposed to be mowing today and then helping me with that busted fence on the northeast corner of the property."

Mom didn't look happy with that proclamation. The twins were her babies, after all.

"Chuck, they'll grow out of it," she argued. "It's just a phase."

"A phase that started when they were ten and hasn't ended yet." My dad opened a cupboard and grabbed his favorite coffee mug. "Thank goodness for Jake. He's up at the crack of dawn, feeding the animals before he heads to the school. And did you see how helpful he was to me during hay baling season? At least I'll have someone willing to keep up the place after I'm gone."

"What am I?" I asked. "Chopped liver?"

"No, honey." He paused and gave me a kiss on the forehead. "You're the one who's probably going to end up taking care of us all."

Oh boy.

"You've been busy setting up the antique store, and doing a fine job of it," Mom said. "Exactly what we needed you to do, and we're grateful."

"Yep. You just find yourself a hardworking husband, RaeLyn," Dad said. "Someone who can help Jake keep the ship afloat after we're gone."

And here we were again, talking about marrying me off.

"Why are we going on about everyone dying?" Bessie Mae looked back and forth between my Mom and Dad. "I'm twenty-five years older than either of you, and I don't plan to kick the bucket anytime soon."

"I like to be prepared," Dad said. "That's all. Now, why are we talking about car thieves? What's happened?"

I explained that Tilly was missing from the auction house, sharing every detail about my phone conversation with Harlan.

Creases formed between my dad's bushy brows as he said, "Well, that has to be a mistake."

"That, or Mason isn't who he is pretending to be," I countered. "What if that whole dinner routine last night was just to throw us off track so he could take the prize? He was bidding against us, after all."

Mom shook her head. "That's just silly. Mason wouldn't do that. It has to be someone else."

"Maybe it was that blond," my dad said. "The one who's married to Harlan Reed."

"*Was* married to Harlan Reed," Mom added. "They've been divorced for several months. Meredith was wife number four. I know the whole story, if you want details."

"Right now I just want Tilly." I slumped into my seat at the breakfast table and released my hold on my coffee cup. The idea that I'd lost the truck and six thousand dollars was almost more than I could manage this early in the morning. Why now, after all we'd been through?

It wasn't fair. . .any of it.

CHAPTER SIX

"I know you want Tilly home, safe and sound, honey." Mom gave me a sympathetic look. "And the good Lord knows that. I have no doubt He'll bring her back here where she belongs."

I fell silent as my mind went back to all of the goings-on at the auction house yesterday, particularly after winning the bid. I played through the whole thing in my memory, trying to make sense of it, especially the parts involving Mason. And Meredith.

And that's pretty much where my imagination stopped, whenever I thought about the two of them, seated together, and her asking for a six-thousand-dollar check from me just after.

Had I been set up by this dastardly duo? It certainly looked that way, no matter how differently my parents and aunt felt. Mason and Meredith could very well be a team, working some sort of scam. Should I call Harlan and let him know?

"Am I the only one who found it odd that Meredith tried to get me to give her a check?" I said after thinking it through. "You're sure she's the auction owner's wife?"

"*Ex*-wife," Mom chimed in. "And I don't trust Meredith as far as I can throw her. From what I've heard, she's from Dallas."

"We can't trust her. . .because she's from Dallas?" I knew my mother frowned on city folks, but this was taking things a bit too far.

"No, we can't trust her because she was tangled up with Harlan Reed, who met her when he went to Dallas to pick up some auction items from her."

"My stars, you know a lot about the two of them," I observed.

I knew Harlan to be a kind and respected businessman in the area, so Mom's concerns totally threw me.

"Harlan Reed is what your papaw used to call a *rounder.*" Dad gave me a knowing look, then leaned in close. "He gets around."

"I see." That did cast him in a new light.

"That man has been married more times than I've been to Brookshire Brothers," Bessie Mae added.

"That's a lot of wives," I said. After all, Bessie Mae looked for an excuse to go to our local grocery store at least four or five days a week, if not more.

Mom leaned back in her chair, a thoughtful look on her face. "He's caused more damage than a tornado in springtime, and we know how dangerous those are. That man has left a trail of broken hearts over the years. As I said, I have details, if anyone cares to hear them."

"With four wives, I'm thinking this is going to be a long story." My dad leaned back in his seat. "Can we have the *Reader's Digest* version?"

"I stopped counting after the third wife," Bessie Mae said. "So I don't know a lot about Meredith."

"I know enough to know she's a piece of work." Mom stirred her coffee, then took a sip.

"Goodness. How do you know all of these things?" I asked.

Mom gave me a look that said, "Trust me," followed by a whispered, "I'm on the prayer team at church. I know *all* the things."

"Are you saying this woman goes to our church?" If so, why had I never noticed her before?

"Heavens, no." Mom fanned herself. "Wife number one, Gloria, goes to our church."

"Gloria *Pappas*?" How did I not know she was once married to Harlan Reed?

Mom offered a curt nod. "Yes, ma'am, she was married to that awful man for seven years. After he broke her heart, she decided it was better to go back to her maiden name. I fully supported her decision."

"And she keeps up with his goings-on?" My dad asked.

Mom reached for her coffee cup. "Oh yes. She was particularly invested in wife number two, as you might imagine, since she's the one who took Gloria's place. But then the craziest thing happened. Sheila—that's the second wife—was diagnosed with cancer not long after Harlan left her for another woman."

"Oh dear." This story wasn't getting much better.

The tight expression on Mom's face relaxed. "Yes, such a sad story. But you know Gloria—"

"Not really," I confessed.

"She has a heart of gold, so she ended up taking care of Sheila until she passed a year later. Would you believe Harlan didn't even bother showing up for her funeral?"

"Gracious." The man *was* a cad. "Then came Meredith?"

"No." Mom shook her head. There was the one in-between, but that's the wife we don't speak of. We just call her Number Three."

"Why?"

"There are certain things we just don't talk about."

"Even on the prayer team?" I quirked a brow.

Mom pretended to zip her lips. Good gravy. If this one was beyond the help of the prayer team at First Baptist, Number Three must surely be a piece of work. I'd hate to meet up with her, at least with Mom around.

"Anyway, she didn't last long," Mom said. "And then came Meredith."

"Number Four." If my math was right.

"Yep. But she left the marriage several months ago, according to Gloria. And trust me when I say this was the first time one of the wives ever left Harlan, and not the other way around. But I'm not saying I blame her."

"Not sure I do either," Bessie Mae said. "Though it breaks my heart to hear about couples breaking up."

Mom nearly lost her grip on her coffee cup, and a bit of the liquid splashed onto her hand. She wiped it off with a paper towel. "All I know is, Harlan Reed apparently owes Meredith a lot of money. When they split, she was supposed to get half of his worth. Texas is a community property state, you know. Both parties automatically get half of what they mutually own."

"Unless there's a prenuptial agreement," I chimed in. "Right? Surely Harlan Reed had one of those. A man with that many wives would surely require a prenup." I couldn't imagine he would be foolish enough to go into a fourth marriage without one, especially since he owned a valuable business.

"Maybe." Mom shrugged. "Hadn't thought of that. But the long and short of it is, Meredith feels like she's owed."

"And that's why she tried to get me to make out a check and give it to her?" I asked. "Because that's still wrong, no matter how much money he owes her."

"Agreed. And we'll never know if she planned to keep that check or pass it off to him. Just thought you'd appreciate a little backstory."

The prayer team was really coming in handy for backstory on Harlan.

"Well. . ." Mom released a sigh. "Here's the thing. Gloria still loves him. He was the only husband she ever had, and she's been standing in faith, believing he'll come back to her."

"Mom!" I gasped. "Are you saying Gloria would still have him, even after all of this?"

"Sounds like she's got a bad case of the I-Love-Yous, honey." Mom shrugged. "Sometimes you can't help who you fell in love with, even if it's a scoundrel like Harlan Reed."

At this very moment, Meredith was looking like a bigger scoundrel, but I didn't bother saying so. I hated to interrupt my mom's twisted story. But I couldn't imagine Wife Number One would still want Harlan back, not with three other wives sandwiched into the story.

"Harlan won't stay single long." Dad pushed his chair back. "Mark my words." He reached for his baseball cap on the hook by the back door and excused himself to go out to start the mower, which he planned to use in front of the twins' window.

"And now Harlan's back on the prowl," Mom said. "According to Gloria."

"Searching for Wife Number Five, no doubt," Bessie Mae said. She rose and carried her coffee cup to the sink, then started rinsing it out.

I was having a hard time keeping up with wives one through four but didn't say so. I didn't want Mom to have to repeat this story.

"So, you do me a favor, RaeLyn." Mom reached over and grabbed my hand. "If you go back up to the auction house, keep your wits about you. Don't be swept in by that, that. . ." She released a slow breath.

Okay, I now saw where she was going with this. "Mom! Are you afraid he might hit on me?"

"Pretty girl like you?" She gave me a pensive look. "You can count on it."

"I will run in the opposite direction, I promise. After knocking him upside his head." My older brothers had raised me right. I could defend myself if the situation called for it.

She withdrew her hand, then her face lit up. "I have an idea. Take Mason with you. If Harlan thinks you and Mason are a couple, he'll leave you alone."

"Mom!"

"You're right." She released a sigh. "That won't work. Meredith was married when he hit on her. Harlan has never been stopped by competition, even someone as handsome as Mason Fredericks."

"Good grief." Though she wasn't wrong about the handsome part. Mason did look like he stepped off the cover of *Tool Time* magazine. But I would never ask him to go up to the auction house with me. I wasn't sure the guy could be trusted, after all.

Mom headed back outside, and Aunt Bessie turned her attention to the breakfast dishes. I couldn't stop my mind from wandering. Our conversation was making me nervous about having to go back to the Big Red Bid on my own. Maybe I could talk one of my brothers into going with me. Or Dad. He would give Harlan a piece of his mind, if need be.

No. Suddenly I knew exactly who I would take with me. My girl Tasha. She would know exactly what to do. And best of all, she could probably calm me down and help me think more rationally. Tasha always seemed to have that effect on me.

But first, I had to take care of one teensy-tiny thing. In the back of my mind, I still wondered if Mason was telling me the truth when he said that he barely knew Meredith. There was one way to know for sure.

I grabbed my phone and signed onto Facebook then went straight to his account.

And that's when I saw—very clearly—that the two of them were, in fact, friends. Well, at least on social media. She had even left a post near the top of his page, right there in public view, telling him how great it was to hang out with him at the auction.

And in that moment, I had the strangest feelings creep over me. Had Mason come back to Mabank after all of these years to be with Meredith? Were the two of them a duo? Is that why she had left Harlan Reed, to develop a relationship with Mason Fredericks?

Were they simply hiding that fact so that they could walk off with Tilly? My Tilly?

The idea left me feeling absolutely ill inside.

I rose and paced the room, ready to figure this out once and for all; then I picked up the phone to call my best friend. . .just as my two youngest brothers shuffled into the kitchen in search of food, grumbling about the noise coming from the mower outside their bedroom window. My thoughts were so diverted to the matter at hand that I barely paid attention.

This much I did see: Bessie Mae dove right in, fixing pancakes and sausage for those lazy boys and catering to their every whim. Heaven help them if Dad came back in while they were chowing down on all that food.

I punched in Tasha's number and walked out onto the back porch so that I could better hear the conversation. Off in the distance, the sound of the mower rang out, and before long I saw my dad round the corner of the house on the riding lawn mower.

My gaze swept over the acreage in front of me. Duchess, my favorite horse, ambled up to the gate, and I walked over to pat her on the head as the call went through.

Tasha answered on the third ring. "Well, good morning. It's kind of early, isn't it?"

"Depends on who you ask. I've been up a while, but Dallas and Gage just crawled out of bed."

"And Logan?"

"Tucked away in his hidey-hole. We never see him until later in the day. His whole life is a mystery to me."

"A handsome mystery."

An awkward silence hung in the air between us as I contemplated the possibility that my best friend might be interested in my loner brother. Weird.

"Anyway, I'm calling because I need someone to go with me to the auction house."

"Right now?" she countered. "I'm barely awake."

"Yep. Someone stole Tilly."

"Wait. . .what?"

I spit out the bare minimum of details, and twenty minutes later, Tasha's tiny truck squealed into my driveway. She bounded out and rushed my way with a *Let's get going!* expression on that animated face of hers.

My quick attempt at dressing for the day had me looking a little wrinkled and worn, but the same could not be said of my bestie. She had me beat in the looks department. There was no arguing that point. With her saucy red hair and bright green eyes, she captivated even the dullest of passersby. But today, her bright attire really caught my eye.

This gal had a penchant for over-the-top clothing. She treated her body more like a Macy's store mannequin than anything else, but with a figure like that, no one could fault her. Everyone else in Mabank was comfortable in their jeans and button-ups, but not this gal. Why fit in when you could stand out with a little shimmer and shine?

Okay, a lot of shimmer and shine.

And today she shone like a bright copper penny in a blouse that even Dolly Parton might have considered too much.

Tasha held out her arms and did a little twirl, showing off the glittering blouse and fancy jeans, complete with jewels embedded. I hadn't seen jeans like that for at least a decade. Or two. But who was I to question another woman's fashion choices?

Five minutes after that, the two of us were on our way to town in her truck.

With the bright morning sun streaming in the window, Tasha's fiery red hair seemed a more vibrant shade than usual, the kind that really stood out in a crowd. This gal had what mom called "attention-gettin' hair."

She also had the sweetest freckle-faced charm of anyone I knew, which only added to her likability.

"So, bring me up to speed," Tasha said as she glanced my way. "You won the bid on Tilly?"

"Yes. Then Mason came to dinner, and the next thing you know, Tilly's missing!"

"Wait." She tapped the brakes as we neared a turn in the bumpy road. "Mason Fredericks came to your house for dinner?"

"Yeah." I sighed as I realized I'd left him out of the details in our phone call. "He actually bid against me on the truck. Said he wanted it for his business. Seemed like an appropriate explanation at the time, but now I'm not so sure."

"I haven't seen him since he went off to college." A thoughtful look came over her. "I heard he was coming back to open a car shop of some sort."

"His dad's old place. He flips vintage cars and trucks. Well, he's going to. I think he's only been back a few weeks so far."

"Oh, that's cool."

"Anyway, last night he seemed totally fine that I outbid him. But this morning, I got a call from the auction house owner saying the truck had been stolen."

"And your thoughts immediately went to Mason?" she asked.

"Yeah, and for obvious reason. He told me that he would send a tow truck driver to the auction house this morning to get Tilly and bring her home."

"Sounds like a sweet guy, not a thief. Maybe that's just what he did. Maybe Tilly's on her way to your house right now?"

"Nope." I shook my head. "I called him first thing. He was sound asleep. Hadn't even talked to his tow truck driver yet to give him instructions."

"So, Tilly just disappeared from the auction house parking lot?" She tapped the brakes and swerved to avoid a pothole in the road.

"Yes. Which is behind a locked gate, no less. And she doesn't run, so it's not like someone drove her off. Though I did leave the keys on the dash, so I suppose someone else could've had her towed if they figured out how to get past the gate."

"I'm sure it's just a misunderstanding. This will get ironed out, RaeLyn. These things always do." Her driving evened out, and she turned her attention to the road as we approached a curve.

"I hope so. But I left out the part of the story where he was sitting with the Empire State Building."

"The Empire State Building?" She shot a curious look my way.

"Sorry. Statue of Liberty. I always get those two confused."

"Now *I'm* really confused too. But let's let that part slide until we have more details, okay?"

"Okay." I released a loud sigh. She would probably think I was crazy anyway. But right now I just had to figure out if this dastardly duo had stolen my Tilly, and the sooner, the better!

CHAPTER SEVEN

We reached the edge of Cedar Creek Lake and started the drive across on the bridge, the bright sun shining down on us and causing the water to shimmer. I did my best to push my errant thoughts away, at least for now. I'd often been accused of having an overactive imagination, and it sometimes got me into trouble. So I needed to stay calm and not let it run away with me.

Instead, I turned my attention to the north side of the bridge. The early-morning sun rippled across the waters of the lake, a beautiful sight on any day but particularly mesmerizing at this time of day. I allowed it to soothe me as I watched the rays of sunlight at play.

That somehow led to a conversation about Clayton Henderson's new place on the far side of the lake, which seemed to get my bestie riled up.

"You heard he's got a big grand opening coming up next weekend, right?" Tasha rolled her eyes with such vigor that I could imagine her driving us backward off the bridge. "Can you believe it?"

"Yeah." Though I hadn't given it much thought. No more than I'd given any of his other business ventures over the past several years anyway. Clayton Henderson owned everything else, why not a B and B too? What did it really matter anyway? We needed all of the successful businesses we could get in the area, after all. Keeping Mabank healthy and thriving was important.

"There's a rumor going around that Clayton's got financial troubles," she said.

I countered with, "Sure doesn't act like it."

But then again, maybe that's why he stopped bidding on Tilly when he did.

"You know I've always wanted to open a B and B," Tasha said.

And there it was, the real reason why his new place of business bothered her so much.

Tasha went off on a tangent about the property she hoped to buy in Gun Barrel City on the lake. "It's been a part of the five-year plan for four years now, which means I'm down to the final year and no closer to my goal, which really stinks. You know?"

"Right." I knew. She'd talked about little else for the past year. And this girl with her five-year plan! Who was that organized?

Okay, I was pretty organized myself. I'd been plotting and planning the opening of Trinkets and Treasures for months now, as well as saving money for Tilly's purchase. Maybe Tasha and I were more alike than I realized, minus the snazzy clothes and bright red hair.

"Just about the time I save enough money to start looking at properties, I find out Clayton Henderson is opening his new place in Gun Barrel City. Ugh. I just can't keep up."

I understood her concern.

No matter how hard people tried to compete with Clayton, he always one-upped them.

Take that time Papaw gave a thousand-dollar offering for the new furnace at church.

Clayton gave ten thousand, right on the heels of my grandfather's offering, knowing full well he would get all of the accolades.

That was just the kind of man Clayton Henderson was. A showboat. And everyone in the county knew it. So, why my friend was trying to compete with him, I could not say. Still, I hated to see her discouraged.

"I'm dying to see what he's done with the place," she said. "If I'm going to have my own B and B, I'd better see the competition."

"There are plenty of opportunities around the lake for more B and Bs,"

I argued. "You can still build one too. Yours will be cuter. . .and probably more affordable for the common folk like us."

She glanced my way, feigning offense. "Hey, who's calling me common?"

"Sorry. You know what I mean."

"I do." She sighed and turned her attention back to the road as we reached the city side of the bridge. "But the point is, he always seems to beat everyone to the punch. Life is so unfair. Why do some people get to be so rich and the rest of us so. . ."

We weren't poor. Middle class would be more like it.

"Maybe common was the right word after all," Tasha said after a moment's pause. "Even if I find just the right piece of property, I can't begin to compete with the place he's built. It's top of the line. Mine will just be. . ." Her words trailed off.

"Tasha! You're the most creative, colorful person I know. Anything you come up with is going to be light-years better. You'll make it eclectic. You'll make it your own. And people will come back to stay there time and time again because of its uniqueness."

"From your mouth to God's ears," she said.

"No, from His mouth to *your* ears," I countered. "He's the one who gave you this dream; He will be the one to fulfill it. And besides, Clayton doesn't always get his way."

"Oh yeah?" She gave me an *I don't believe you* look.

"Yep, it's true. He bid on Tilly too, and I outbid him. That should make you feel better."

"Wow. No way." She looked my way, eyes widening. "You beat out the richest guy in town at the auction?"

"I did."

"How much did you spend anyway?"

"Too much." I sighed. "Six thousand dollars."

"Whoa."

"Exactly. And the idea that someone else took off with what I paid for makes my stomach hurt."

"We'll find her."

"I hope so. Because now I have no vehicle and a near-empty savings account."

"Oh, RaeLyn." She gave me a sympathetic look. "This truck really means a lot to you, doesn't it?"

"You have no idea. And did I mention I have no car now?"

"I'll drive you wherever you want to go. Just call me anytime." She changed lanes without using her signal, and I bit my lip to keep from mentioning it. This girl drove like I folded my clothes—haphazardly.

"Do you think Clayton might've stolen Tilly? I wouldn't put it past him." She dove into a lengthy conversation about what a no-good businessman he was, but I had to stop her.

"We have no proof he did anything like that," I countered. "Just because he bid against me doesn't mean he stole her."

"I guess." Still, she didn't look convinced.

We pulled into the parking lot at the Big Red Bid a few minutes later. Harlan emerged and took one look at Tasha and I, and the worry lines on his brow straightened out. Suddenly the fellow had a swagger in his step and a twinkle in his eye as he ambled our way. Hopefully it was just the effect of my BFF's colorful blouse.

Nope. Nada. He was aiming his attentions straight at me. And I didn't even sparkle, not one little bit. Was Mom right? Did this fella have some kind of interest in me?

His eyes locked onto mine, and I broke out in a sweat. I didn't have the energy to fend off a creep today, so I decided to be forward in my approach to the problem at hand, to keep him focused.

"Mr. Reed, I'm here to talk about—"

"Call me Harlan." A smile tipped up the edges of his lips, and the morning sunlight picked up wisps of gray in his thick mustache.

"I'm here to talk about Tilly."

"Tilly?" His eyes narrowed.

"The truck that disappeared this morning," I explained. "Do you have any news yet?"

"No. I was hoping you did."

"Have you called the police?" These words came from Tasha, who was suddenly all business. "I would have called them first thing, myself."

"No." He shook his head. "I was giving you an opportunity to reach out to the tow truck driver to make sure he didn't take it without letting you know. Someone towed it away."

"I called Mason right after I talked to you. He was sound asleep. Said he never contacted the tow truck driver. So. . ." I shrugged.

"Well, that stinks. I was hoping they just showed up earlier than planned."

"Me too."

"Though I still couldn't figure out how he got past the gate." Harlan pulled his phone out of his pocket, gave it a quick glance, and then shoved it back into place.

Before I could say anything else, a shiny silver Lexus pulled into a parking spot next to where we were standing.

Tasha gave it a close look and then groaned aloud. "Really?"

I glanced over to discover Clayton Henderson emerging from the driver's side. He took several decisive steps toward us, his attention on Harlan.

"I'm here to pick up the '67 Buick Riviera, Harlan."

Ah. He must've won that after we left the auction.

"Brought the little woman so she can drive my car home." Clayton raised his hand and waved toward his Lexus, signaling his wife to join us.

The passenger side door of the Lexus opened, and she stepped out into the morning sunlight. I'd always liked Nadine Henderson, though she did seem a bit aloof at times. Not that her husband ever really let her get a word in edgewise. And what was up with that "little woman" comment? Was the guy always this demeaning to the ladies?

As if to prove my point, he gave me a curt nod.

"So, you won the bid on the Chevy truck after all," he said, more statement than question. "Are you here to pick her up?"

"I wish." My response was guarded. "Tilly was stolen out of the parking lot this morning before I could get her towed to my place."

His eyes widened. "Stolen?"

"Yep." I took a cleansing breath and narrowed my gaze, determined to keep a close eye on his expression to see if there were secrets lurking behind that cocky expression.

"That's crazy."

To my right, Tasha cleared her throat, then reached into her purse for a cough drop.

Clayton turned to acknowledge her. "Tasha. How've you been?"

I couldn't help but notice the smirk on her face as she responded, "Great. Terrific. Awesome. Never better."

"You could've stopped with great. How's the B and B of yours coming along? Did you ever find the right piece of property?"

"I have not. But I will."

"Awesome. The more the merrier. Oh, and in case I forgot to mention it, we're having an open house out at our new place on Saturday. Nadine's making hors d'oeuvres, and we're doing a big giveaway for a free one-week stay. You should all come." He glanced at his wife. "Honey, get them a brochure."

Nadine scurried off to their car and came back with a multicolored trifold brochure, which she passed our way. I saw the look on Tasha's face and decided I'd better take it. Nadine also gave one to Harlan, who folded it and tucked it into his pocket.

Harlan turned his full attention to Clayton and Nadine, leaving Tasha and I standing alone in the parking lot while they walked toward the office together.

"See how it is?" The look of exasperation on Tasha's face shared her truest feelings. "The man just walks in, and everyone stops what they were doing to wait on him first. It's infuriating."

I had to admit, it was a little ridiculous. Harlan was talking to us first, after all. Now he couldn't seem to remember that we existed. Clayton just seemed to have that effect on people.

A few minutes later, Clayton drove off in the '67 Buick, his wife trailing behind him in their fancy Lexus. And Harlan was free to turn his attention to us once again. After Tasha gave him an earful about making us wait.

With the wave of a hand, he appeared to dismiss her concerns. "Well, if you folks are sure you weren't the ones who hauled off that truck this morning, I have no choice but to give the sheriff's office a call. Let's do that right now."

Minutes later the rhythmic wailing of sirens pierced through the quiet morning air. Somehow that sound only made the realization of what had happened even more glaring.

Knowing that Tilly was gone hit me like a sucker punch to the gut.

My emotions kicked into overdrive as the Henderson County cruiser pulled into the parking lot.

A deputy stepped out of the car, his dark, crisp uniform making this even more official. He took several steps in our direction, clipboard in hand, and my nerves tightened my stomach into knots.

"Morning, folks." He introduced himself as Officer Warren, then tucked the clipboard under his arm and looked back and forth between us. "What've we got here?"

"Stolen vehicle," Harlan said.

I tried to dive into an explanation but got tangled up in the story—delving way too much into the part about my grandfather's death than was probably necessary.

"Whoa, whoa." Officer Warren put his hand up. "Are you saying there's been a homicide too?"

"No." Harlan and I spoke in unison.

"No one died," I explained. "We've called you here so that we can report a truck that's been stolen. That's all."

But somehow the words "that's all" seemed too trivial a response. My family had already lost Tilly once. The idea that we might have lost her again was almost too much to bear.

CHAPTER EIGHT

"What's she's trying to say," Tasha interjected, "is that the missing vehicle once belonged to her grandfather, who passed ten years ago. The truck was up for auction here yesterday, and she won the bid. But before she could have it picked up, someone absconded with it."

The officer gave Tasha an admiring look, then glanced my way. "From now on, let her do all of the explaining."

Tasha beamed like a proud mama.

Officer Warren and Harlan dove into a conversation about the safety measures used at the auction house.

"Don't you have a security guard?" the officer asked.

"No, we keep most of the stuff inside in locked storage," Harlan responded. "And we just had everything rekeyed less than a month ago. Only the vehicles stay outside, and they're behind the gate, which has its own automated locking system."

"Is that new too?" Warren asked.

"Yep. C'mon and I'll show you."

Harlan started by showing us the gate with its fancy locking system. "It's open right now, obviously, but when I got here this morning it was closed and locked."

"You're sure?" Warren asked.

Harlan nodded. "Yeah, I opened it just like every other day. Never would have guessed someone messed with it. Very strange."

"Who else has access to a key?" Officer Warren asked.

"Ben. He's worked for me for years. But he's never once done anything to make me suspect him of anything wrong. And he's the one who noticed the truck was missing. He pulled in just after I did this morning and noticed the truck was gone."

"Anyone else have access?"

Harlan seemed to lose himself to his thoughts for a moment. "Well, maybe my ex-wife still has a key. I guess that's possible. She used to work here."

"Meredith?" I asked.

He nodded. "Yeah. Don't get me started."

I turned to face the officer. "Well, speaking of Meredith, something odd happened yesterday when I came out to settle my bid."

"What's that?" He looked up from whatever he had been writing down.

"Meredith was here with a clipboard, acting like she worked here. She tried to get me to write her a check."

"Yeah." Harlan's brow furrowed and wrinkles formed around his eyes. "Heard all about that from Ben. I'm mighty glad you didn't give Meredith that check."

"Me too, but why was she here?"

"Well. . ." He kicked the gravel on the ground below with the toe of his boot, his gaze trailing down. A pause followed, but then he looked my way. "Let's just say some folks can't be trusted, and leave it at that."

"Do you think there's any chance she might have been working with someone else?" I asked. "Like. . .a partner?"

"A partner?" His eyes narrowed and then his mouth rounded into an O. "I see where you're going with this. You think she's involved with someone? Like. . .a man?"

"Well, I don't know. I'm just asking. You said she can't be trusted, so. . ."

Officer Warren scribbled something down on his notepad then looked at Harlan. "Mr. Reed, do you think there's any chance at all she took the truck when she didn't end up with that check?"

Harlan shrugged. "I guess anything's possible. She's got experience with tow trucks and knows some of the drivers around town. So, I guess it's feasible she might've hired one on the sly and then opened the gate for them."

"How could she pull that off, though?" Tasha asked. "Why would they believe her that the truck was hers?"

"Meredith is the kind of woman who uses her. . ." He paused and appeared to be thinking. "Charms. To woo men, I mean. I could totally see her contacting a tow truck driver from outside the county, someone unfamiliar with our marital situation, to pick up that truck for her."

"But why *that* truck?" I asked. "She could have picked any truck or car she liked."

"Because she knows how this works." Harlan sighed. "Some of these vehicles—like that particular make and model—go for a lot less at auction when they're really worth a lot more. She could have won it, flipped it, and sold it for a lot more."

"Ah."

Ben had said that Tilly was worth a lot more than six thousand dollars, hadn't he?

"So, maybe she had this planned the whole time?" I said. "If she didn't win the bid, she would just come and take her."

On the other hand, how did Meredith know that Tilly would be staying overnight in the lot. . .unless someone told her.

A shiver ran down my spine as I thought about Mason's quick offer to have Tilly towed to my house this morning. He knew all the particulars, didn't he?

I did my best to wipe those thoughts from my mind as Harlan suggested we all walk over to where the truck had been parked overnight.

He then led us across the parking lot, and we all followed. I swallowed hard when I saw the empty spot where Tilly had been sitting just yesterday. My heart twisted as I relived that moment when I'd first seen her, first touched her. Now she was gone.

"Whoever took her, took her from this spot," Harlan explained. "It would've been a tricky tow, for sure."

"What about a security camera?" Tasha asked. "Maybe the whole incident was recorded."

"I've got one inside and another near the office. But nothing that shows up in this particular corner of the yard. Never felt I needed it because the gate stays locked."

"Well, that figures," Tasha interjected. "But this might be a good day to go buy one."

"Right." He raked his fingers through his hair, and I wondered—my toupee suspicions growing—if the whole head of hair might lift clean off his head.

Nope. It stayed put.

"I'll be looking into that, I promise," Harlan said. "But somehow someone got in here and moved that truck out without anyone knowing, and my first thought is that it must have been Meredith."

Officer Warren looked up from his clipboard. "I'll need the name and contact information for this woman, if you have it."

"Yeah, I've got it," Harlan said. "And just so you're aware, she's a classic, not a junker."

"The woman?" Officer Warren's brows arched.

"No, the truck," Harlan explained. "We're talking about an antique Chevy, not some junker. If Meredith took it—and I guess we have to consider that possibility—she will sell it off for a wad of cash. . .a lot more than what was paid for it yesterday. It's likely she'll go out of the county, maybe even out of the state, to do that, though."

"But we can track the VIN number, right?" I asked.

"Maybe." He rested his weight against the car behind him. "But it's nothing to change out a VIN number. If you know what you're doing. And trust me when I say that Meredith knows how to sneak around and get away with things." He paused. "That I've seen firsthand."

I groaned as I pondered the notion that she might do just that.

"Do you have unsettled financial issues with Mrs. Reed, Harlan?" Officer Warren asked.

Harlan glanced down at the ground, then back up again. "Nothing worth mentioning. Anyway, come into the office, and I'll get the information."

We all tagged along behind him once again, this time heading inside to the offices of the Big Red Bid. Harlan gestured for Tasha and I to take a seat in the waiting room, and he led the way into the inner office with Officer Warren following.

"What do you think, RaeLyn?" Tasha asked. "Sure sounds like Harlan is right. It had to have been his ex-wife. She was bidding against you, she tried to take money from you, and she had a key to the gate. And she knows people in the towing business who could have helped her."

"Sounds pretty cut-and-dried," I admitted. "Hopefully we can track her down and find Tilly quickly."

"No, ma'am." Officer Warren's voice sounded from behind me, and I realized he had joined us once again. "You'll leave that to us. We don't need you snooping around her place. Some folks would think nothing of harming a trespasser. That's the last thing we need right now."

"Oh, I wouldn't trespass," I said. "I was just thinking of driving by her place to see if the vehicle is there."

"I'll do that, first thing. But I'm guessing she's moved it to a remote location, probably out of Mabank, as Mr. Reed said. I'm guessing that truck is out of the county now."

"She's got family in Kaufman," Harlan said as he joined us once again. "A brother."

Officer Warren asked for that brother's address, and Harlan said he'd have to look it up.

Then the police officer turned my way. "Okay, Miss Hadley, let's talk about the truck. Can you give me details? Any distinct features or modifications that could help us identify it?"

I described Tilly to the best of my ability—the once-vibrant red color, now faded to a rusty shade. The worn leather seats, and the custom chrome grille my grandfather had installed years ago. As I spoke, Officer Warren jotted down notes.

"She's a 1952 Chevy 3100," I responded. "Part of the Advanced Design series."

He gave me an inquisitive stare. "You know a lot about this truck."

"Oh yeah. She was my papaw's baby. He took care of her."

"So, pristine condition, then?" He scribbled this down, and I stopped him.

"Oh no. Papaw died ten years ago, but just before he passed he sold her to a collector in Kaufman. He needed the money to pay for his cancer meds at the time, but it nearly wrecked us to let Tilly go."

Even speaking the words aloud now brought back the pain of that decision. I was young at the time, only a sophomore, but watching my grandfather go through chemo—and feeling the pain of losing Tilly in the middle of it all—still wrecked me.

We should have tried to save her.

Ultimately, we couldn't even save him. And the pain of that still haunted me.

Tasha rested her hand on my arm. "I had forgotten that part, RaeLyn. It was all so sad."

"It really was." I fought the temptation to sigh aloud. A lump rose in my throat as I relived the moment our family had watched Tilly being driven away by her new owner.

Officer Warren wrote something down, then glanced my way. "So, what is the vehicle's current condition, then?"

"Rusty. The interior seats have some tears. And the glove box was busted open. The lock had been messed with and the whole thing pried loose."

"Anything else?"

A few dents and dings but nothing that couldn't be fixed," I said. "When I saw she'd come up for auction, I rushed right over to see her. I knew that these older model trucks don't last long on the auction block. They're highly collectible."

"Other than the woman you've already mentioned, do you have anyone else in mind who might have wanted to steal the truck?" He gave me a pensive look. "Anyone at all who seemed interested in her?"

I hesitated, considering whether to mention the suspects that had been swirling in my mind. Instead, I opted for a more cautious response. "There were others bidding on her. We had quite the bidding war, actually. But I won in the end."

"Beating out the richest guy in town," Tasha said. "That's something."

Warren gave me an inquisitive look. "You know the other bidders personally?"

"Yeah." I hesitated. "Well, sort of." I filled him in, shifting my attention to details about Wyatt Jackson in particular.

"So, this elderly man seemed interested in the truck?"

Harlan chimed in with a loud, "Oh yeah. I can't believe he stopped bidding on her when he did, to be honest. He came early and went through the truck from side to side. Said he had to have her or die trying."

"Wyatt had a longtime feud with our family," I explained. "I never really understood it all, but my parents seem to think he's the most obvious person to steal the truck."

I carried on, giving the officer details of Wyatt's home, where he lived, and so on.

"Anyone else stand out?" He asked when I came up for breath.

"Well, there's always Mason Fredericks."

Creases formed around Warren's eyes, and he appeared to be thinking this through. "Mason Fredericks, the guy who owns the new car shop up the street?"

"Yeah."

Warren still didn't look convinced but jotted down his name. "What makes you think he might want the truck?"

"He bid against me and was the last one to tap out. I felt sure he might win her in the end, but I did."

"That doesn't make him a truck thief."

"True." I hoped he was right. Surely my suspicions of Mason were unfounded. The man had just eaten my aunt's chicken and dumplings last night. Surely he couldn't rob me blind with a belly full of my aunt's chicken and dumplings and dewberry cobbler on his lips. Right?

"Actually, Mason and Meredith were sitting together at the auction," I interjected. "And I found out this morning that they're Facebook friends. So maybe they're..."

"Working together?" Tasha interjected. "RaeLyn thinks they're working together."

Harlan groaned aloud. "More likely she's using him like she uses everyone else."

"Well, we'll follow up, starting with going by Meredith's place," Warren said. "If we need to involve Fredericks, we will."

I felt a sick feeling in the pit of my stomach as I realized how awkward this could get. If I was wrong about Mason's involvement, he might never forgive me if the police questioned him.

The officer nodded, his expression maintaining a level of professional skepticism. "All right, Miss Hadley. I'll get this information in the system. In the meantime, keep your eyes open. We'll do the same."

"So, that's it?"

"We'll do our best to find the truck, I promise."

With a curt nod, he returned to his cruiser, leaving me standing there, staring at the empty space that once held Tilly. The investigation had begun, but I couldn't shake the feeling that the road to find her would be a long and winding one.

CHAPTER NINE

Right after we left the auction house, I got a call from Bessie Mae, asking me to pick up a few things from Brookshire Brothers on my way home. Tasha had no place else to be, so she didn't mind a bit. A few minutes later, we were perusing the store, talking through everything that had just taken place at the auction house.

"I think they'll find her, RaeLyn," Tasha said as she gave me a compassionate look. "We'll pray. She'll turn up. Just wait and see."

"I hope you're right." I did believe in the power of prayer, and it was definitely going to take some to see this thing through. Finding Tilly the first time was nothing short of a miracle. I'd stumbled across the ad in the local paper two weeks before the auction. If God had arranged all of that—and my winning the bid—surely He could take care of this.

I pushed my cart from aisle to aisle, trying to remember all of the things that Bessie Mae had asked for. She needed ingredients for chicken-fried steak, which she planned to make for dinner.

I did my best to check off items as we made our way from the meat department to produce. Then we headed to the baking aisle to grab ingredients for Bessie Mae's famous oatmeal cookies.

"If she's baking, I might have to hang around awhile," Tasha said.

"Never could turn away your aunt's cookies."

"Me either. If she keeps going, I'll end up twice this size." I strained to reach the baking soda, which was on the top shelf.

Tasha—a good five inches taller than me—nudged me aside and grabbed it for me. "Here you go, short stack."

"Thanks a lot. And for your information, I'm petite, not short. There's a difference."

"You're five foot three."

"And?"

"And as cute as a bug in a rug." She tossed the baking soda into the cart. "What else do we need?"

"Oats. They're on a different aisle, with the other cereals."

We turned into the breakfast foods aisle, and I saw something that made me lose my breath. Mason. And Meredith Reed. Together, in the cereal aisle. Okay, so maybe they were more than just Facebook friends if such a thing could be judged from their comfortable conversation. Maybe all our suspicions about the two of them working together weren't so unfounded after all.

I veered back toward the far end of the aisle, planting myself behind a large display of walnuts.

"Why are we hiding?" Tasha asked. She peered around the display and then looked back at me. "Is that Mason Fredericks?"

"Yeah."

She gave him another look then glanced my way, wide-eyed.

"RaeLyn Hadley! You didn't bother to mention that he was married when you told me he had come over to your house. That's a pretty important detail to leave out. I don't mind you having a crush on a guy, but not a *married* guy!"

"What makes you think he's married?"

She gave them another peek. "Well, for one thing, the two of them are picking out breakfast cereal together. And look at how that woman is hanging on his every word. She's cuckoo for Cocoa Puffs over him."

I gave the duo another look.

Ugh. She was hanging. And giggling. And flirting. I didn't even know Meredith Reed, but I didn't care for what I saw. And in this moment, I wasn't terribly crazy about Mason either. If they were working in tandem, they sure weren't doing a very good job of hiding their real relationship, now were they?

Or were my eyes deceiving me?

I squinted to give them a closer look. These two weren't behaving with the usual casual camaraderie you would expect from a couple of friends but, rather, something a bit more intimate. Well, at least from Meredith's end.

Warmth flooded my cheeks when I saw the twinkle in her eyes as she stared up at him and then giggled at something funny he said.

Okay, enough of this nonsense. Suddenly I couldn't get out of here fast enough.

I decided to skip the oats. Bessie Mae could make cookies another day. I turned and headed toward the registers at a pace that would've made a track star jealous.

"So?" Tasha struggled to keep up with me. "We're leaving, just because he's shopping with his wife?"

"That's not his wife. That's Meredith Reed, the one we were talking about just now. The one who tried to take the check from me."

"Harlan's ex? Really?"

I nodded.

"With Mason Fredericks?" Tasha turned back to face me, her mouth falling open. "So, they are working together after all! They look pretty cozy, I must say."

"I sure hope not, but you never know. He said he only met her casually when she showed up at his workplace to ask some questions about cars. But I looked her up online and she's friends with him on social media. I honestly don't know what to believe right now."

"I'm pretty good at reading body language, and she's definitely interested in more than his cars."

"Ugh."

Right now I just wanted to get away from him—from them.

As I headed toward the checkout line, my concerns deepened. Whoever Meredith was—or wasn't—she certainly knew how to captivate Mason Fredericks.

"I'm just saying, they seemed mighty friendly," Tasha said. "Did you see how she was resting her hand on his arm? That's a wife move. Or a girlfriend move, at the very least."

"I guess." I released a slow breath as we approached the line at register three. "If they're married, then he pulled off an Oscar-worthy performance in front of my family last night. He was as sweet and normal as ever."

"Normal, as in steal-your-best-friend-and-move-her-to-Waco normal?" she asked. "I might've been a sophomore the year all of you graduated, but even *I* remember that. You didn't take it well, as I recall."

"I'm just saying, he was the old Mason. All the good parts anyway. And he insists he didn't talk Stephanie into moving away. It was just a coincidence that they ended up at the same college."

"Sure it was." Tasha shrugged. "Well, forget about Stephanie. She's water under the bridge."

I turned to face Tasha, astounded at her word choice. "Why does everyone keep saying that?"

"Saying what?"

"Water under the bridge."

"Oh." A little shrug followed on her end. "Well, the part with Stephanie is, right? Anyway, I still say Mason and this Meredith chick have got to be more than casual acquaintances. Don't you think? Was it my imagination, or were they sharing a cart?"

Okay, I was done. I'd heard enough. I just needed to get through this line and. . .

Ugh. I'd forgotten the milk. Bessie Mae had specifically asked for a gallon of whole milk, which she planned to use to marinate the chicken-fried steak.

Which she couldn't make unless I went to the dairy department.

So, I eased my way out of line and pointed my cart that way.

"What are we doing now?" Tasha whispered. "Going back in for the kill?"

"Going back for milk so Bessie Mae can make the chicken-fried steak for dinner."

Tasha batted her eyelashes in my general direction. "Did I mention chicken-fried steak is my favorite?"

"You said you liked cookies." I nudged myself over to let an impatient shopper through. "But you're more than welcome to stay if I just live through this shopping trip first. Did I mention that I have to work for a couple of hours in the barn? We're still not ready for the grand opening, and it's a week and a half away."

"Don't worry. I'll help. I'm great at organizing."

She was, at that. And I would take her up on that offer as soon as we got out of here.

I took several tentative steps toward the dairy where I caught a glimpse of Mason and Meredith on the far end, looking at packages of sliced cheese. Well, terrific.

I did my best to stay focused on the task at hand, getting the gallon of milk, but even from here I could hear ripples of girlish laughter from Meredith.

I strained to catch a few snippets of the conversation but couldn't hear much. The sight of them together caused my mind to race with all kinds of over-the-top scenarios.

Was theirs a connection that went beyond casual friendship?

"She's giving him her business card," Tasha whispered. "So, maybe they're not a couple after all."

"Okay. . ." Had I misinterpreted this whole thing? "Maybe he was just being nice to a near stranger?" I suggested. That idea seemed to congeal as she headed off to another aisle with her cart, and he grabbed a small handheld basket from the edge of the cheese counter.

They definitely weren't sharing a basket.

And they surely weren't married.

Probably not even dating.

I'd let my imagination get the best of me. I hoped.

And why all of this bothered me, I could not say. I held no claim to Mason Fredericks.

Still, it seemed too much of a coincidence that he and Meredith were both here—together—on the same day Tilly had gone missing. Were these two up to something? If so, what?

I made my way to the front of the store and paid for the groceries, and then we headed out to the parking lot.

Where I discovered Meredith Reed getting into her white SUV. A Lexus. Did everyone in town own a Lexus except me? I didn't own a vehicle of any kind. Not until I got Tilly back anyway.

I didn't really let my imagination go too much further. I needed to get home and pass these things off to Bessie Mae, then head out to the barn to work.

When we arrived home, Bessie Mae was dozing in her recliner, open Bible in her lap and a muted John Wayne movie playing on the TV. No doubt she would fuss at me when she awoke for not bringing ingredients for the cookies.

I quietly put away the groceries. Mom came in the back door looking winded. "We're out in the old barn, if anyone needs us," she said. "We've got a mare about to foal."

This certainly got my attention. "Really? Which one? Delilah or Jemima?"

"Jemima. Logan's out there with her now."

"Logan's here?" Tasha's face lit up.

"Must be home from the bank early," I observed.

"Yeah, he came as soon as we texted about Jemima." Mom reached for a bottle of water from the fridge. "And Jake's on the way."

"What about Dallas and Gage?" I asked.

"Working on the busted fence."

"Well, that's good."

"Yeah, they'll be moving the cows back to that pasture once they're done. I think it's best if they keep doing what they're doing and leave the foaling to the rest of us."

"Right." I paused. "I'm headed to the barn to organize for the opening, but text if you need me. I'll come running."

"I saw her running in the grocery store earlier," Tasha added. "She's very fast."

After putting away the groceries, Tasha and I headed out to the barn to work. Things were really coming along out here, but I still had so much to do. We made the trek out there together, and I opened the barn door.

"Wow!" Tasha gave me an admiring look. "It's coming together, RaeLyn! It's starting to look like a real store."

"Thanks. That's the idea. We've been working hard, but there's still so much to do."

"Well, I'm here now, so let's get to it."

As we worked on organizing the kitchenware, my thoughts kept drifting back to Mason and Meredith. Why did they seem so cozy? And why hadn't he called me back to ask how it had gone at the auction house? Wasn't he the least bit curious? I would be.

"Penny for your thoughts."

"They're not worth that much." I sighed as I set an antique colander aside. "Just fretting. I can't believe Tilly is gone and I'm out six thousand dollars."

True compassion shone in my best friend's eyes. "They'll find her, RaeLyn. You heard what that officer said."

"Yeah, I heard. I also heard the part where Tilly's going to be worth a whole lot more than that, which means that Meredith—or whoever stole her—is going to be rich if we don't get her back in time."

"We'll pray that she's located."

"Yeah." But all I could do was sigh as I thought it through. Had I really just sacrificed my life savings for a pipe dream?

About an hour into our work session, both of my parents came in to share the news that Jemima was now the proud mother of a tiny new foal, a male. Logan came with them and shared all sorts of fun details about the newest family member. I couldn't help but notice that Tasha's cheeks flushed pink as soon as she saw my brother. So weird.

"Where's Jake?" I asked.

"Headed back up to the school," my dad responded. "Apparently there's a big game this afternoon. But I'll be looking in on Jemima and the foal."

He and Mom dove into the story of the foal's birth with great animation—as my family members were prone to do—and I promised to stop by and see the new baby when I wrapped up my work in the barn. The animal lover in me could hardly wait.

After that we switched gears, and Tasha took the reins of the conversation. Before long she had them all laughing at some funny story. Tasha seemed to have that easy way about her, the kind that drew people in.

"You still working at Fish Tales, Tasha?" Mom asked after they all stopped laughing.

"Yep. Head cashier." She laughed. "My dad told me to start telling people that. I just do whatever they need me to do. You know how it is with a family business."

Yep. We all knew.

"And you're off today?" Logan asked.

"I'm on at three. What time is it?" She reached into her back pocket and came out with her phone.

Logan glanced at his watch. "Two fifteen."

"Oh, yikes." She shot a glance my way. "Sorry to organize and run."

"No, I'm so grateful you came with me today," I said. "You always have a way of making everything better. In case I don't say it often enough, I'm really glad to have you in my life."

"And I'm glad to have you." She threw her arms around my neck and gave me a big hug. "Now, I'd better skedaddle."

And just like that, she was off to work at her parents' restaurant. Poor girl never even got to have any of Aunt Bessie Mae's chicken-fried steak.

Logan headed out at the same time, mentioning something about needing to make a call. He'd been noticeably quiet about last night's date, but I sure didn't want to push him. He deserved his privacy.

"So, how did it go at the auction house this morning?" Mom asked after they left. "You never told us."

"We didn't make much progress," I explained. "But the police did show up and took a report. I found out that the front gate was locked all night, so whoever took her knew how to get through the gate."

"Interesting." My mom clucked her tongue.

"So, someone who works there?" Dad asked.

"Maybe." I shrugged. "Harlan thinks it's his ex-wife."

"Oh my." Mom grabbed a rag and went to work dusting a nearby shelf unit. "Well, shame on her—or whoever else might've done that. We've waited too long to get your papaw's truck back for someone to waltz off with her."

Suddenly something hit me. "Y'all, I just remembered something that might be of interest."

"What's that?" Mom stopped dusting and looked my way.

"Remember that guy Ben who took my payment yesterday? He told us that Wyatt was looking in the glove box before the bidding started. In fact, he said that he'd given him the keys so that he could look the truck over top to bottom."

"Nothing too suspicious there," Dad said. "People do that all the time."

"Except that when we came back out, the box was wide open and the lock mechanism didn't work. I could tell it had been forced but didn't think much of it at the time. Could've happened years ago, for all I knew. But what if Wyatt was on the prowl for something and couldn't find it, so he decided to take off with the truck to do a little more digging?"

"We'll never know for sure what was—or wasn't—in the glove box," Mom said.

"And how did he get past the locked gate?" Dad added.

They made good points. "Still, it makes me wonder if Wyatt was searching for something specific. Something important."

We continued to share our thoughts about the truck, and before long the door to the barn opened and Bessie Mae walked in, looking a bit disheveled.

"Hey, just letting y'all know that dinner will be ready around six thirty. I've got the steak marinating."

"Sounds great." Dad offered a smile. "Thanks, Bessie."

"Mm-hmm. And since someone forgot to pick up ingredients for oatmeal cookies, I decided to whip up a lemon dewberry pound cake."

"Yum." I flashed a smile. "My favorite!" At least she was versatile.

"What am I missing out on?" Bessie asked as she looked around the shop. "Y'all have been busy out here."

"Working hard," I said.

"And talking about the missing truck," my dad added. "The police took a report, but they still don't have any suspects."

"Well, of course we do." She gave my dad a pensive look. "You said Wyatt Jackson was in the room bidding against you, right?"

"Yeah."

"You know the backstory there better than anyone, Chuck. If anyone would want to steal from this family, it's Wyatt Jackson, especially when you take our whole history into account."

"Wait, what backstory?" I asked. "What history? Could you be more specific?"

Dad raked his fingers through his thinning hair. "Well, remember, I told you there was more to the story with Wyatt Jackson?"

"You did."

"Welp. . ." Dad kicked the floor with the toe of his boot. "What I didn't tell you was this: Wyatt Jackson is your great-uncle."

CHAPTER TEN

"Wait...what?" This made no sense at all. How could Wyatt be related to Papaw and Aunt Bessie? "Somebody's got a lot of explaining to do."

Mom kept right on dusting, now moving down to another shelf unit. Had she heard this story before?

"Wyatt and your papaw were best friends as boys." My dad leaned against a nearby bookshelf. "When Wyatt was in his teens, his parents were both killed in a house fire."

"His parents, meaning someone in our family line?" I stopped working on the kitchenware and plopped down into a folding chair.

Dad shook his head. "Nope. Paul and Neda Jackson. They owned that property a quarter mile east of here, where Wyatt lives with his wife to this day. The one where you said you used to pick berries with Mason."

"This is making no sense at all, Dad," I countered. "I mean, I know that's the Jackson place, but I don't get the rest. If he wasn't related to us, then how is he my uncle?"

"*Great*-uncle," Mom called out.

"Your great-grandparents—my grandparents—took Wyatt in and gave him a home when his parents died," Dad explained.

"He became part of the family," Bessie Mae added.

Dad nodded. "Wyatt was the same age as my dad—maybe a couple months older—and they became like brothers, so I'm sure it seemed like an ideal setup."

"I was really little at the time," Bessie Mae chimed in. "But I loved having another big brother to watch out for me. It was a great life. And they were very close, almost like twins, which made it even better."

"It's just so weird no one bothered to mention this before," I said. "Was he officially adopted?"

"Nope." Bessie Mae shook her head and appeared to lose herself to her thoughts for a second. "My parents were just given—I think it's called power of attorney. Something like that. But he stayed with us for quite some time."

"The fact that he was never adopted came up later as a topic of great interest when Wyatt decided to file suit to claim some of the land later on," Dad explained. "The court held that he had no legal claim."

"Seems kind of sad, considering they had loved him like a son," I said.

"Maybe Wyatt really felt he deserved a portion of the land," Mom chimed in, as she laid the rag down on the register counter.

"I'm sure he did," Bessie Mae responded. "And there was a time I might've agreed that he deserved it. But after what he did to our family. . .well, I wouldn't give him a dime if he asked for it, then or now."

"What did he do?" I asked. "Someone fill me in, because I'm feeling a little lost."

Mom started organizing some dishes on a shelf unit nearby, but I could tell she was still listening intently.

Dad pulled up a milk crate and sat down next to me. "There was a big falling-out, and Wyatt moved on from the family when he was seventeen."

"The boys were in their junior year at Mabank High School," Bessie Mae explained. "Wyatt was saving up to buy a truck when your papaw won a football championship that came with a cash reward from a car dealership in Dallas."

I knew Papaw was famous in these parts for his moves on the football field, but didn't recall anything about a championship.

"Wyatt didn't have those same skills," Bessie Mae added. "He tried out for the team but didn't make it."

"So, these wannabe brothers had a falling-out. . .over football? And that led to a lawsuit over the land?"

"Hey, we take our football very seriously here in Texas," my dad said.

Oh boy, did I know it. I was a cheerleader for the Panthers football team my junior and senior years, after all. I'd spent nearly every fall and winter weekend at one game or another.

"The falling-out wasn't really about football," Bessie Mae explained. "It was over the truck. Your papaw won that prize and took advantage of the opportunity to buy the very truck Wyatt had been saving up for."

"Ouch."

"Wyatt was very hurt," Bessie Mae said. "He lost out on the truck altogether and ended up with a broken-down used car someone in the church passed his way."

"I can see how that would have hurt him," I said. In fact, I felt a bit sorry for him after hearing this. No wonder he wanted Tilly so badly.

"To make matters even worse, there was a big chess championship a few months later, and Wyatt was a shoo-in. Everyone in town knew it. But he was so distracted by a fight he'd just had with your papaw that he ended up losing that game. That was a real kick in the shins."

"What were they fighting about that was such a distraction?" I asked.

Bessie Mae's nose wrinkled. "I guess I skipped part of the story. The chess championship happened the day after we all learned that Wyatt and a girl in town were...well..." She glanced down at the ground, then back up again. "Expecting."

"Good gravy." I shifted my position in the uncomfortable chair. "This story has more twists and turns than a country road."

"And people think life in a small town is boring." Dad chuckled as he shifted his position on the milk crate.

"So, my almost-great-uncle Wyatt got a girl pregnant, and the news broke the day before this big chess championship, which was on the heels of Papaw winning the truck."

"Yes, and I feel sure Wyatt was determined to win that championship to prove that he had as much worth as Charles, if that makes sense."

It made perfect sense to me. But with all of these other details added in, Wyatt didn't stand much of a chance of coming out looking like a hero, even if he had won.

"You left out a key part of the story, Bessie Mae," Dad said.

"Did I?" Fine lines creased her forehead as she appeared to be thinking it through.

"Yep." He nodded and glanced my way. "Your papaw was dating that same girl at the time all of this happened. In fact, everyone in town thought they would get married."

"Oh yes." Bessie Mae's lips curled up in a smile. "I believe I did leave out that part, didn't I?"

I could hardly believe it. "Whoa. No wonder they were fighting."

"And to complicate things further..." Bessie Mae's voice lowered to a whisper. "She was the pastor's daughter. And our parents were founding members of the church, so it reflected poorly on the whole family."

"The church judged all of you for what Wyatt had done?" That hardly seemed fair.

"Yes, ma'am. That's how it was, back in those days." Bessie Mae reached for the broom and started sweeping the floor at my feet. "And there were many who would've seen us all booted. But my mom wasn't having it. She planted her backside in the pew and said they would have to use a crane to pull her out of there."

"Oh my." That took some chutzpah.

"Almost caused a church split, as I recall. But things settled down once Wyatt agreed to marry the girl. They had a shotgun wedding." Bessie Mae's lips curled up in a delicious smile as she paused from sweeping. "I was a junior bridesmaid."

"That about sums it up." Dad chuckled and stood up.

"This is crazy." I paused to think all of this through. "So, Papaw got the truck and Wyatt got the girl," I said. "And now Wyatt wants the truck too?"

"He had his heart set on it years and years ago." My aunt shrugged. "And from what I can tell you firsthand, he's never been very happy married to Corina. Or she to him."

"Well, that's just sad." I paused. "Whatever happened to the baby?"

"That's the saddest part of all. The baby, a little girl, passed away just weeks after she was born."

This news rendered me silent. Suddenly I felt very, very sorry for Wyatt Jackson. Even if he was—sort of—my great-uncle.

"Do you think it's possible Wyatt stole Tilly from the auction house to get back at Papaw?" I asked.

Dad nodded. "I've been thinking about this all day, and it's the only thing that makes sense. Wyatt seems like the most viable suspect to me."

"Want me to call Corina and ask her if she's seen it?" Bessie Mae asked.

"You still know her?" This surprised me.

"Well, of course. She sits on the third pew, far right, every Sunday."

"Wait, are you talking about Ms. Rena Sue?" I asked. "I thought she was widowed."

With a wave of her hand, my aunt dismissed that notion. "She's definitely not a widow. And she's not going anywhere. She's stubborn, that one. Kind of like my mama in that regard."

"My goodness," was about all I could manage.

"Wyatt, on the other hand, hasn't shown his face in that church since they booted him out all those years ago, though I'm sure he would be welcome now. Let's just say he's one to hold a grudge," Bessie Mae said, "and leave it at that. He said he'd never grace the door of that church again, and he hasn't."

And there it was, the story I'd never known.

Now I had to get Tilly back. "For sure, please call Rena," I said. "Or better yet, maybe we just drive up to Wyatt's place tonight and look around?"

"No." Dad shook his head. "I don't trust that man. He's liable to come out with a shotgun."

"I'm not going anywhere near his property," Mom agreed. "And don't recommend either of you do either. But I agree we should call Rena."

And so that's what Bessie Mae did. Just a few minutes later, with Mom, Dad, and I gathered around her in the kitchen as she tenderized the meat for the chicken-fried steak, she called Rena Jackson.

Who, it turned out, was apparently in the beginning stages of Alzheimer's and couldn't seem to remember who Bessie Mae was.

My aunt did manage to ask about the red truck, and a very animated Rena told her that red had always been her husband's favorite color.

And that was about as far as we got with that bit of sleuthing. I'd just have to figure out plan B if I wanted to know more about Wyatt Jackson.

CHAPTER ELEVEN

After taking a peek at the adorable new foal, I spent the rest of that evening writing my weekly column for *Mabank Happenings*. I chose to write a promo piece for the church, a big to-do about our upcoming Easter celebration, an early morning service that the whole community was invited to attend. Hopefully the article would bring in bigger numbers. Attendance had been down over the past few months.

After I clicked the SEND button, I settled in for the night, but I had trouble sleeping. When I did fall asleep, I had the strangest dreams about Papaw as a younger man. He and Wyatt were engaged in a boxing match, duking it out for the girl. In my dream, Papaw won the girl, but Wyatt—who suddenly looked a bit like John Wayne—drove off in that shiny red truck.

The next morning, I woke up with my thoughts in a whirl. Despite my parents' warnings, I found myself fighting the overwhelming temptation to drive by Wyatt's place to have a little look-see around the place. I knew right where it was. But I didn't feel safe going alone. Maybe with time I'd garner the courage.

We talked more about him over breakfast, and Bessie Mae brought up one more piece of information that she thought might be helpful. "I remember Wyatt always loved the color red, so Rena was right about that. He specifically wanted that truck to be red because it reminded him of his mama somehow."

"And Papaw?"

"I think he picked the red one just to spite Wyatt."

"Man." I hated to hear that the grandfather I adored might've had a mean streak. Or, at the very least, a bitter streak. But knowing that Wyatt had stolen his girlfriend did help me understand his desire to irritate Wyatt by choosing the red truck.

"What we really need is someone who knows Wyatt well," I said. "Not back in the day, but now."

"Rena's obviously not going to be much help. And we've already seen that he's an old loner. He never comes to any of the senior events or anything like that." Bessie Mae took a seat at the table, coffee cup in hand. "The Wyatt I knew as a boy loved being around people, but apparently he's become an old stinker. A hermit."

"Sad, what time and bitterness will do to you."

"No, what's sad is what he's done to life," she said. "He's had every opportunity to live and love and be nice. And he's squandered those opportunities."

Still, I felt a little sorry for him. He'd lost his parents, after all. And his friend—his brother—had taken advantage of him by deliberately choosing the very truck that he'd wanted.

I had a weird feeling wash over me as I thought about this. I was reminded of Mason, moving off to Waco with my friend. When it happened, I felt like they were going to have a blessed life, and I was going to be. . .I don't know. . .alone?

"Maybe you should go talk to Dot." Mom's voice roused me from my pondering. "She knows all the things, especially about Mabank and Gun Barrel City."

"Oh, good idea." Dot wasn't just the head of the chamber of commerce, she was also head librarian at the local library. The woman was a wealth of information. Hopefully she could help me out with info about Wyatt Jackson.

So, at my mother's prompting, I decided to head into town to the

Mabank Library. And I hoped to talk my aunt into coming with me. After her recent comments about not getting out much, I realized she needed to be included more, and this would provide the perfect opportunity. She argued that there was too much work to be done around the house, but I knew better. The house could wait. And Mom could certainly fix her own lunch.

"I think it would do you good, Aunt Bessie."

An inquisitive look followed on her end. "Why is that, girlie?"

"You said you don't get out much."

With the wave of a hand, she tried to dismiss my concerns. "Oh, that was just a joke, silly. I was making that up. You know that I get out all the time. I was at Brookshire Brothers a couple days back and church on Sunday."

Still, I'd learned that most jokes, even the really funny ones, usually had a sprinkling of truth to them. Maybe my aunt was sincerely feeling left out of family activities. This was one way I could keep her in the loop, by taking her with me. Besides, she and Dot probably would have a lot of information to share about Papaw and Wyatt, once they put their heads together.

After a bit of arguing over her baking schedule, she reluctantly agreed, and we put together a plan of action to visit Dot at the library. Mom needed her car to make a run to a women's ministry meeting at church, so we took Aunt Bessie's older-model Pontiac sedan. I didn't drive this boat of a vehicle very often, but it was definitely a different experience from driving my VW Bug or my mom's SUV. This thing was a cruise ship.

"Want me to drive?" my aunt asked as we walked out toward the carport.

Um, no. I most certainly did *not* want Aunt Bessie to drive. The last time she drove us to lunch after church we almost ended up in the ditch at the corner of 198 and Market Street. The woman could barely see the road anymore.

So, I climbed behind the wheel, happy to be of service. And we made the trip into town with no problems—unless you counted the point where I hit a hole in the road that sent my aunt flying several inches into the air. All was forgiven and forgotten by the time we got to the highway. Bessie Mae commented on the lovely weather, and I countered with how pretty the bluebonnets looked in all of the fields to our right.

"Well, honey, you're blessed to live in a little slice of heaven like this," she said. "I might be partial to Mabank, having grown up here, but you won't find anyplace prettier than the lakes and fields and such."

She was right about that. And the gently rolling hills provided more than just lush greenery in the springtime and bales of hay in the fall. Underground natural gas deposits had provided income for many in the area over the past few decades. Of course, that was all tapering off now, but we did our best not to dwell on that.

"When I was a girl, I'd go to the lake with Wyatt and your papaw, and we'd swim for hours. Mom wouldn't even worry a bit if we were gone all day swimming." A pause followed and then, "Remind me why we're going to see Dot?"

"She's the president of the Cedar Creek Chamber of Commerce," I said. "And knows a lot about the goings-on in town, so I was hoping she could help me figure out who might have been interested in stealing Tilly."

"Oh, right. She's always planning this event or that event. She's the perfect person for that job."

"She is." And I could hardly wait to talk to her. If anyone could fill me in on the happenings in or around Mabank, it was usually Dot.

"She's going to try to sign you up for the chamber, mark my words." Bessie Mae gave me a knowing look.

"Me? Why?"

"Your new antique shop—Trinkets and Treasures. She'll want you to be a chamber member, for sure."

I'd never given that idea a moment's thought but wasn't opposed to the idea. It might be nice to be in a community with other business owners so that we could pool our efforts and have networking opportunities. I would have to give that more thought.

We turned into town, and Bessie Mae pointed out the new restaurant going in on Market Street. "I tell you, every time I come into town that building is something new. When I was young it was a Sears and Roebuck. Then it was a five-and-dime. Then a homemade pottery shop. That didn't last long. Now they're turning it into an Italian restaurant."

"Hopefully the restaurant will last a good long while," I said. "We need good restaurants that stay put. It gets old, driving to Athens or Kaufman for a night out." I paused and then added, "Not that any of those places even comes close to your home cooking, Aunt Bessie."

A lovely smile tipped up the edges of her lips. "Well, thank you, honey. That warms my heart."

Still, I liked the idea of that new Italian restaurant staying put. Bessie Mae wasn't one to make chicken parmigiana or fettuccine Alfredo, two of my personal favorites. Though, if I was being honest with myself, this restaurant would probably end up being a Mexican cantina by month's end. The businesses, like the townspeople, just continued to evolve over time, accepting the changes as gracefully as they could without giving in to despair that the town might be dying off. Heaven forbid that should ever happen. We wouldn't let it.

Here in Mabank we had an overabundance of community spirit. Folks were friendly, and there was a palpable sense of camaraderie, which showed itself off in so many of our regular events—festivals, parades, and so on. We absolutely loved coming together to celebrate our shared heritage and history. I hoped that never changed.

I smiled as we made our way down Market Street, deep in thought. Mabank was such a charming small town, this quaint street lined with ever-changing businesses.

As we drove past the bakery, we saw Miss Annie, one of Bessie Mae's best friends, in front of her shop. She was wearing her bakery apron, covered in splotches of flour, with her hair pulled up in a twist as she fought to get the key in the door of her shop.

"Slow down, honey," my aunt said. "I need to tell Annie something."

I tapped the brakes, and Bessie Mae rolled down her window. Moments later the two ladies were engaged in lively conversation about an upcoming quilt show, to be held at the Methodist church—chosen for its larger fellowship hall.

"I want you to bring a bunch of those homemade cinnamon rolls, Annie," Bessie Mae said. "They'll sell like hotcakes."

"Oh, I plan to," Annie countered. "And I'm bringing a bunch of muffins to boot. Folks'll buy me out, and my sweets will put them in the mood to shop for quilts."

"Which will help our missionary fund," Bessie Mae added. "Which is the point of all of it, to raise funds for those sweet folks in Nicaragua."

And that's just how it was here in my hometown. The warmth of southern hospitality was everywhere, spreading all the way across the globe. Even strangers were greeted with a broad smile. Unless they dared to criticize. Then we sent 'em packing.

"I can't seem to get my key to work in the lock." Annie waved her keys to show them off. "It's the silliest thing. I left a baking project half-done to run to Brookshire Brothers, and now I'm locked out."

I pulled over to the curb and got out to help her open the door.

She thanked me, and we were soon on our way again.

I drove another block up the road to Market Street and turned to the right. We approached the library parking lot seconds later. I pulled in and started looking for a place to park.

"I've got permanent plates now, honey," Bessie Mae reminded me. "'Cause of my rheumatism."

The woman could probably dance circles around all of us, but I knew she quietly struggled with a lot of hip and back pain. So I followed her instructions and pulled into the handicapped parking spot.

Before we could get out of the car, my aunt looked my way with a hint of sadness in her expression. "What did she look like, RaeLyn?"

"Who?" I turned off the car and pressed the keys into my purse.

"Tilly. What did she look like, after all these years?"

"Oh." I paused to think it through. "Rusty. Old. Doesn't much resemble her former self."

"Sounds like me." She chuckled, but I could see pain in her eyes behind that laughter. "I guess Tilly's a lot like us."

"What do you mean, Aunt Bessie?" I slipped my purse strap over my shoulder and reached for the door handle.

She shrugged and gazed out of her passenger door window. "I'm just saying, I know what it's like, to be past my years of usefulness."

I didn't mean to gasp aloud, but there it was. "Past your years of usefulness? Bessie Mae Hadley, tell me I didn't just hear you say that." Tears misted in my eyes, and I realized this conversation had just taken a turn. "You? Of all people!" I then went into a lengthy list of all the obvious ways she kept our family afloat. After listing them, I was quick to add, "But even if you couldn't do any of those things, you would still be valuable to us—and cherished by us—because you're part of the family. You're the matriarch, Aunt Bessie."

That brought a smile to her face.

She dabbed at her eyes and adjusted the rearview mirror to see her reflection, then wrinkled her nose. "Welp, I don't have a plastic surgeon handy, so I guess I'll just have to go in there looking like this."

"You look lovely," I said.

Seconds later, I exited my car and went around to help Bessie Mae out. Then we headed inside the 1950s storefront that served as Mabank's public library. Right away, the familiar scent of old books greeted me. Paired with the scent of polished wood, it offered an aroma that almost felt inviting, especially to a bookworm like me.

The library hummed with a plethora of hushed conversations, coupled with the occasional creak of floorboards underfoot. I blinked to adjust my eyes to the lighting and then sought out Dot, Mom's BFF. Her connection to the library seemed as timeless as the volumes of books that always surrounded her.

I passed by rows of well-stocked bookshelves, fighting the temptation to dig around in the fiction section. Finally, I located Dot behind the circulation desk. She glanced up as I approached and tucked a loose strand of that gorgeous short silver hair behind an ear. Her blue eyes held a hint of mischief as she said, "Well, hey there. Heard you ladies might be stopping by."

"Mom called?" I pulled up a chair and gestured for Bessie Mae to sit, but apparently we'd already lost her to the true crime section. So I took the seat across from Dot, slinging my purse strap over the back of it.

"Yep. She says you've got a problem. Someone took off with Tilly?" The warm smile and twinkle in her eyes faded a bit as she posed the question.

"Yeah." I couldn't stop the tears that sprang to my eyes as she mentioned Tilly. "Terrible timing too."

Dot pulled a tissue from the holder on her desk and passed it my way. "Don't worry, sweet girl. We'll find her."

"I hope so. But we definitely need some help. Mom says you're the best, so we've come to you."

Dot's cheeks flushed. "Well, I don't know about that, but I did hear you were looking for information on Wyatt Jackson. Is that right?"

"Yes." I nodded and thought through my next words. "We were hoping you would know more about him. From what I gather, he had a falling-out with the family years ago, even filed a lawsuit against us."

"You're not the only ones," Dot countered. "He sued the city, he sued the county, and he even tried to sue the state at one point. I wouldn't be surprised if the man came up with some excuse to sue the president of the United States."

"For pity's sake." I took a seat. "Is there anyone he hasn't sued?"

Dot chuckled. "Well, neither of us, but let's don't give him any ideas."

"Why do you suppose he's so intent on always getting what he wants?" I asked.

"I was younger than Wyatt by a good twenty years or so, but he always fancied himself an entrepreneur. He was one of those guys who always thought he was more than he really was, if that makes sense."

Kind of like Clayton Henderson, I wanted to say but didn't.

"He started up a hobby shop once. It made sense, for a man who loved chess as much as he did."

"Oh, that's right. Aunt Bessie said he was well known for his chess moves and came close to winning a championship his senior year."

"Yes. I think the hobby shop was his attempt to keep his legend alive in the community, as it were. He had some beautiful sets for sale. Marble and everything. But the shop didn't last. In the end, he went to work as a locksmith."

Oh, wow. Now that she mentioned it, I did remember that Wyatt Jackson had a little locksmith shop that he ran out of his home. Not that we had ever done business with him. My dad usually handled those sorts of things himself.

"Maybe it's because he lost his parents?" I said after a moment of thinking it through. "Could be he was trying to prove something to them, that he'd made something of his life. You know?"

"Sure. Or. . ." She paused and appeared to be thinking. "Maybe because he got kicked out of so many different social circles when he got Rena pregnant. And to make matters worse, I don't know that he ever really loved her. I think he just wooed her—or trapped her, really—to hurt your grandfather after that incident with the truck."

"Wow."

Dot shrugged. "That's my theory anyway. I can't really prove it. I just always felt like the man had a chip on his shoulder or was trying to prove some sort of point to folks."

"Maybe in reality he just felt like he'd never measure up." These words came from Bessie Mae, who had returned with an armload of books. She held up a hardback with a dull cover. "What do you think of this one, RaeLyn?"

Sleuthing 101? I laughed. "Is that our handbook for figuring this out?"

"Sure." She opened it to the table of contents and read the names of the various chapters. "Says here we should create a suspect list. Who've we got so far?"

"Yes, who else besides Wyatt?" Dot asked. "You should make a list."

"Really?" I looked back and forth between them. "What is this, Sleuths R Us?"

"Why not?" Dot laughed. "I'm game."

"Remember the Duke's role in *Stagecoach*?" Bessie Mae set the book down on the table in front of me. "That was his breakthrough role. The rest of his career came as a result of him saying yes to that one role."

"What's your point?" I asked.

"Just saying, this case could be your breakthrough."

"Good grief." Still, I did want to figure this out, and that was going to require a lot of thinking on my part.

CHAPTER TWELVE

"Maybe I've been watching those whodunit shows for too long," Dot interjected, "but they always write down the suspects and then eliminate them one by one. Who else have you got on the list?"

"Well, let's see. . ."

I quickly shared the names of the suspects and the clues I'd gathered so far. Dot listened attentively, her gaze unwavering as she penciled down the names on a piece of library stationery.

"So, Meredith Reed. I can't believe she tried to take a check from you. And it's even crazier that she has a key to that gate. I wonder if Harlan just forgot to get it from her during the divorce proceedings." Dot paused and appeared to be thinking. "Of course, that was a pretty tumultuous time, so I can see how it might have been overlooked."

"I was equally as bothered by the idea that she might have connections with tow truck drivers who might have been willing to help her," I said. "And if she ends up selling that truck and making a bundle of money off of her after not paying a penny for her in the first place, I'm really going to be upset."

"I don't blame you." Dot gave me a sympathetic look. "Hopefully it won't come to that. Now, we're also looking at Wyatt Jackson for obvious reasons that date back for decades. And. . ." Dot lowered her voice. "Of course, Clayton Henderson. I wouldn't trust that guy as far as I could throw him. He wants to own everything in town."

"Terrible man." Bessie Mae shook her head. "Don't trust him one little bit."

"I haven't really paused to give Clayton much thought," I said. "But I would add Mason to that list too. Since he seems to be so chummy with Meredith."

"Mason Fredericks is chummy with Meredith Reed?" Bessie Mae's eyes widened. "Oh my. That's a twist I didn't see coming."

An explanation was due, so I offered it. "I saw them together in the grocery store. They were in the baking aisle."

"And that makes him a truck thief?" Dot quirked a brow. "Because he's shown interest in a woman who likes to bake?"

"A woman who tried to take a check from me who was once married to Harlan. I think it's very suspicious. One minute he's bidding against me, then all chummy with me, then he turns up at the store with the very woman who tried to weasel me out of six thousand dollars? You know?"

"Oh, I think I know, all right." Dot leaned forward, her eyes crinkling at the corners. "But I'm pretty sure Mason Fredericks doesn't have anything to do with the disappearance of the truck. But before we go any further, let's talk about what all of these folks have in common."

"They all love vintage red trucks," Bessie Mae chimed in. "That much is a given."

I rose and began to pace the small area between us, an idea taking root. "It would be great if I knew all of the folks in town who are avid classic car and truck collectors. Maybe if I had a list like that I could see if any of our suspects' names were on it."

"You mean people that show off their restored vehicles at car shows?" Dot asked.

"Yes. I know we have a lot of them in the area," I said. "There are always antique car shows going on around the lake."

"That's because folks in my age group tend to frequent the area, and they love that sort of thing." Bessie Mae flipped through the pages of the book in her hand.

Dot lowered her voice as she added, "Of course, hardly anyone tops

Clayton Henderson when it comes to these car shows. That man's got more vehicles than he has common sense."

"Really?" I asked.

"Oh yes. It's quite the challenge for the others to even come close. He comes in first most every time. Some of the competitors have stopped coming because they believe the whole thing is rigged."

"Oh boy." I fought the temptation to roll my eyes. Still, I could imagine how important it must be for a man like Clayton Henderson to come in first in everything he did.

"Does he ever show trucks?" I asked.

Dot nodded. "Sure. He even flipped a really rare '42 custom Buick truck one year. From what I understand, he flips 'em, shows 'em, and then sells them for top dollar online."

"Where online?" Bessie Mae asked.

"I'm not altogether sure, but I would be glad to do some research." Dot jotted something down on that paper of hers. "If I figure anything out, I'll get back to you, I promise. But he's always showing cars at one event or another, including the big one coming up this weekend."

"There's a big car show coming up this weekend?" Bessie Mae's eyes lit up. "Really?"

"Over in Gun Barrel City," I explained. "I did an article on it last week. Folks are coming from all over the state to show their vintage cars and trucks."

"And Clayton is one of them," Dot added. "I believe he's got three cars listed on the roster."

"Oh, wow. How do you know all of this?" I asked.

"Chamber, honey. Chamber. And I pay close attention to these car shows because we've got hundreds of thousands of dollars at stake when they all bring those vehicles to town at the same time. Those folks eat at our restaurants, shop in our stores, and gas up at our service stations. So, these types of events are good for all of our businesses."

"Oh, wow, I never thought of that." I paused to think through her words. "It makes me want to host some sort of event to bring in more people to the area. Maybe an antique week?"

"That would be amazing," Dot said with a nod. "I'm sure other stores would be happy to participate. It would be fun in the spring."

"I don't know." Bessie Mae wrinkled her nose. "They'll clog up our streets with traffic and leave their litter everywhere."

"Might be worth it," Dot said. "There's always cleanup after the car shows, but like I said, they bring in revenue that's badly needed in our little town."

"So, question—the point of the car shows isn't just to brag about how great your vehicle is?" This surprised me. "Some of these folks are trying to attract high-dollar buyers for their flipped vehicles?"

"Sometimes." Dot shrugged. "I mean, I love to go to the car shows just to look around and meet the car enthusiasts."

"That sounds like fun." Bessie Mae looked my way. "We should go, honeybunch."

"But I've got so much work to do before our grand opening." I chewed my lip as I thought it through. With only ten days left, I needed every minute.

"Maybe one of the boys will take me." My aunt diverted her gaze back to the book. "I just think it would be so fun to see all of those old cars all done up again. It'll take me back in time, I think."

Well, when she put it like that.

I offered Bessie Mae a warm smile and found myself wondering if I should offer to take her. It would probably do us good. And who knew? Maybe there would be clues waiting for us there. I was a supersleuth, after all, hot on the trail to find my beloved Tilly.

After a moment of thoughtful silence, Dot leaned back in her chair, fingers tapping on the worn-out desk. "I'm not sure I have anything to help in the library, but the chamber of commerce keeps records of car show participants. I guess it's a good thing you know the president of the organization personally."

"Guess so," I countered.

"Come with me, honey. Let's see what I can find." She put a BE BACK SOON sign on her desk and led the way to the door, then called out to her coworker, "Be back in fifteen, Kelsey. Have something to take care of."

Kelsey nodded and went back to helping a customer.

I followed Dot as she bounded through the open door and into the parking lot. Seconds later she was moving toward the sidewalk, her steps confident and purposeful. Despite the difference in our ages, I could barely keep up with her.

Though well into her late '60s, Dot's slender frame hinted at a past life as an athlete—a fact she often shared, especially during local sports discussions. It really showed on days like today, as she outpaced me—one long stride for every two short ones of my own. I felt sorry for Bessie Mae, who lagged behind by a few yards. I decided to slow my pace so she wouldn't feel overlooked. I slipped my hand through the crook in her arm and offered a bright, encouraging smile.

"Never could keep up with Dot," she huffed. "That woman's a machine."

Indeed.

We finally arrived at the chamber of commerce office just a few doors down on Market Street, but Dot was already inside. She went straight to her computer and flipped it on.

"Give me just a second, honey." Seconds later, her fingers danced across the computer keyboard, until she finally found something of interest.

It didn't take long to come up with a list. A long list. Apparently Henderson County had a plethora of antique car and truck collectors who had registered their vehicles for the upcoming car show in Gun Barrel City.

Her nose wrinkled as she peered at the screen. "So, it looks like we've got all sorts coming—from flippers to mechanics to high-dollar owners looking to sell."

"Sounds like it's going to be a big deal," my aunt observed.

"It is. That's why they're using the parking lot of the Walmart. It's going to be huge. And like I said, this is all good news for our businesses, which will benefit from the additional influx of people."

On and on she went, giving us all the details about the upcoming show and how it would benefit our little town. Before long we knew who and we knew what. We knew when and we knew where. All that was lacking for most of these folks was the why part. But it was pretty clear why most of them were participating in the upcoming show—they loved old cars. They loved showing them, bragging about them, sharing them, and drawing interest from others.

Dot's eyes sparkled with the joy of discovery as she shared about one car owner and then the next. This gal was a treasure trove, and I was glad to have her on my side. I should probably just hand her the reins of our little sleuthing operation and let her solve this crime single-handedly.

"What kind of person collects cars?" Bessie Mae asked when Dot finally paused for breath. "Sounds like kind of an expensive hobby."

"Oh, lots of them," Dot explained. "We're talking about super-dedicated individuals who live, eat, and breathe antique vehicles."

"Basically, these folks are the ones who keep those antique cars and trucks in front of people so no one ever forgets just how beautiful they once were," I added. It all sounded very intriguing to me.

"You're really making me want to go." Bessie Mae pulled up a chair and sat down, still looking a bit winded from our walk over here.

"Oh, you should," Dot said. "The shows are a great place to showcase the vehicles and to hobnob with the owners. But mostly they're trying to pass on the passion to the next generation."

"Is it a contest?" Bessie Mae asked. "Like, do they win prizes and such?"

Dot nodded. "Yes, I forgot to mention that. There are real judges, and they make their evaluations based on a number of criteria—everything from the vehicle's craftsmanship to presentation and authenticity."

"In other words, they can't just fix up an old car any old way they like?" Bessie Mae asked. "They have to make it look just like it would have back then?"

Dot nodded. "Exactly. And if they do, they can win top dollar in their various categories. It's also a real source of pride for the car and truck owners to win these awards. They also win prizes from businesses like auto repair shops, hobby shops, and even car dealerships."

"Kind of like Papaw did all those years ago."

Dot smiled. "I guess you're right. Hadn't thought about that."

"Well, if I didn't already want to go, I'd be sold, just based on what you've said." My aunt looked my way. "What do you say, RaeLyn? Are you game?"

"Sure. I'll work extra hard between now and Saturday at the antique shop so I've got some free time." I turned to Dot. "We're working fast and furiously to get the shop open by the sixth. That's a week from Saturday."

"Oh, I know, honey. Your mama's been telling me all about it. It's going to be great. And I'm always happy to hear about another business opening in the area. That makes my heart so happy. You have no idea."

"Go for it, Dottie." Bessie Mae offered a playful nod. "This is your window of opportunity to talk RaeLyn into joining the chamber."

True to form, Dot dove into a lengthy explanation of all the reasons I needed to consider adding Trinkets and Treasures to the Cedar Creek Chamber of Commerce roster.

I didn't really understand much about how the chamber worked, but she was happy to fill me in.

"They provide networking opportunities, RaeLyn," Dot explained. "Joining will put you in close communication with the other business owners, and you can learn a lot from them. We've got a very helpful bunch, and many of them have tons of experience to share."

"Like what?" I asked.

"Oh, you know. Some of these folks are entrepreneurs just like you."

"Is that what I am?" I'd never considered that notion before. Was I just like my great-uncle, ready to start business after business? Hopefully mine would stick around longer.

"Well, sure, honey." She gave me a sympathetic look. "Maybe you just don't realize it yet, but you really are. You've got that entrepreneurial spirit that we love to see in our chamber members."

"I don't know that much about growing a business," I confessed. "At least, not yet."

"Well, hang on for the ride, kiddo, because the chamber will help with that too. We've always got someone leading a workshop or a seminar to share business strategies, marketing trends, and all sorts of other business practice info."

That sounded good to me. I really knew very little, as I'd already shared.

"Not that you have to be a business owner to join," she was quick to add. "We have individual memberships for about a quarter of the cost. Oh, and organizations and ministries can join too. It's really advantageous for everyone in the community."

At this point I kind of felt like I was listening to an informercial. I had a feeling Dot had given this speech before—possibly a hundred times or more, based on how smoothly the words came rolling off her tongue.

"There are a ton of benefits for you, RaeLyn," she added. "Like, cost-saving opportunities on essentials like insurance, legal services, or even accounting."

"I hope I don't need legal services," I said.

"No, but if you ever do, being a member of the chamber of commerce will come in handy. We've got lots of people who are skilled in that area. Best of all, we're a great community group. We're such good friends, all of us." She paused, and her smile faded for a moment. "Well, most of us. There are always a few bad apples in every bunch. But you'll get along just fine, RaeLyn. You're so relational. That's a bonus."

"She is, isn't she?" Bessie Mae beamed with pride.

"The best part of being a member is that we help promote each other. The chamber provides a platform for your store to gain visibility, which is especially helpful in those first few months. We'll share all about you in our newsletter and on the chamber's website."

"This is sounding better by the minute, Dot," Bessie Mae said. "What else?"

"Oh my goodness, so many things come to mind." Dot rose and began to pace the room. "We're always doing marketing initiatives. We do a lot of joint advertising campaigns, social media campaigns, and things like that. And of course, you'd be included in local business directories. That's a plus."

"That sounds great, Dot." I didn't really need any more encouragement. She could ask me to sign on the dotted line right here and now, and I'd do it. I loved the idea of actively engaging with my community. And by the time she was done with the rest of her spiel—which included lots of chatter about community events, fundraisers, and collaborative projects—I was ready to dive in headfirst.

"I don't know if you know this or not, but chamber members have a say in local business-related decisions. There's power in the collective voice, and you'll soon be a part of that."

I felt like puffing my chest out. Soon, I would be part of a group that could make a difference in my little town. Suddenly my dream of opening the antique store seemed bigger than myself, even bigger than my own little family. I could literally play a role in keeping Mabank alive and well, ready for the next generation. And that felt mighty, mighty good.

CHAPTER THIRTEEN

"Who knows, honey?" Bessie Mae smiled as she rested her hand on my arm. "You might one day run for mayor of Mabank! Wouldn't that be something? One of the Hadleys overseeing the whole city? Boy, would your papaw ever be proud of that."

"I. . .I don't think so, Bessie Mae. I'm not exactly the mayor type. I have a hard time standing up in front of my Sunday school class to share a prayer request."

Bessie shook her head. "I'm just saying, if you do well at this business, it could lead to bigger and better things. Like the Duke, in that first movie."

"Point is, you'll be contributing to the overall economic health and vibrancy of our little community," Dot said. "And that's a blessing—for you and for us."

Suddenly I felt a zeal I hadn't experienced before. "I can hardly wait to get started."

Dot's smile widened, and she reached to pat my hand. "It's going to be great. I'll come out to the grand opening of your store and bring some other chamber members. We'll make a big splash."

"Please do," I said. "And if you know anyone who has antiques to put on consignment, let me know. I suspect our store is going to look pretty sparse during the first few weeks, so the more the merrier."

"This is what I love about working in community," Dot said. "These people are your eyes, your ears, your mouth. They are truly on your team."

In that moment, I was struck with an idea. "I've got it! You just hit the nail on the head, Dot."

"How so?" She looked up from the computer screen.

"I love this idea of reaching out to others for help. What if I did that at the car show? What if I went and handed out MISSING posters with Tilly's picture on them, along with the VIN number and other details about her. That way people can be on the lookout for her."

"That's perfect!" Dot exclaimed. "Maybe someone in that circle has seen her."

"You should offer a reward, honey," Bessie Mae chimed in. "Missing posters often have a big reward."

"I wish I could, but I spent most of my money bidding on her." I did my best not to sigh aloud for emphasis as I was reminded of that.

"Well, the Lord will make a way." My aunt patted my hand. "He always does."

"Yes, He does." And I felt sure He would once more.

"You never know," Dot said. "You might get all of those car enthusiasts together, and one of them might be privy to some information about your missing truck. Stranger things have happened."

"And they could share the information about Tilly with others in the community. That way if the person who stole her took her outside of this general area, the word would be spread beyond Mabank, Gun Barrel City, and so on."

"Exactly. Now you're catching on." Dot gave me an admiring look. "Your skills are increasing already."

"Yeah, before long I'll open my own detective agency." A laugh followed at the idea of that.

"I'll be there in my official capacity as president of the chamber," Dot said. "So, anything you need from me, just ask."

"You've given me so many ideas already. You really are a wealth of information, Dot. Every town needs someone just like you." And I meant it. This woman was a gem.

She smiled and thanked me. And in that moment, I was struck with an idea. "Can you give me a list of contacts for businesses on 198 near the Big Red Bid?"

"Sure, hon. Why?"

"I want to contact all of them to see if anyone noticed Tilly being towed off early on Saturday morning. I'm thinking someone along that stretch of 198 must have seen something. You know?"

"Sure. I think that's a fine idea, but there are a lot of businesses between Mabank and Gun Barrel City. You know? Might be quicker to visit with the owners on Saturday at the car show. Most will be there representing their businesses."

"You think?"

"I know." She gave me a little wink. Besides, it'll do you good to get to know the other business owners anyway. Introduce yourself and your antique shop. Nudge your way into the circle."

That made sense, though the idea of meeting so many people made me nervous. Still, I needed a list, which she was happy to provide.

"I'm ready for some lunch, RaeLyn," Bessie Mae said. "The tearoom is only open for another hour and a half. Want to go?"

That sounded great to me. I loved the chicken salad sandwiches at the tearoom.

We invited Dot to join us, but she had to get back to the library. As we parted ways, I couldn't stop thinking about all I had learned. Maybe I would somehow stumble across a car enthusiast to help me find Tilly.

Minutes later, carefully situated in the driver's seat of my aunt's oversize vehicle, I pulled out of the parking spot and attempted to take a right onto Main Street.

In front of me, a car coming from the opposite direction decided to take a left-hand turn into the parking lot of True Value Hardware. Good thing I tapped the brakes just in time. The old man behind the wheel didn't even seem to notice me as he doodled his way into the parking lot.

"That was a close call," Bessie Mae said. "Who drives like that?"

"Who, indeed. Wyatt Jackson, that's who." I made a quick decision to pull into the parking lot behind him. Seconds later, I was parked one row away from Wyatt, who had pulled into a handicapped parking space.

"Why are we at the hardware store, honey?" Bessie Mae asked. "I thought we were going to lunch at the tearoom."

"Oh, we are, sorry. It's just that I noticed something." I pointed to Wyatt's '93 Ford pickup truck.

"I hate it when folks park illegally like that," my aunt said. "He doesn't even have proper tags for that spot."

That wasn't the part that bothered me. He probably had one of those hanging placards to attach to his rearview mirror.

The Pontiac's engine hummed softly as I observed Wyatt Jackson get out of his truck and take a few steps toward the front door of the hardware store. The sun beamed down, casting long shadows across the pavement. Wyatt moved at a slow, deliberate pace, his steps seemingly burdened by the weight of age as he shuffled along, cane in hand.

His features seemed even more weathered today, his face etched with wrinkles and deep lines.

"Oh my stars!" Bessie Mae let out a little gasp. "That's Wyatt Jackson, right there in the flesh."

"Yes. I noticed him as he turned in, which is why I followed him."

I kept a watchful eye as he navigated the step up to the sidewalk. His struggles were evident, and for a moment, empathy warred with the suspicion that crept up inside of me. Still, I needed answers and needed them quickly.

"What's the plan, honey?" My aunt turned to face me, wide-eyed. "Do we follow him inside to see what he's up to?"

"I guess." Though the idea made me a little nervous.

"Well, count me in. I watch *Murder She Wrote*. I know how these things go. And you know what Duke would say. . ."

"A man's gotta do what a man's gotta do." We spoke the words in unison.

"Yep." Bessie Mae swung open the door and started climbing out, even before I'd opened my door.

My aunt might be eighty-two, but all talk of rheumatism faded as she sprinted from the car. She was as spry as a teenager at this very moment. Perhaps sleuthing would do her good after all.

As I climbed out of the car, I found myself more determined than ever to unravel the mystery surrounding my grandfather's stolen truck. And with Bessie Mae by my side, I felt confident.

We followed a distance behind Wyatt as he entered the hardware store.

I did my best to keep him in view. The bell above the entrance chimed as my aunt and I stepped inside, and I nodded at a worker who called out, "Welcome to True Value. Let me know if I can help you."

I doubted he could help me track an old man's steps but didn't say so.

Bessie Mae grabbed a cart and tossed a package of batteries inside.

"I needed those anyway," she whispered. "Might as well look legit."

Half an aisle later she'd tossed in a garden hose, a new faucet for the kitchen sink, and a toilet plunger.

"In case we have to fight him off." She waved the plunger in the air.

All righty then.

Wyatt made his way toward the automotive section, and I followed, lagging a few yards behind.

I pretended to be interested in something on the shelf in front of me. Duct tape? Really? But my eyes never really left him for more than a moment at a time. The poor guy moved so slowly, and appeared to be in pain.

"He's really looking old," Bessie Mae whispered, her words hoarse. "Not all of us have aged well."

She could say that twice and mean it. My aunt had aged with grace and ease. Wyatt, on the other hand? Well, I found myself struggling internally as I watched him creak his way along. His frailty caused me to wince in pain, just watching him. Just as quickly, though, suspicions cut in.

Wyatt examined a display of car accessories, holding a car part with his weathered hands.

"What's he got? Can you tell?" Bessie Mae whispered.

"Yeah, a rearview mirror. Just like the kind we would need for Tilly."

"Thief! Should I tackle him?"

"No, Bessie Mae." Though, I might pay money to see that. "We're going to get out of here."

"Over my dead body!"

He glanced our way, and my aunt lifted the toilet plunger to cover her face.

Clearly, she wasn't ready to give up just yet. So, we trailed him from aisle to aisle, watching his every move. He didn't seem to notice us. Maybe his vision wasn't what it used to be.

When he reached the tool section, Wyatt paused to examine a display of wrenches. At this point, my suspicions grew. I found myself grappling with the possibility that he was purchasing tools to fix up Tilly.

Whatever he planned to use those tools for, he'd found what he wanted. Wyatt abruptly made his way toward the checkout area.

Bessie Mae opted for the self-checkout, a catastrophic error in judgment on her part. The woman was no good with anything electronic. True to form, she double scanned the toilet plunger and—just about the time Wyatt headed out the door into the parking lot—entered a heated dispute with a young store worker.

By the time we'd made our purchases, any window of opportunity to confront Wyatt had passed. We stepped outside just as his truck pulled out of the parking lot.

"Well, that was fun." Bessie Mae giggled and hefted her bag of purchases from one arm to another. "I say we do that again, real soon."

"Trail a suspect, you mean?"

"Yep. And come to the hardware store. I don't get over here nearly enough. Did you know you can buy old-timey bubble gum and soda pop at the hardware store?"

"I did not."

"Well, you can. I saw it in the checkout line just now. And you know what else?"

"What's that, Bessie Mae?"

"I think after we have our lunch at the tearoom, we should drive by Wyatt's place and not tell your parents a thing about it."

CHAPTER FOURTEEN

Well, then. If she wanted to drive by Wyatt's place, we'd drive by Wyatt's place.

And that's exactly where I was headed when the call came from Mom, saying we needed to get home quick because Carrie was having contractions.

So, home we went, frantic anticipation leading the way. Our little investigation would just have to wait for another day when we weren't preoccupied with a baby.

Only, by the time we got there, Carrie's twinges had proven to be false labor—Braxton-Hicks contractions, she called them. So, I took the opportunity to head out to the barn to work for a few hours to clear my head and heart.

This day had proven to be more complicated than I had imagined. And we still had no answers about Wyatt, except to say that he was apparently not listed among those showing cars on Saturday. Though, based on the rearview mirror in his hand at the hardware store, the man was currently working on a vehicle.

My Tilly, perhaps?

I did my best to divert my attention to the antique store. There was still a lot to be done, after all. So, I dove into action, moving shelf units from here to there, labeling products, and dividing items by category. I'd always been pretty good at decorating, so this was the fun part, deciding what would go where. . .and why.

The practicality of moving things around was grueling. And after a couple of hours, I was tired and hurting all over. Time to give up on this project and give that new foal another peek. Watching him toddle around put a smile on my face and almost made me forget my aches and pains. Almost.

When I got back to the house for dinner, I was a sweaty, dirty mess but happy with the progress I'd made. It was getting easier to see what I still needed to do to pull off this dream of mine in time for the grand opening a little over a week out.

I slept like a rock that night but had the weirdest dream about old cars. In the dream, I was buzzing down 175 in a '57 Chevy convertible with Mason seated at my side. Stephanie was in the back seat, hollering about the wind in her practically perfect hair. For whatever reason, Meredith Reed was in the back seat with her, putting on lipstick and spitting out quotes from John Wayne movies. Weird.

When I awoke, I had a headache and the sniffles. Probably from all the dust I'd stirred up in the barn. At this very moment, I didn't feel motivated to go back and continue my work, but someone had to do it. So, just after breakfast, while the morning was still fresh and new, I trekked back out to the barn once again, Riley moving along beside me, my ever-faithful companion. Today would be spent taking serious inventory. So I brought my laptop, spreadsheet file ready to go. I didn't relish this part, but it had to be done.

As I made my way past the gate into the field, the horses meandered my way to greet me. I was particularly fond of Duchess, the oldest mare. She had proven to be a favorite with everyone in the family, even after facing a couple of major health scares over the years. I was so grateful she was still with us.

Off in the distance, Dad and the twins worked together to move the cows from one field to another to graze.

"You should be helping," I said to Riley, who glanced up at me with a woeful expression that read, *Who? Me?*

"I know, I know. You're a cattle dog in name only."

And she was. This sweet old girl wasn't much for ranch work, but she sure loved to roam and play. And spend time with me, her favorite hobby.

I didn't have much time to think it through, with so much to do. The morning hours were spent frantically in the antique shop, going through every item on every shelf, adding them to my inventory list by category.

I'd made good work of organizing the store's various areas yesterday and was finally able to fine-tune that. Once that was done, it was absolutely getting easier to see which areas of the store were still short on items. I wasn't altogether sure what to do about that, other than put out a plea for consignment items, and quickly.

Hopefully folks would take me up on that and actually bring items for me to sell. I would love to have some handmade elements—like quilts or personalized knitted items. Those always sold well.

I was so busy that I forgot all about eating anything for lunch. A text from my sister-in-law alerted me to the fact that Mom and Bessie Mae were getting worried about me.

I'LL BE THERE IN ABOUT TEN MINUTES, was all I could manage.

Twenty was more like it. I found myself distracted, staring at my phone at a notification that had just come through on Facebook.

From Stephanie.

My heart skipped a beat as I saw the friend request had been accepted, and even more as I realized I had a private message waiting from her.

HEY, YOU! were her first two words. WERE YOUR EARS BUZZING OR SOMETHING? I WAS JUST TELLING CONNOR ALL ABOUT YOU THE OTHER DAY. I HAVE SO MANY GREAT MEMORIES OF OUR YEARS TOGETHER.

Okay, how to respond? My mind raced as I pondered the possibilities, finally landing on: GREAT TO HEAR FROM YOU.

GREAT TO HEAR FROM YOU TOO. HOW'S LIFE IN MABANK?

WE'RE BUSY ON THIS END, I typed. GETTING READY TO OPEN AN ANTIQUE STORE IN OUR BARN. IT'S CALLED TRINKETS AND TREASURES.

No WAY! she wrote back. I'LL HAVE TO TELL MAMA. SHE'LL BE STOP-PING BY TO SHOP, NO DOUBT.

THAT WOULD BE GREAT. I paused. YOU'RE LIVING IN IOWA NOW?

YEP. AMES. MY HUSBAND IS A PASTOR AT A LOCAL CHURCH. IT'S A GREAT LIFE.

Whoa. The star quarterback was now a pastor? Surprising.

I never thought I'd love a place as much as Texas, but I've fallen in love with Iowa. Go figure. She followed this with a smiley face.

I'm so glad you're happy, Stephanie. I stopped short of adding, "You deserve it." There was still a teensy-tiny part of me that wondered why the Stephanies of this world always seemed to get the best—the high school prom king, the star quarterback, the cozy life in Iowa.

She was Papaw.

I was Wyatt Jackson.

"For pity's sake, RaeLyn," I muttered aloud to no one but myself. "Just say it."

And so I did. I typed the words, You deserve it. And I felt them, all the way to my toes.

She responded with another smiley, and I told her I had to go. The family would wonder what had happened to me.

I finally showed up in the kitchen just as the others wrapped up their lunch, platters of sandwich meats, cheeses, and breads. I helped myself, then took a seat at the table, deep in thought.

"How's it going out there?" Carrie asked.

"You look tired, baby girl." Mom clucked her tongue at me. "This grand opening is going to be harder than you thought, isn't it?"

"Well, I'm just figuring out that we have way too much of some things and not enough of others. I've never seen so many little knickknacks in my life. But we have a real shortage of larger, more valuable items—like collector's items—and you usually see a lot of those at an antique store. I'm sure they'll come in, but right now it all feels a little sparse."

"I'm still going through those old road signs and gas station signs and other things we found in the old barn," Dallas said. "I've been looking them up online to see how to price them."

Wow. Did one of the twins really just say he was working. . .without being coerced? I would have to circle this date on the calendar so I'd never forget the day it happened.

"When Jake gets home from the school, I'm going to have him go up into the attic at our place," Carrie chimed in. "Remember, I told you that we came across some boxes up there last year? I think there's a lot of the old family stuff left to go through. Maybe you'll stumble across something valuable in that stash."

I'd forgotten all about those, to be honest. But the idea that there might be more to sell brought me hope. It also got Bessie Mae excited. Carrie and Jake's place was her family home, after all. She would probably love a trip down memory lane.

"I wonder if we'll find any of my dolls that I had as a kid," she said. "I always wondered what happened to those."

"Well, if we do, we certainly won't put them up for sale," I promised.

"We certainly will," she countered. "They'll bring in top dollar, and I could use the money for a cruise." A little smile tipped up the edges of her lips. "There are lots of crimes to solve on cruises, I would imagine. You'll have to go with me RaeLyn."

"So, now you're a crime solver?" Carrie looked back and forth between us. "That sounds like fun."

"Yep. We're the Hadley Sleuths, at your service." Bessie Mae offered a funny little curtsy. "Selling antiques and solving crimes, all while baking the best cobbler you ever tasted."

"Then writing articles in *Mabank Happenings* exposing our suspects after the fact," I added.

Funny how my life was expanding. I was shop owner, future chamber-of-commerce member, journalist, and now supersleuth. If I kept adding credits to my résumé, I'd have to get bigger business cards.

Oh, who was I kidding? I didn't have any business cards. But maybe one day I would, especially if I joined the chamber.

"There's no need to wait for Jake to come home from work," I said to Carrie. "I'm happy to go into your attic and look around."

"Really?" She didn't look convinced.

Neither did Mom.

"I don't know if that's wise, RaeLyn," she said.

"I've been up many a ladder in my day," I argued. "I'm pretty sure it's not going to be a big deal to look around and see what I can find."

And boy, was I ever glad I did. Half an hour later I'd dragged down six big boxes of stuff, which Bessie Mae and Carrie were going through, piece by piece. We were startled—and frankly, relieved—to see so many of our grandparents' items in those boxes. Maybe I wouldn't have to take as many consignment items after all.

I started looking through the first box and was surprised to find yearbooks from Mabank High dating back several decades.

"Oh my goodness, these aren't supposed to be here," Bessie Mae exclaimed. "They're definitely not for sale. I think these are all family yearbooks."

"Are you and Papaw in these?" I asked.

She nodded. "I think so. I'm so glad you stumbled across these, honey. I haven't seen them in ages."

"Well, let's give 'em a look."

We started flipping through the oldest ones, dated in the early '50s. The vintage pages were creased and worn, and the black-and-white images were now a distinct sepia tone.

"Oh my stars." I smiled as I saw the picture of Papaw standing next to Tilly wearing his football uniform. "It's Tilly!"

"Fresh and new, straight off the lot in Dallas." Bessie Mae let out a whistle. "Man, she was a beauty."

"Wasn't she?" I gave the picture a closer look. Papaw was beaming ear to ear, but in the background, in the very center of the crowd of onlookers, I saw another face, one with a twisted frown.

"Oh, wow. Wyatt Jackson." I pointed. "He looks mad."

Bessie Mae leaned down and squinted. "Yeah, remember what I told you. This was the day he lost that truck to your papaw, and he was none too happy about it."

We continued thumbing through the rest of the yearbooks, and I had to laugh when I saw the ones from the early '80s, when my parents were young.

I'd never seen my dad with an '80s rock perm before. And mom's wavy hair made her look like Farrah Fawcett. Well, according to Bessie Mae. I wasn't exactly sure who Farrah Fawcett was.

We finally pushed the yearbooks aside and looked through some of the other boxes. I paused when I found one of Bessie Mae's porcelain dolls.

"Oh!" She let out a cry and grabbed one with long blond curls. "You found them. Good for you, RaeLyn!" She hugged the doll and carried on with such joy, sharing story after story about her childhood antics with this doll.

Before long I found two more. One of them had tangled hair and looked like she'd seen better days. I couldn't get much money for her, even if I did sell her. But I couldn't do that to Bessie Mae. She needed to keep these babies.

"I say you put them in your room, Aunt Bessie."

She looked up from the one she was holding. "You think?"

"Absolutely. They can be a lovely reminder of your childhood."

"Well, if you say so." A lovely smile lit her face.

We found a few more items in the box, including a couple of Christmas tree ornaments and a vintage nativity set.

"Should we keep this or sell it?" I asked.

"Oh my stars." She latched onto one of the little pieces—a wise man. "I used to play with these when I was a little girl. I would move them all around on the fireplace mantel."

That settled that. We would keep it and set it up at Christmas. Anything that brought a twinkle to my aunt's eyes was staying.

I thought we'd finished with the box but felt something down in the bottom. I reached down and pulled up a little piece from a chess set. I held up the marble king and gave it a closer look. "Oh my. Look at this."

Bessie Mae stretched out her hand, and I passed it off to her.

The loveliest smile lit her face. "Oh, wow. I recognize this. It went with a chess set that Wyatt always used. That set was one of the few things that survived the fire when his parents died."

"Why do you suppose the king is the only piece left?" I asked.

She shrugged. "No idea. It's funny, the things you find in an attic. Isn't it? I can't imagine why that wasn't tossed years ago, since the rest of the set is missing."

I flipped it upside down and found a tiny piece of tape on the bottom. I had to squint to make out the word penciled on it.

Checkmate.

I showed it to Bessie Mae. "Why would it say *checkmate*?"

"I have no idea." She gave it a closer look. "Very strange. But that's definitely Charles' handwriting. I'd know it anywhere."

"Not Wyatt?" I asked.

She shook her head. "Nope. Your papaw always did that funny little thing with his k's."

"But Papaw wasn't the chess player, right?"

"Right." She turned it over in her hand. "I have no idea why this is here."

"You said Wyatt had a hobby shop that sold marble chess sets?"

"For a while, yes. But that shop didn't last. These marble sets are beautiful, but unless they're incredibly rare or made by a well-known company, they're not terribly valuable. A couple hundred dollars, maybe. But it is odd that we would find this here, and now."

Odd, indeed.

But I couldn't allow myself to get preoccupied by that little king. I had to keep my eye on the prize and go through the rest of these items.

We found all sorts of things for the shop, which gave me great hope. I texted Dallas to see if he and Gage were done with their chore. Hopefully they would haul this stuff out to the barn for me. Minutes later Dallas showed up, ready to help.

Before I left Jake and Carrie's place, I stopped off to give the new nursery a look.

"This was my room as a little girl." Bessie gave the space a wistful look. "I have so many beautiful memories of this space from those days. But it looked nothing like this."

"I just love what you've done with the space, Carrie." I gave the room an admiring look. "You're really good at this decorating thing. If you weren't twelve months pregnant, I'd put you to work in the shop so it could look this nice."

"Eight months and one week, but thank you for the compliment. What do you think about the colors?"

I gave the walls a closer look, taken in by the soft cream and sage colors she'd chosen. "I love that accent wall. Sage green is a favorite of mine."

"Me too." She laughed. "I think Jake's getting a little tired of it, though. "I asked him to paint the new kitchen cabinets the same shade and he groaned." A smile turned up the edges of her lips. "I want to get the kitchen finished before the baby comes." She rubbed her belly. "And I think sage green is perfect for the cabinets."

"And I was sure you showed me this same color when we were talking about the master bath walls," I chimed in.

"Yes." She sighed. "I like sage green."

"Me too," Bessie Mae said. "But all I have to do is look out the back door, and I see it on all sixty-three acres. Why add more green to the inside of a house?"

Carrie's smile faded, and she set the paint can down. "Oh."

"I like it." I offered what I hoped would look like an encouraging nod. "It's soothing."

Aunt Bessie wasn't really one to offer decorating advice, but I would never say that to her face. She and Mom kept our family kitchen decked out in the same duck theme my mother had integrated in the 1980s, long before I was born. The older ladies in the Hadley clan didn't take change well, and I had a feeling Bessie Mae wasn't keen on all the changes happening here at Carrie and Jake's place either.

"You know, back when I lived in this house, we never gave a minute's thought to decor. If we had food on the table and enough beds to cram all of the kids into, that was all right by us. These days young folks decorate like they're planning to be on a magazine cover." Bessie Mae rolled her eyes.

"I think it's nice." I shot a quick glance my sister-in-law's way. I could read the discouragement in her face. "When I get a house, I plan to decorate it to the hilt."

"Yeah, in Texas decor," Carrie added. "I can almost imagine it now. Cowboy boots and heavy wooden furniture."

"Yep. And no one can stop me."

I had dreamed of a house like that since childhood. I knew just where I would put it on our property: on the southwest corner. We didn't use that field for the cattle, and it had such a lovely view of the bluebonnet field. A gorgeous Texas-themed house would be perfect on that corner.

I didn't have long to think about it because Jake arrived home from ball practice a few moments later and helped Dallas and Gage load all the boxes of stuff into the back of his pickup. Together, they hauled all of those items out to the shop for me, for which I was very grateful.

Several minutes later, my nearly clean space in the barn was loaded again with stacks and stacks of boxes to go through. And though this might've seemed overwhelming earlier, it actually got me excited now. I didn't mind diving right in. In fact, I was thrilled about the possibilities of having more to offer our upcoming customers.

Jake helped me go through them while talking at length about the spring baseball lineup at Mabank High. I pretended to be interested, but baseball wasn't really my thing. Finally, I'd had enough.

"You excited about the baby coming?" I asked when he paused for a breath.

"Yeah." He stifled a yawn. "Just exhausted. Carrie's always got me painting or sanding something."

"I heard the new kitchen cabinets are going to be—"

"Sage green. Just like the baby's room. And the master bedroom walls. And the trim around the top of all the doors in the house." He laughed.

"Hey, I think it's nice that she's trying to make that place her own. It was really good of Carrie to agree to move onto the family property."

"Yep." Jake pointed to a box that was still sealed shut. "Hey, what's in this one?"

"Oh, I think Bessie Mae said it was all of Papaw's old papers—business stuff. Ranch ledgers. Stuff like that. It wasn't supposed to come out here. I think Mom wanted it at the house to go through."

"Let's make sure before I haul it back." He pulled out a pocketknife to open one of the boxes.

Sure enough, the box was filled with stacks and stacks of papers. Some looked business related. There were a few tax returns, some dating back to the 1960s.

But, way underneath it all, we came up with something rather surprising.

"What's this?" Jake held up a manila envelope. He reached inside and pulled out several more white envelopes.

I gave them a closer look. "Letters? They're addressed to Papaw from Clayton Henderson. That's weird."

I opened one and read through it, curiosity getting the better of me. Then I looked my brother's way and said, "Whoa. Jake, you're going to want to look at this."

CHAPTER FIFTEEN

I passed the paperwork off to my brother, who gave it a close look before speaking.

"This is some sort of contract between the two of them," he said as he glanced up from the pages.

"Right." I took it back and looked over the details of it, trying to make sense of it. "Did you realize Papaw had a business deal with Clayton once upon a time?"

"Sounds vaguely familiar. I was really young when everyone was talking about it. Or, arguing about it, as the case were."

Jake and I talked about the document at length but finally decided to show it to Dad and Bessie Mae. They would know best. A short while later we made our way to the house. We walked inside to find the place eerily quiet and still. I wasn't sure where my parents had gone, but Bessie was probably catching a little catnap in her room. That wouldn't be unusual at this time of day.

Jake headed to the fridge to grab a drink, and I tiptoed down the hall to her large converted bedroom.

The soft creak of the door hinges announced my entrance into Bessie Mae's domain. The air in her room was thick with the warm scent of tea rose, an outdated fragrance that had become synonymous with my aunt.

The garage, once home to dusty tools and the lingering scent of motor oil, had been transformed into a cozy haven, perfect for her. The quilt on the bed always made me smile. She'd stitched it herself, by hand, years ago and wouldn't think of swapping it out with something more modern. Why mess with perfection?

I had to smile when I saw her porcelain dolls on the bed, propped up against the pillows. It brought tears to my eyes as I thought about how special they must be to her.

My gaze swept the room, which was adorned with John Wayne memorabilia—posters, framed photos, and even a life-sized cutout of the Duke himself, watching over the space. The woman was pretty passionate about her guy.

I glanced at the far corner, where I caught my aunt catnapping in her favorite recliner, an '80s-themed relic in a lovely shade of country blue. Should I wake her or leave her be? I decided to ease my way out of the room so as not to disturb her.

She must've heard me because she stirred in the chair and let out a little grunt, followed by a, "Well, hey, sweetie. Didn't see you there."

"Hey, Aunt Bessie Mae," I responded quietly. "Didn't mean to disturb you."

Bessie yawned and gestured for me to join her. I took a seat on the quilt chest at the foot of her bed.

"I was just catching a little rest before starting dinner." She rubbed at the back of her neck. "But I really need to invest in a neck pillow."

"You have one, remember?" I walked to the closet and peered inside. Every square inch of this space was filled with her stuff, most of which dated back to long before my birth.

I finally found the neck pillow on the top shelf and walked it over to her. "I got it for you for Christmas last year, remember?"

"Did you?" She yawned again. "I think I'm just tired, honey."

"If you're worn out, I can cook dinner tonight," I offered. "I don't mind a bit."

"Oh no, honey. It's my joy to cook for everyone. You know that."

I did, but I also knew it must be exhausting. And I was pretty good at spaghetti.

Jake popped his head in the door. "Oh, here you are. Did you ask her about the contract?"

I shook my head. "Haven't had a chance to tell her about it yet."

"Tell me about what?" Bessie Mae sat up in the chair, now wide awake. "What did I miss? What contract?"

We brought her up to speed on the papers we'd found, and she asked to see them.

Jake passed them her way, and she looked them over with great interest, flipping from page to page.

"Oh my goodness, yes. I remember all of this now." She turned one of the pages over to read the back side. "They were going to go into business together once upon a time. It's all coming back to me now."

"Papaw and Clayton Henderson?"

"Yes, Clayton was young at the time and just starting out. I think Charles took an interest in him and wanted to help get him up and running. But, as I recall, things went awry not too far into the deal."

"So, what kind of business was it?" I asked. I had no recollection of it whatsoever.

She attempted to stand but almost tumbled back into the chair.

"Just rest, Bessie Mae," I said. "Don't get up on our account."

"Pooh. I'm fine." She glanced at the papers again and a hint of recognition lit her face. "I remember now. They were going to open some sort of fishing resort for tourists with cabins and such. Your Papaw was the best fisherman."

"I remember fishing with him more times than I could count," I said. "But I don't remember anything about a business."

"He wanted to open a place alongside the lake, on the Gun Barrel City side. I think he pitched the idea to Clayton, who was just starting to buy up real estate. They were going to build it together. There were going to be inexpensive cabins to rent, boat rentals, that sort of thing. People could come and stay in these quaint little cabins and fish all day if they liked. Or take their boats out on the water. He had all sorts of plans, perfect for everyday folk."

A host of memories flowed over me all at once. "I have a vague recollection of Papaw once telling me that he had wanted to open cabins along the lake. But I sure don't remember Clayton being in the story. Are you saying it never happened?"

"No, they didn't end up moving forward on the joint venture." Bessie stirred in the chair and tucked the neck pillow into place. "But, my goodness, what a dreamer your papaw was. He wanted a place with a private fishing pier that extended out over the lake. You know what I mean? A peaceful place where folks could cast their lines and while away the hours without a care in the world."

"Sounds dreamy."

"Perfect for vacationers. I also remember that he wanted to offer guided fishing excursions."

"That sounds like so much fun. And Papaw would've been perfect for that," I said.

"I never knew a better fisherman," Jake chimed in. "He taught me everything I know."

Bessie Mae nodded and settled back into her chair with a contented look on her face. "He was the best. And he knew all of the other seasoned fishermen in the area too. They could've guided newcomers to the best spots for fishing, for sure. I think he even talked about doing boat trips to explore the waterways. Sunset rides, I think he called them. More scenic in nature."

Wow. Papaw must've been more fascinated with the lake than I'd realized. "Sounds like he really thought this through."

"Oh, he did." Bessie Mae attempted to stand once again. "It was his big dream."

Jake rushed over to help her up. "So, what became of the idea?"

"Clayton bought the property but then reneged on the deal. I think there was some sort of dispute about the terms of their agreement, so it all fell apart. Now, you two follow me into the kitchen. I've got to get going on our supper. We're having meat loaf."

"Yum." I loved my aunt's meat loaf.

When we arrived in the kitchen, she pulled the ground beef out of the fridge and reached for the other ingredients she would need.

While she worked, Jake and I skimmed a few more of the letters, finally landing on the last one in the batch.

"You're right," I said after giving it a closer look. "They were arguing over the terms. Clayton wanted a larger share of the profits and actually threatened Papaw with legal action unless he agreed."

"That Clayton Henderson is no good." Jake shoved the letters back into the manila envelope.

"Yep. Tried to tell you that yesterday," Bessie Mae said. "I've never had a good feeling about him, even when he was young. Some folks just can't be trusted."

I paused to think that through. "Well, if that's the case, I'm glad they didn't end up doing business together. We probably would've ended up losing the whole ranch."

"You're probably right, RaeLyn." She looked up from the meat loaf, which she'd just pressed into the loaf pan. "If I know Henderson—and I'm pretty sure I do—he would've found some way to make it his own. That's how he is."

It was, indeed.

"So, what happened to the property they were going to turn into a resort?" I asked.

And then, just as quickly, it hit me.

"Oh my goodness. The new B and B he just opened is on the piece of property where Papaw wanted to build his cabins?"

"Yes." She popped the meat loaf into the oven, then turned our way, wiping her hands on her apron. "There's now a million-dollar home on that very spot where your grandfather wanted to build affordable log cabins for everyday folks to rent."

Mom walked in the back door, carrying on about the new foal. She went into the half bath to wash her hands, then came back out again. "What did I miss? Something to do with Clayton's new place?"

"Oh, we just put it together that he and Papaw once wanted to turn that property into affordable cabins for tourists," Jake said.

"Yep. I remember." She paused and her brow wrinkled. "But that went south in a hurry, and Clayton won out, as always."

"Sometimes life's just not fair." My aunt sighed. "But God is the one who will have the final say. That brings me some degree of peace when injustices happen."

"Have you been out to his new place?" Mom asked. "I've been tempted to go look. There's an open house this weekend, and everyone is talking about it."

"I heard all about it from Clayton," I said. "Did I tell you that he and Nadine turned up at the auction house the morning Tilly went missing?"

"You didn't." Mom's eyes widened.

"Yeah, apparently he won a bid on a '67 Buick Riviera."

"Nice car," Jake said, then excused himself to head home to check on Carrie.

"We should go to his open house," I said after Jake disappeared out the back door. "I want to see this piece of property where Papaw dreamed of building a business."

"Only he never got to see his dream come to pass because Clayton one-upped him." Bessie Mae opened the fridge and pulled out a bag of potatoes. She gestured for me to join her at the sink, and before long I was peeling those potatoes and she was chopping them up into pieces.

"Why do you suppose the Clayton Hendersons of this world are the way they are?" I asked. "Like, why do they always have to outshine the others? What are they trying to prove?"

"Clayton Henderson wasn't always the high-and-mighty man you see now." Bessie filled the pot of potatoes with cool water and set it on the stove. "He was the son of the richest man in town and took some bullying because of it."

"Yes, he came from family money," Mom said. "He was in my grade in school, you know."

I did know that at one time but had apparently forgotten.

Bessie nodded. "I remember what he was like as a boy. Back then I worked in the school lunchroom. He would sit on the far side of the room at lunch because the other kids were so hard on him."

My heart went out to him, for a moment anyway.

"Then one day he just decided he'd had enough, and he started fighting back. Next thing you know he's star baseball player, valedictorian of his class. . .all the things." Bessie shrugged. "I was really proud of him for all of that. I didn't start questioning his actions until he started buying up all of the businesses in town and putting his name on front."

"Yeah, there's something wrong with a person who feels like he has to have it all."

In that moment, the image of my once-upon-a-time best friend, Stephanie, flashed in front of my eyes and those usual feelings of angst crept over me. Just as quickly, I pushed those contrary feelings away.

"She deserves it," I whispered to no one but myself.

And I meant it.

CHAPTER SIXTEEN

And there we were, Saturday morning—the majority of the Hadley clan—at our first-ever antique car show. I wasn't sure what I'd expected, but the parking lot of the Walmart was buzzing with activity, filling a usually low-traffic corner of the lot with hundreds of people.

We strolled along under the lovely March sunshine across that bustling lot, where a symphony of revving engines upped the anticipation. This, coupled with all the lively chatter, seemed the perfect undercurrent to the morning's activities. Owners and enthusiasts all seemed to bond over their shared love of all things vintage, at least in the car world.

I held tight in my hands the MISSING posters I'd created, showing Tilly—in her current state—as well as the details of when and how she had gone missing. Hopefully someone in this crowd would have information for me. I hoped.

Rows and rows of colorful vintage cars gleamed under that bright sun, their shiny exteriors polished to perfection for a day such as this. It was a vibrant tapestry of colors and conversations, giving the place an electric feel. Or rather an internal combustion engine feel.

I'd expected to be blown away but not like this. Amidst the chrome, laughter, and sound of engines purring, I immersed myself in the vibrant world of the Cedar Creek antique car show—which turned out to be a mosaic of passion, history, and freshly polished vintage automobiles in pretty much every make and model.

Mom flipped over the 1967 Mustang in a shiny turquoise. Dad was keen on the '70 Plymouth Barracuda in a rich shade of green. Bessie Mae couldn't stop swooning over the '66 Chevy Bel Air. She said it took her back to her younger years.

No doubt. I hadn't even lived during those eras but found myself drawn in as if I had. These cars had the power to transport us back in time.

The car owners were almost as exciting as their vehicles, always ready to chat and brag about their babies. Most had flipped their cars and trucks, and that's probably why I located Mason Fredericks nearby—all decked out in jeans, a button-up, and well-worn boots, talking to an older fellow standing in front of a '72 Pontiac.

And passing out cards for his new business.

Of course he would be here. It just made sense. I'd seen the guy's eyes sparkle many times—like when he gazed at Bessie Mae's chicken and dumplings—but never like they did today. He was like a kid in a candy shop here, among his people. And in that moment, I felt very happy for him.

He didn't seem to notice me, but I didn't blame him. The guy was too busying examining the engine of the Pontiac and carrying on about how spectacular it was.

Mom gave me a nudge with her elbow when she saw him. "Hey, there's Mason."

"Yeah. In his element, apparently."

I decided to follow his lead and start handing out flyers. My family decided to move on without me, but I didn't mind. I was here on a mission to find Tilly.

So many of the people I shared the flyer with commented on what a great make and model Tilly was, but no one seemed to have any information.

I finally stumbled across the manager of Brookshire Brothers, which was located just a couple of blocks away from the Big Red Bid. Maybe he had seen something that morning.

I shared the story of what had happened and then asked, "Did you, by chance, see a rusty red Chevy being towed by the grocery store on Tuesday morning?"

He scratched his head. "Well now, it seems like maybe I did. I see lots of vehicles coming and going from the auction house, many pulled by tow trucks. Wouldn't be unusual."

"That's great! I need particulars."

My hopes went straight up and then crashed back down again when he added, "Wait. Did you say Tuesday? I came in late on Tuesday morning. I had a dentist appointment." He flashed his shiny white teeth. "Veneers."

"Nice."

"What kind of truck did you say it was, again?" he asked.

"A '52 Chevy 3100. Originally red, but pretty faded out and rusty." I handed him one of the Missing flyers.

He gave the flyer a look and then glanced my way. "Aw, man. I remember when your grandfather used to drive her up to the store. That was years ago, long before I was manager. Back in those days we would actually carry the groceries out to the vehicles for our customers and load them. I loved loading up his in the back of that beautiful truck. How long has it been since he passed away?"

"Ten years back," I explained. "Tilly was sold shortly before he passed, but I bought her back on Monday night at the auction. Or, rather, I should say I won the bid, paid for her, and arranged for transport on Tuesday morning."

"If you get her fixed up, you should bring her to the next car show."

"Well, I have to find her first. That's the point. She went missing the same morning she was supposed to be towed to us. But the auction house cameras didn't pick up that stretch of the parking lot."

"Bummer. But I'll keep my eyes and ears open. In the meantime, you should connect with Freddy over at Quick Tow. That's the biggest towing company in town. Maybe someone paid him to haul that truck." He pointed at a fellow who, like Mason, was also handing out business cards. I didn't recognize him, but approached and shared my story.

When I asked if he had hauled Tilly, Freddy shook his head. "Definitely would've remembered that. I love those old trucks. Hope you find her again."

"Thanks." I lowered my voice. "Hey, you know the other tow truck drivers in the area?"

"Sure. I know most of 'em. And several in surrounding counties too."

"Any that might be willing to work a job like this. You know, under the table?"

Creases formed between his brows. "Most of the guys I know are on the up and up, so I doubt it. There are strict laws that govern what we do, and we're required to carry hefty insurance, so. . ."

"Even for big cash money, it wouldn't be a temptation?"

He shrugged. "It would be too big a risk. A driver could lose his license to tow if he was caught hauling off a vehicle that was stolen. You know? It wouldn't be worth it, even if someone offered a pretty penny."

Yeah. That made sense.

I took a few steps away from him and tried to get my bearings. Who should I approach next? Surely someone here could help me.

Before I could come up with a plan, Dot came rushing my way, arms loaded down with clipboards.

"What'a y'all think? Pretty great, huh?"

"Yeah, it's very. . .colorful." I gestured to the row of vehicles in front of me. "And the cars are great."

"I thought you might want to see Clayton's," Dot said. "He's got three in the running."

"In the running?" I asked.

"Well, sure. Did I forget to mention there are big prizes to be had? Winners get bragging rights and money too. Like I said the other day, folks come from several counties away to these events."

"Ah. That's right," I said.

"Stay till the end and you'll see. And in case you're interested, there's plenty of other stuff going on too. We've got a live band coming in at eleven, and there are more food trucks than I can keep up with." She gestured to the far end of the lot, where children were gathered. "There's also an area with face painting, balloon animals, and such. They've even got mini car rides."

"That's nice," I said. "I can't believe it's taken me this long to come to one of these. It's fun for the whole family."

"Sure is. I just saw Bessie Mae, and she's having the time of her life. Your mama too. I think everyone should come to these events—from kids to seniors."

"I can see why."

"It keeps the passion for cars going through multiple generations, which I think is sweet." Dot beamed. Then she leaned my way. "But we're not just here to have fun, are we? We're here to solve a riddle. We've got to figure out which of our suspects is most likely to have taken off with Tilly. And, as luck would have it, all of them are here today, gathered in this same parking lot."

"Well, that's convenient," I said. "Because my sleuthing skills are somewhat lacking."

"This is as good a day as any to figure it out." She offered me a wink and then disappeared into the crowd, pausing only to pick up a couple of clipboards she dropped along the way.

I did feel better about the fact that all the players were here. Hopefully the pieces to this puzzle would come together soon.

Before I could give it more thought, I caught a glimpse of Harlan. He walked toward me, sipping on a cup of coffee and pausing as he drew near.

"Hey, I didn't expect to see you here. Any word on your truck?"

"No." I shook my head. "I was going to ask you the same question."

He shifted his coffee cup from one hand to the other. "I figured the police would be in touch with you if they heard anything."

"I've been trying to find business owners near the auction house so that I can talk to them in person. I'm thinking someone must've seen something. Maybe I can jar someone's memory."

"Good idea. I'm still puzzled about how they got past the lock on the gate. That's a mystery to me."

"You still think your ex-wife. . ." I paused and decided not to finish the sentence.

"I suppose anything's possible. If Warren questioned her, I didn't hear anything about it. Did you?"

"No, but maybe I should ask him about that."

I didn't bother to tell him that I'd already seen Meredith at the grocery store with Mason. That might be too much. Instead, I decided to change the subject.

"Are you here as a buyer?" I asked.

Harlan shook his head. "Nope. I came because a lot of these cars were once auctioned off at my place, then flipped. I like to see the trans-formations, you know? It's a lot of fun to see them spring to life again."

I nodded but found myself distracted as Harlan gazed at me a little too intently.

Thank goodness Bessie Mae and Mom approached with sodas in hand. Harlan headed off to look at a vintage Chrysler and then disappeared into the crowd.

My aunt passed a soda my way, and I took a sip, happy for the cool liquid. Before I could thank her, Tasha joined us, dressed in a bright lime-green blouse and jean shorts.

She rested her hands on her hips as she looked my way. "Did you see the flyer Clayton's handing out to everyone?"

When I shook my head, she pressed it into my hand. I read the infor-mation about his fabulous B and B and was duly impressed. His flyers were a lot more professional than mine, for sure.

"Oh, that's right. I'd forgotten he's having an open house for his new B and B today."

"Well, I didn't forget," she said. "And I'm off work this afternoon, so I'm planning to go. I want to scope out the competition. It's at two, if you want to come with."

Mom took the brochure from Tasha and looked it over. "Look at how he's described it, y'all: 'Nestled on the shores of Cedar Creek Lake, the brand-new Henderson House Bed-and-Breakfast stands as a testament to all that is good and right with the world.'"

"Good gravy." Tasha slapped herself on the forehead. "What's he building, a house or a cathedral?"

"From looking at this picture, I'd have to say a little of both." Mom gazed more intently at the paper in her hand. "Listen to this: 'Henderson House is designed with refined elegance and simple, understated luxury, a harmonious blend of modern comfort and classic charm.'"

"Ugh!" Tasha turned her gaze away from us.

"'As guests approach the property, a sense of tranquility washes over them.'" Mom handed me the brochure. "Man. Sounds great. And look, it says we can tour the facility and have hors d'oeuvres and drinks. We should do it!"

Now, I knew my mother wasn't a drinker, so she wasn't in this for the refreshments. She must have something else in mind. So I asked her about it.

"Okay, I'll confess, I want to do a little snooping." Mom laughed. "I'd like to see this man's new place. Curiosity killed the cat, you know."

"Well, just call me Fifi, because I want to go too," Bessie Mae said. "Nothing's more fun than looking at a brand-new fancy house."

"One you don't have to pay the mortgage on," Tasha said. "But I say we go together. I mean, I'm still not happy with the fact that he has an actual B and B while it's still just a dream for me." She released an exaggerated sigh. "But it wouldn't hurt me to check out the competition."

Bessie Mae reached for her sweater. "What time should we head that way?"

"Oh, it's not for hours yet," Mom said. "We've got plenty of time to enjoy the car show and have some lunch before we drive over there."

Mom cleared her throat a little too loudly, and I realized she must be trying to get my attention. I followed her gaze to discover Wyatt and his wife Rena looking at a vintage Chevy truck to our right.

"That's a similar make and model as our Tilly," I said. "In fact, it's the very same model."

"Totally different color," Mom quipped. "Not sure I like it in copper, do you?"

"No, I don't." But it did intrigue me to see Wyatt so immersed in conversation with a man who owned a truck that looked so much like mine. Surely this wasn't my Tilly, all done up in a shiny coat of copper paint.

No, there was just no way. That eighty-something-year-old man could not have stolen my vehicle all by his lonesome and then flipped it this quickly. I was letting my imagination run away from me.

Still, he seemed nervous this morning. Furtive glances my way, as well as nervous hands shoved into his pants pockets, clued me in to an ulterior motive. Something with this guy wasn't quite right.

"Go get 'em, girlie." Bessie Mae gave me a little nudge. "I'm going to take a peek at that white Mustang. It was always my dream car." She and my parents headed off to look at the sports cars, and I turned to discover Tasha had also left me alone. She was deep in conversation with Dot about something.

With the brochures tucked under my left arm and my soda in my right hand, I made my way to the Chevy. As soon as he saw me, Wyatt shuffled away, his arm linked in his wife's.

The owner struck up a conversation with me, all smiles as he sang the truck's praises. "She's a beaut, ain't she?"

"Definitely." I gave the truck a closer look and noticed some subtle differences between this one and Tilly.

"I call her Penelope. Or Lucky Penny. She goes by both."

That explained the color.

"Where'd you get her?" I asked.

A wistful look came over him. "Oh, I've had Penny for years. I've been showing her at least four or five years now. She's won all kinds of awards. She was passed down through the family."

So much for thinking I needed to look at the VIN number.

Okay, so I went ahead and glanced at the VIN number under the pretense of checking out the interior through the front window.

"Let me open 'er up for you." He swung wide the driver's side door and gestured for me to climb inside.

Once I got in there, tears instinctively sprang to my eyes. Sitting here, I could almost feel my grandfather's presence. It might not be the same truck, but it was the same experience.

"I see those tears." The elderly man gave me a sympathetic look. "This isn't the first time someone has had a reaction like that to Penelope. She has that effect on people. I get a little emotional myself."

I laid the Missing flyers on the dash and held tight to my drink as I looked the car over. I was terrified I might actually spill the drink and ruin this beautiful interior, so I decided I'd better get out of here.

Through the front window I saw Mason approaching. He took one look at me in the driver's seat and hurried my way.

I was tempted to bolt but paused when he offered a bright smile and a wave. He drew close and leaned into the open driver's side door. "Hey, you look mighty good behind the wheel of that thing."

"Thanks. It's the same make and model as Tilly, so I'm feeling a little nostalgic."

"I see those tears in your eyes."

I swiped at them with the back of my hand, embarrassed. Then I climbed out of the driver's seat and closed the door. I thanked the owner for letting me look her over, then took a couple of steps away before realizing I'd left the flyers on the dash.

I had no choice but to turn back around and fetch them. Mason hovered close by as I grabbed them and tucked them under my arm.

"What have you got there?"

"Oh, these?" I placed the flyers in his hand.

He looked them over and said, "Great idea. I'm sorry she's still missing."

"Thanks." Was he, though?

I took a sip of my soda and kept walking, wondering which direction Tasha had gone. "Would you help me hand them out?"

"Sure. To who?"

"Anyone who might know something. But, specifically, businesses along 198 near the auction house. I'm thinking someone might've seen the truck being towed away that morning."

"True." He offered a smile. "I'm glad to see you, by the way. I didn't know you guys were coming."

"We didn't either," I admitted. "It was kind of a last-minute thing. Figured if I'm ever going to find Tilly, I need to start hanging out with people who might be interested in her."

"That makes sense."

Off in the distance, I caught a glimpse of Meredith Reed. She was adorned in an over-the-top way, her somewhat low-cut floral dress drawing almost as much attention from the guys as the hot pink sports car she now stationed herself in front of. If I didn't know any better, the woman was begging to be photographed. She tipped her head from side to side and appeared to be posing.

Mason glanced her way, muttered "Great," under his breath, then looked back at me.

"You're in your element here," I observed.

"Boy, am I. I just talked to the owner of an antique station wagon about possibly restoring it for him. He needs bodywork and engine restoration."

"That's a big commitment."

"Hope he calls me. I'd love to tackle it. This is what I live for." He paused. "Well, not live for, but you know what I mean. I'd love to do it."

Meredith's shrill laughter rang out as she talked with the sports car owner. She whipped out a tube of lipstick and a tiny mirror and made a production out of dolling up her lips. . .which she painted the same hot pink as the flashy vehicle she now rested her hand against.

The owner didn't seem to mind. In fact, he asked if he could take a picture, and she willingly obliged.

I shot a glance at Mason, to see if he'd noticed.

Nope. He was gazing intently at me, a relaxed smile on his face.

All righty then. Maybe he wasn't on my suspect list anymore after all.

CHAPTER SEVENTEEN

Off in the distance, I noticed Harlan watching Meredith's every move. He seemed put off by her flirtatious actions, and I didn't blame him. No doubt he was still holding a grudge that she'd left him. Poor guy wasn't used to being the one left behind.

Meredith gave her ex-husband a curt nod and muttered "Harlan," as he passed by them.

To which he responded, "Meredith," and then walked away.

Mason looked their way, his brow wrinkling. "She turns up every-where, doesn't she?"

"I'd say."

He gave me an inquisitive look, and I could tell I'd struck a nerve. "What do you mean by that?"

"Well, you were sitting together at the auction, and she was bidding against me too. So I thought maybe…" A pause followed as I tried to think of the right words. "Thought maybe you two were a team. You know?"

He stared at me, wide-eyed. "RaeLyn Hadley, if I didn't know any better, I'd say you were jealous of Meredith Reed."

"Jealous? Me?" My heart thump-thumped at the accusation. "Of course not. Don't be silly."

"I told you I barely know her."

"You're Facebook friends."

"Well, I accepted her friend request, sure. I'm nice like that. But, why are you stalking my Facebook page?"

"I wouldn't call it stalking, exactly. We're old friends. I was just. . ."

He gave me an inquisitive look. "Snooping?"

"I guess."

"Inquiring minds want to know why." His eyebrows elevated mischievously.

"No reason. Only, you also went grocery shopping with her too. So, there is that."

His eyes narrowed to slits, and he leaned forward to whisper, "Are you *spying* on me now, RaeLyn Hadley? Should I change the locks on my doors?"

"No, I just happened to be in the baking aisle at Brookshire Brothers the other day when the two of you—"

"Bumped into each other and said hello. And that was the end of that. If you'd stuck around, you would've seen that she went her way and I went mine."

Okay, I actually *had* seen that, but I wasn't planning to tell him.

"We were starting to think maybe the two of you were a team, working together," I explained.

"A team?"

"When you're missing a vehicle, everyone begins to look like a suspect."

"Wait a doggone minute here." He paused and a hint of suspicion flashed in his eyes. "Are you saying you suspected me of taking Tilly? Now you think I'm a thief?"

I shrugged, unsure of how to respond. "I mean, you did want her at the auction."

"Well, sure. But I've already explained that I wouldn't have bid against you if I'd realized that was your grandfather's truck. And when you said 'we' a minute ago, who else are you referring to? Who was with you at the store? Because I'm pretty sure anyone in your family would've seen it for what it was, just a friendly exchange. The Hadleys know me better than that."

"Tasha said it was obvious, the way Meredith was hanging on your every word, that you two were an item."

"Tasha Dempsey was with you?"

"Yeah."

"She never really liked me very much." He raked his fingers through his hair. "Ever since high school."

Should I explain that she was just sticking up for me all those years? That's what a faithful friend did.

"Have the two of you started some sort of spy agency I need to be aware of?" Mason asked.

"No." I groaned. "Well, maybe, but not like that. She just happened to be with me and saw you with Meredith, and she thought—actually assumed—that Meredith was your wife."

"Now I'm *married* to her?" He slapped himself on the forehead. "I've never been married to anyone, least of all her. You can wash that thought right out of your overactive imagination right now."

And there it was, the accusation about my imagination. He always did think I was a little too animated.

She's the last person on earth I'd be interested in," he said, then paused and appeared to be thinking. "Though, I will admit that she might have some interest in me that goes beyond just talking about antique cars. She's been private messaging me nonstop since the day of the auction, and I've gotten a weird vibe from those messages. But I can assure you, I had nothing to do with the truck disappearing, and I'm not even remotely interested in her. Rest easy on that."

I didn't want to rest easy, but before I could give it any more thought, Tasha joined us, eyes wide and a broad smile lighting up her face. "Hey, did you see they've got food trucks?"

Mason looked her way with what appeared to be a forced smile. "Tasha, how have you been? Long time no see."

"I'm good." She gave him a pensive *I don't trust you* look. "But I skipped breakfast so I'm starving. They've got chopped beef."

"For breakfast?" I asked.

She laughed. "Why not? With a big glass of lemonade. Sounds perfect."

I had to admit, the tempting aromas that wafted up from the line of food trucks to our right were drawing me in too.

Before I knew it, we were ordering. Tasha got the beef and lemonade.

I opted for a funnel cake and Dr. Pepper. Nothing like a sugar rush at ten in the morning. Mason ordered a corn dog and some chili cheese fries. And before I could say, "No, please don't," he'd paid for the whole thing.

"Hey, I like hanging around him," Tasha said as we ate together moments later. "We should do this more often. Unless he's really married, of course." She gave him a closer look. "*Are* you married?"

"I can assure you I am not, despite what you think you saw." He took a bite of his corn dog and looked away.

She glanced at me, eyes widening. "You told him that we saw him with the Statue of Liberty at the grocery store?"

"The Statue of Liberty?" Now he really looked confused.

"It's kind of a long story," I said. "We'll share it on another day."

"O–okay." He took a bite of his corn dog and pointed to some folding tables under the tents nearby. "Want to sit awhile? Get out of this heat?"

"Sure!" Tasha flashed him a broad smile. "Let's do that."

She led the way, nonstop chattering, and plopped down at the closest table. He waited for me to join them and then sat directly across from me.

Tasha looked my way and winked.

Good grief. Was she trying to set me up with this guy now?

We settled into a comfortable conversation, and before long we were talking about church, which provided a lovely distraction from our earlier conversation.

"I'm so excited about the Easter service coming up." I used my napkin to dab the powdered sugar off my lips. "It's going to be great. Tasha's leading the children's choir. You should come."

"It's a special gift I have." She took a bite of her food then talked around it. "Teaching children to sing off-key like I do."

"She's actually got a really nice voice," I said. "And don't let her fool you. She's great with kids."

"So are you," Tasha countered. "They love you more than me, but I try not to let that get to me."

I shrugged. The children were pretty amazing, and they did seem to love me.

"You should totally come." Tasha took a swig of her drink and gave Mason a look that said, "I doubt you really will, though."

"Sounds great," he countered as he tossed the stick from his corn dog into a nearby trash can. "I've missed being in church. It wasn't the same in Waco. I went to a megachurch there. Tried to fit in but never really found my spot."

"We've got ten spots with your name on 'em," Tasha said. "If you really want to fit in, I mean."

"Are you really thinking about coming back?" I asked.

He looked surprised by my question. "Sure. Why not? It's my old stomping ground."

"We have a new pastor now. Did you know?"

"Heard that."

"And the youth group is thriving."

"I'm twenty-six."

I laughed. "I know. I'm just catching you up. But since you're so old now, you might be interested in the seniors' ministry. The fifty-five-and-up crowd meets the first Tuesday of every month for potluck and board games. And they go to Dairy Queen for ice cream after."

"Very funny. I'll find my Scrabble board and bring it with me."

"Hey, you're really good at croquet, as I recall."

"Not a board game," he countered, "and we only played it once, on a dare."

This led us into an intense conversation about how much better I was at croquet than him.

"Wow." Tasha looked back and forth between us as we argued about who was the better player. "You two are. . .wow."

I wasn't sure what she meant by that. But I had to admit, joking and laughing with Mason felt good. Comfortable.

After we finished our food, it was time for the winners in the various categories to be announced. By now we'd hit the noontime hour and I had perspiration running down my back.

We found my parents seated in lawn chairs near the front of the stage. Dot took to the stage to announce the winners, and I found myself captivated as she went category by category, announcing every winning car and truck.

Turned out the man with the '52 copper Chevy took first place in the antique truck category. Go figure. And, of course, Clayton swept the field, placing or winning with all three of his vehicles.

"See what I mean?" Tasha muttered. "The man's unbeatable."

Man. Dot wasn't kidding, was she? He really did seem to get whatever he wanted.

Still, everyone clapped politely as he took the stage. He asked for the microphone and made an announcement about the open house at his new B and B.

"We start at two o'clock, folks, and you're all welcome. Come for a tour and hors d'oeuvres and the best view of the lake you'll ever see."

Tasha looked my way. "We're going, right?"

"Yeah." But I wasn't sure what we were going to do between now and then. There wasn't really time to go home and change, though I was pretty damp by now.

Behind me, I heard a group of people talking about Clayton as he exited the stage, trophies in hand. I strained to make out what they were saying but was pretty sure I heard, "You know he's in financial trouble, right?"

I leaned in closer, hoping to catch more, but could not.

"You okay over there?" Mom asked.

Her words startled me back to attention. "What? Oh. . .yeah. Sorry."

I would have to ask her later if there was any truth to that rumor. If I'd heard correctly anyway.

Mom suggested we hang out at Dairy Queen, and several minutes later we found ourselves crammed into a booth, talking up a storm about everything we'd just seen at the car show and licking on chocolate-covered dip cones. Tasha kept us all entertained with funny stories, and Mason held up his end of the conversation too. The whole thing felt. . .perfect. Absolutely perfect.

Until my phone dinged.

I reached into my purse to grab it, wondering who might be texting me.

The words WANT TO GO OUT ON A REAL DATE? filled the screen.

I looked across the table at Mason, who had—somehow—sent the text on the sly. When I didn't respond right away, he added, I PROMISE NOT TO BRING THE STATUE OF LIBERTY. WHATEVER THAT MEANS.

I couldn't help the laughter that followed.

"What's so funny over there, honey?" Mom looked up from her

ice-cream cone, eyes narrowed in confusion.

"Oh, nothing." I felt my cheeks flush but hoped my mom would think it was from the heat.

I started to shove my phone back into my purse but decided I'd better answer him first. I didn't want to keep the guy waiting. So, I typed Sure and sent it soaring across the table to his phone.

He looked down and smiled, then tucked his phone into his back pocket.

I was about to put mine away too, when I noticed a notification from Facebook messenger.

From Stephanie.

I excused myself to go to the ladies' room. Once there, I read her message: I'm so glad you got back in touch with me. I've really missed you. Missing everyone in Mabank, actually.

I responded with Aw. Then I added, I just saw half of Henderson County at the antique car show.

And she came back with, That sounds like fun. Was Mason there?

My heart skipped a beat. Did she really just go there?

Yes, actually. He just moved back to Mabank. He opened a vintage car shop at his dad's old place, so he came to check out the antique cars.

I heard his father died. Mama keeps me up-to-date with some of the goings-on. I don't know if you heard, but my parents split up.

Yes, so sorry to hear that.

A moment went by before she responded, Things with my dad were a lot rougher than I let on. Anyway, Mama's in Athens now, and doing fine. But she stays in touch with her friends in Mabank, including Dot. Do you remember her?

Um, yes. Yes, I did.

Yeah, she's a family friend, I responded. We were just with her too.

Oh, right. Well, Dot told Mama about Mason's father dying. The whole thing was so sad.

It was a terrible accident on I75. Involved an 18-wheeler.

Awful. She paused. I still think about Mason from time to time. He was such a great guy. But. . .

Okay, was Stephanie really going to leave that "but" hanging in the air between us?

A few seconds ticked by before she came back with, HE NEVER REALLY GOT OVER YOU. I GUESS YOU'VE ALREADY FIGURED THAT OUT, RIGHT?

Wait, what? I sat, staring at the phone screen. OVER ME? I finally typed.

WELL, YEAH. THAT'S WHY WE BROKE UP. I GOT KIND OF TIRED OF HEARING ABOUT RAELYN THIS AND RAELYN THAT. I FINALLY TOLD HIM HE SHOULD JUST WORK UP THE COURAGE TO TELL YOU. HE WAS NEVER HAPPY IN WACO, SO I'M GLAD TO HEAR HE'S COME BACK HOME.

I continued to stare at the screen, unsure of what to say in response. Before I could pull my thoughts together, she came back with, GOTTA GO, THE BABY'S CRYING. BE SURE TO ADD ME TO THE GUEST LIST WHEN YOU GET READY TO SEND INVITATIONS. I CAN'T THINK OF ANYTHING I'D LOVE MORE THAN TO COME BACK HOME TO SEE TWO OF MY FAVORITE PEOPLE TIE THE KNOT.

Guest list?

Invitations?

Tie the knot?

For a second, I felt sure I was having some sort of surreal, out-of-body experience. The woman had not just implied that Mason Fredericks and I would one day get. . .married? Had she?

I scrolled back up to reread the whole thread. Sure enough, that was the implication. But why?

Before I could think it through, my phone dinged again with a text from the man himself.

EVERYTHING OKAY IN THERE? Mason asked.

I responded with a laugh emoji and a thumbs-up.

Though, to be honest, I wasn't quite sure how I felt right now.

CHAPTER EIGHTEEN

When we wrapped up at Dairy Queen, Mason headed off to work on a car at his shop, Dad headed home in his truck, and Mom, Bessie Mae, Tasha, and I made the drive to the new Henderson B and B just over the lake in Gun Barrel City.

I gave directions, using my phone as a guide, and we chatted as my mom drove.

Bessie Mae kept her attention riveted out the passenger window, only glancing up to say, "My goodness, the wildflowers are just breathtaking this spring, aren't they?"

I didn't blame her for being mesmerized. Nature had truly painted a masterpiece in our area this year. The magical days of bluebonnet season were often eye-catching, but this was beyond the norm. Fields were heavy in those gorgeous blue flowers. And nestled between were Indian paintbrushes, equally as beautiful in their own way.

These fields were scattered throughout the country, but many of them we found as we turned down the country road leading to Clayton's new place.

I could hear Tasha's breathing intensify, the prettier the landscape became. "You okay over there?" I asked.

She didn't look okay but managed a quiet, "Mm-hmm."

Tasha might be irritated that Clayton had landed such a spectacular view for his B and B, but I found myself completely immersed in the breathtaking beauty of this quintessential Texas experience as we drew closer to his new home. No doubt tourists would love this home, if for no other reason than the spectacular view.

I kept a watchful eye on the field as the flowers seemed to stretch toward the horizon, creating a symphony of color. In that moment, I decided that God must really love the color blue, to share these flowers so freely with us. He was a celestial painter, creating blossoms that were individual masterpieces.

As we drew near the property, I caught a glimpse of a nearby pond. The reflection of the flowers shimmered in the tranquil waters, which seemed to double the enchantment.

I thought about Stephanie, up there in Iowa. Should I send her a picture?

I pulled out my phone and quickly snapped one, then attached it to a message that read, TEXAS!

She wrote back right away with a *SIGH* followed by THE MOST PIC-TURESQUE PLACE ON EARTH, AT LEAST IN THE SPRING.

She wasn't wrong. These fields were a vibrant tapestry beneath the boundless Texas sky.

Hey, that sounded pretty good. Maybe I should write an article about the springtime flowers for my next *Mabank Happenings*. God was certainly giving me enough fodder.

Just as quickly, my heart twisted as I remembered that I wouldn't have the opportunity to photograph Tilly in the field of flowers. There would be no "before" picture unless she miraculously turned up. And right now? Well, right now that felt impossible.

A couple of minutes later, we arrived at Henderson House. As we pulled up to the beautiful piece of property on which Clayton had just placed a monstrous home, large enough to sleep fourteen, according to his brochure, I couldn't help but gasp.

"Oh! I've never seen anything like it!" Bessie Mae clutched her hand to her throat. "It's a masterpiece!"

She wasn't exaggerating. A sweeping property it was, filled with the most gorgeous pecan trees lining the curved driveway that arched across the front of the spacious property.

The grounds in front of the drive were simply magnificent as well, with manicured gardens, pink and yellow azaleas, and winding pathways that invited leisurely strolls.

Off in the distance, towering trees provided just the right amount of shade, and strategically placed benches offered peaceful spots for contemplation underneath those beautiful trees. I could almost see myself here, walking this front lawn and praying.

I glanced back down at the brochure for the property and read the line at the bottom once again, but only to myself: *As guests approach the property, a sense of tranquility washes over them.*

That wasn't far from the truth. I already felt calmer here, and we hadn't even gotten out of the car yet.

What really took my breath away, though, was the house itself.

"Whoa." Just one word from Tasha, but it conveyed what we were all thinking. This place was a wondrous build—a solid Texas house with stone, wood, and heavy wooden features. All of the things I loved so much.

It was my dream house. On my dream property. The very property that had meant so much to my grandfather.

I swallowed the lump in my throat as I glanced back down at the brochure to read the description Clayton had chosen: "Henderson House is a picturesque structure, its architecture seamlessly blending with the natural East Texas beauty that surrounds it. The exterior features a combination of stone and wood, creating a warm and inviting facade."

For sure, it was my kind of house, the kind I would build if I ever had the time. Or the money. Or a family of my own.

One day. One day I would live in a house like this, on the lake.

Oh, who was I kidding? Even if I married—and that seemed a long way off, if ever—I would probably end up in a double-wide on my parents' sixty-three acres, like Logan.

Still, a girl could dream, if only for a moment.

Mom pulled into a parking space, and we all got out. As we took the beautifully landscaped walkway up to the double doors at the front of the house, I noticed several other locals pulling into spaces behind us.

"Looks like he's going to have quite the crowd," I said.

"Go ahead. Rub it in. That's fine." Tasha kept her focus on the front door.

As I caught a glimpse of Clayton's three antique cars, which took up residence in the carport to the left of the house, my thoughts shifted to Tilly. Behind the carport stood a massive four-door garage. Guests wouldn't have any trouble figuring out where to park when they visited Henderson House, would they?

Mom gestured to the vehicles and then glanced my way. "Do you think there's any chance he's hiding Tilly here, maybe in that big garage?"

"Could be," I said. "There's certainly enough room." The idea occurred to me that we could check out the garage, if given the opportunity. This was an open house, after all. Perhaps it was an "open garage" too.

When we got to the front door, I read the COME ON IN sign and reached for the doorknob. As I pulled the door open, the loveliest music rang out, informing everyone inside that guests had arrived.

We stepped into the grand foyer, and my eyes went up, up, up to the towering ceiling and the massive rustic wrought iron chandelier above us. Just as quickly, my gaze drifted down to the layout of the space in front of me.

I'd never seen anything like it. The foyer itself was magnificent, but what really caught my eye was the huge living room just beyond it.

Clayton met us in the foyer, all smiles. "So glad you could make it, folks. Welcome to Henderson House."

His wife, Nadine, came up behind him carrying a tray of beverages. "We've got sweet tea or something a bit stronger, if you prefer."

"Tea is fine," Mom said. And we all took a glass.

"Mmm." Bessie Mae grinned after taking a sip. "Fresh brewed and sweet as summer sunshine."

"Thank you." Nadine moved on to offer a glass to an incoming guest, an elderly woman I didn't recognize. No doubt they would have guests from all over the county today.

Clayton led us into the spacious living room, and I gasped as I took it in. I could see out the expansive windows onto Cedar Creek Lake but found myself so mesmerized by the layout of the room that I wanted to keep my focus indoors for a moment. The large room had high ceilings—two stories high, in fact. And it boasted a grand fireplace, constructed of heavy Texas stone. And that gorgeous furniture! There was enough seating for a crowd—from the two sofas to four oversize leather chairs.

Behind me, Tasha let out a groan. I didn't blame her. This was a lot to take in.

The whole place had a rustic aesthetic, but it still looked and smelled like money. Henderson money. I couldn't help but wonder what Papaw would've thought of this, though. It wasn't at all what he'd had in mind.

"It's just beautiful, Clayton," Mom said. "Every square inch of it."

"Well, that's all Nadine." He beamed like a Cheshire cat as he gestured to his wife. "She got the decorating gene, not me." He gestured to her, and she smiled before setting the tray of drinks down on the coffee table.

"I used as many natural elements as I could," Nadine chimed in. "Lots of wood and stone, and comfortable furnishings. I want our guests to feel at home."

"It's. . ." I paused to think of the right word. "Timeless."

"It's almost like we've traveled to Europe," Mom whispered. "Are you sure we're still in Texas?"

"Deep in the heart of!" Clayton gave us a wink that felt somewhat disingenuous.

We were joined a few seconds later by a new crowd of folks from Mabank, some church friends, including Dot. I wasn't surprised to see her here. The woman seemed to turn up everywhere.

Minutes later Nadine was taking all of us on a tour of the home. There were two common areas—the living room and a spacious den, loaded with comfortable furnishings. What really caught my attention was the library. I could almost picture myself seated in the oversize chair in the corner, looking out over the lake while reading a book. With floor-to-ceiling bookshelves, I would certainly have my choice of reading material. They'd stuffed these shelves full of books in every genre imaginable.

And then there was the media room, which looked like a small movie theater. Good gravy. I couldn't even imagine what that massive screen must've cost. Or the rows of recliners.

Mom was most impressed by the kitchen, which had the biggest granite island I'd ever seen.

Bessie Mae's eyes filled with tears as she took it in. "Can you imagine all of the baking I could do here? And that view!" She pointed to the French doors, which led out onto the deck.

"We could catch our own fish and fry 'em up for dinner," Mom said.

"And if we didn't feel like eating in the formal dining room, we could always eat in that cute little breakfast nook." Bessie Mae gestured with her head to the sweetest little table and chairs I'd ever seen.

The decor in this remarkable kitchen was comforting. Inviting. It somehow seamlessly blended heavy Texas elements with a European richness, making me feel like I'd stepped into an upscale restaurant. On the lake. With the best view in town.

A view that had so swept my grandfather away that he'd actually considered working a deal with Clayton Henderson.

Nadine opened the French doors, and we stepped outside onto the expansive deck. I couldn't even imagine living like this, but it would be mighty fine, indeed.

The well-designed terrace had several lounging areas and a firepit in the center. I could just imagine the B and B's guests seated out here, unwinding after a long day and enjoying the gentle breezes off the water.

"Nice, isn't it?" Clayton's strong voice sounded from behind us. "A breathtaking view from every angle. You don't get a view like that just anywhere."

Tasha grunted.

Just for digs, I said, "It's a shame my papaw isn't here to enjoy it."

Was it my imagination, or did Clayton flinch?

He jumped right back into host mode again, his words coming out like a game show host. "Guests can enjoy all sorts of outdoor activities at Henderson House. We've got our own pier, of course. And in the garage we've got kayaks, paddleboards, and fishing rods."

"My papaw was a great fisherman," I said. And left it at that.

Tasha pulled out her phone and took a couple of pictures. I was tempted to do the same.

Clayton turned to give Tasha a half smile. "You can walk out onto the dock and take close-ups of the lake if you like."

"That's okay." She shoved her phone back into her purse.

"I'm just saying. . ." He turned back toward the water. "We set this area up to be as scenic as possible. Guests can explore Cedar Creek Lake at their leisure or just sit out on the little dock at the water's edge. We've got Adirondack chairs out there."

Little dock? He called that little?

"Or you can walk the trails," he added. "Guests can indulge in bird-watching. We've got a diverse avian species here, native to the area."

He lost me about halfway into the conversation about the birds.

So, I decided to do the only thing that made sense. I suggested that Tasha and I head out to the little dock to sit on those Adirondack chairs and look at the peaceful waters of Cedar Creek Lake.

So Tasha and I wandered down to the water's edge and settled into those oversize wooden chairs as if we belonged there, while Mom, Bessie Mae, and some of the other guests visited inside the house. I eased my very tired body into a chair and settled back against it. Until now, I hadn't realized just how exhausted I really was.

After a moment's silence, I decided it was time to bring Tasha up to speed on my private messages with Stephanie, so I broached the subject.

"You'll never guess who's been messaging me," I said.

"Who's that?"

"Stephanie Ingram. Well, it's Anderson now. She's married and living in Iowa. Ames."

"Oh, wow. I knew she moved out of state but didn't know that." Tasha's gaze shifted out to the sunlight rippling off the lake.

"Apparently her husband is a pastor," I said.

"What?" Tasha looked back my way. "Never saw that one coming."

"Me either." I sighed. "It's kind of hard to be mad at a friend whose whole life is tied up in ministry. You know?"

Tasha gave me an inquisitive look. "Why were you mad at her?"

"I always felt like she stole Mason away from me."

"Wait. . .I thought it was the other way around." Tasha turned her attention back to the water but kept talking. "You told me that he stole your best friend from you."

"Yeah, I did always say that." I paused to think through my next words. "Maybe it was just life. You know? Maybe we just weren't meant to be together long term. What's that meme that's going around about how some friends are friends for a season and some for life? Maybe she was a season."

Okay, that caused Tasha to swing around and give me a pensive look. "Well, I'm no seasonal friend, you hear me? You'd better count me in for life, because I'm not going anywhere."

As I gazed into the flashing eyes of my best friend, I had to conclude she was definitely a friend for life.

"You've got it. And don't you dare move off to Idaho. Or Iowa. Or anyplace else," I admonished.

"Me, leave heaven for someplace like that?" Tasha leaned back in the chair and gazed out over the water once again. "I was born and raised on Cedar Creek Lake, and I don't plan to leave anytime soon. I just have to find Mr. Right who's willing to settle down with me in that eclectic B and B I plan to open."

"He's out there, Tasha. I know he is."

"Yeah. I hope you're right." She sighed. "Sometimes it feels like he's not. Other times he's so close I could swear I almost know him already."

"Maybe you do." I shrugged. "Stranger things have happened."

"Yeah. . ." She gazed intently at me. "Like you and Mason getting back together after all these years?"

"I wouldn't say we're back together. We're just. . ."

"Eating chicken and dumplings together. And hanging out at the car show."

"He's a friend."

"Who didn't move to Iowa. And who showed back up in your life when you least expected it."

True. All of that. I couldn't argue that Mason had indeed shown back up rather miraculously.

And now, as I thought it through, I had to wonder if perhaps the Lord had set all that up at just the right time in my life.

For the first time in ages, I was able to actually contemplate that possibility.

CHAPTER NINETEEN

After a couple of quiet moments, Mom called out to us to join them for the tour of the rest of the house. We rose and walked back up to the deck then headed inside where we found the place swarming with people.

Before long, Clayton's wife, Nadine, was offering incoming guests glasses of tea and hand-painted artisan cookies with the letter H on them, then giving us free rein of the upstairs while she tended to those who had just arrived.

"Just don't go in the last room on the right," she said as she gestured to the stairs. "It's not quite company ready. Clayton's using it as an office right now. But have a look-see around the rest of the place and let us know your thoughts. Then please help us spread the word online. We would love to keep this place booked year-round."

"Oh, I'm sure you will, Nadine," Mom said. "Anyone would be blessed for a few days in this lovely home."

"Clayton wanted it to be the best."

Her smile seemed to fade a bit as she spoke those words, and for a moment I thought I saw a hint of pain in her eyes. Just as quickly, Nadine was in hostess mode once more, greeting more guests. We realized we'd better move quickly or the rooms would be packed.

We headed upstairs and made the rounds from room to room. The guest bedrooms were designed with comfort in mind, but every one—and there were at least five that I counted—had tasteful decor and wonderful amenities, including enough bathrooms to keep a houseful of guests content.

The rooms were all on the lake side of the home, and each had large French doors and balconies that framed picturesque views of the sparkling waters. The room that really blew us all away was the master bedroom. I let out a whistle as my gaze landed on the massive four-poster bed and rich bedding in a gorgeous shade of. . .sage green.

Go figure. Maybe Carrie was onto something after all.

"There must be ten pillows on that bed." My mom's eyes widened in wonder.

"And every one covered in an expensive sham," Bessie Mae added. "I can't even guess what the pillows alone must've cost them."

"More than I make in a year at the Fish Tales," Tasha said and then sighed in that over-the-top way of hers.

"Can you even imagine waking up to that view?" Mom asked as we gazed out the French doors onto the sparkling waters just beyond.

Yes. Yes, I could. Waking up to the serenity of that gorgeous lake would be amazing. And having my own fireplace, plush bedding, and a private balcony? Yes, please. This place really was the ideal retreat for relaxation and rest.

"This whole place is just idyllic," Mom said.

To which Bessie Mae responded, "A little too idyllic. Doesn't feel very homey to me."

"And not at all what Papaw had in mind, I'm sure," I said. My grandfather was the farthest thing from fancy.

It was hard to leave the master bedroom, but we finally pulled ourselves away. We walked out into the hallway and found ourselves at the last door on the right.

"This is the room she said not to go in, right?" Mom said.

"Must be," Tasha concurred. "It's closed. The others were open."

Still, I couldn't help myself. I had to take a peek inside. I eased the door open to discover an office, fully decked out with a rich mahogany desk, bookshelves, and all the other items one might need in an office, including a computer and printer.

I wanted to take a closer look to see if I could find anything tying Clayton Henderson to my grandfather. Though, he probably wouldn't keep those documents here. They would be at his house, the one he lived in. Or his office downtown.

"Can I help you?" A voice sounded behind me, and I turned on my heels to discover Clayton Henderson standing in the open doorway less than a foot away.

"Oh, um. . .yes." I plastered on a smile as I pulled the door shut. "Bathroom? Where's the bathroom?"

"You passed several on the way here." He pointed down the hallway. As I walked that way, he opened the office door, looked inside, and then shut the door again.

So far, my sleuthing skills were proving to be pretty lousy.

Instead of going in the bathroom, I headed downstairs to join the others, who had gathered once again in the kitchen. I couldn't help but notice that Meredith Reed was standing alone in the foyer, taking it all in.

Well, standing alone until Clayton joined her, his face lighting up as he caught a glimpse of her in that tight blouse and figure-hugging jeans.

Interesting. Was it just my imagination, or did his gaze linger on her a little longer than one might have expected?

"RaeLyn, look," Tasha whispered. She gestured with her head to Meredith, who was now visiting with Clayton, hanging on his every word in much the same way she'd done to Mason at the grocery store. "Isn't that. . ."

"Yeah." I nodded.

"Meredith Reed." Mom's eyes narrowed. I half expected her to reach for her phone to text Gloria Pappas, but she did not.

Still, it seemed rather odd to me that Harlan Reed's ex-wife would be so cozy with Clayton Henderson. Raised a few question marks in my mind.

Meredith released a little giggle and leaned in close to him to bat her lashes at something he'd said. Off in the distance, I caught a glimpse of Nadine Henderson, as she watched all of this transpire.

In that moment, I saw this situation with clarity. Clayton and Meredith were more than just acquaintances. . .and Nadine knew it. But she had to go on pretending she didn't.

Just as quickly, I reminded myself that I'd thought Mason was involved with Meredith just a few days back. He'd proven me wrong. Maybe I was wrong again.

Another glance at Clayton and Meredith convinced me otherwise.

And at that, Mom decided it was time to head home. Bessie Mae agreed, saying she needed a little nap before suppertime.

We said our goodbyes to the Hendersons and to Dot, then headed out the front door. As we walked to the car, my gaze traveled once again to the carport with those three cars, and to the massive garage behind it.

I turned to Tasha, an idea taking root. "Okay, I'm itching to do something, but I don't want to go alone."

"What are you about to do, RaeLyn?" Mom asked. "Nothing dangerous, I hope."

"I want to get inside that garage to see if Tilly is in there."

"What?" Mom shook her head. "No, honey. You can't do that. They didn't give us permission. What if he sees you?"

"I'll go with you," Tasha said. "I ain't ascared'a no rich fella with a highfalutin B and B."

Okay then.

Seconds later, we were on our way.

Even from the outside, I was impressed by the sheer size of the garage. How many cars did he own anyway? With the three renovated ones out front, maybe the room would be empty.

"Do you really think he would steal Tilly and bring her here?" Tasha asked.

"Maybe. He's got all of these cars out here and. . ." My words trailed off as I saw a side door to the garage. "Perfect. Let's hope it's unlocked."

"Must be our lucky day," Tasha said as the knob turned with ease.

"Almost like it was meant to be," I said and then stepped over the threshold into the dark garage. It took a moment for my eyes to adjust but when they did. . .I gasped.

"Oh my goodness, he does have a vehicle in here. And it's. . ." I squinted to get a better look.

"It's my '67 Buick Riviera, which I'm about to flip so I can show it at the next antique car show."

My heart skipped a beat as Clayton's voice rang out.

He flipped a light on, and I had that instant blindness you sometimes get when you've just stepped out into the glaring sun.

Clayton rested against the wall and gave us a pensive look. "If you don't mind my asking, what are you two doing out here? Still looking for the bathroom?"

I stumbled all over myself to come up with an answer that made sense. "Well, you said there were kayaks and paddleboards and such."

"I did. But they're just for our paying guests. You planning to book a stay? If so, you can have unlimited access to them. Otherwise. . ."

"No, I—"

"It's my fault," Tasha interjected. "I'm in the market for a kayak, and I thought maybe I could see the ones you bought so that I would know what to look for. We should have asked permission first. Sorry."

"Oh, I see." He squared his shoulders and led us to the kayaks, which he described with animation. "These are top of the line, the Lifetime Tide 103 model. Bought 'em at Tractor Supply. If you catch 'em when they're on sale, you can get the pair under a thousand dollars."

"Oh, that's nice," Tasha said and flashed a bright smile. "Thanks for the information. I don't get to Tractor Supply much, so I wouldn't have known I could buy them there. Silly me."

"If you need any other suggestions for your new place—when you get it up and running I mean—don't hesitate to ask." He flashed a convincing look at Tasha, and I almost believed him.

Okay, I actually believed him. Maybe Clayton Henderson had a nice side. When he wasn't trying to outrank everyone else in the county.

And gawking over Meredith Reed.

And ripping off my grandfather.

He walked us out of the garage, all laughter and smiles as he shared other tips with Tasha, who pulled out her phone and started taking notes.

Afterward, he headed back to the house to be with his guests, and we walked back to Mom's SUV, where we found Bessie Mae snoozing in the passenger seat and Mom on a phone call with Jake, who was worried about Carrie.

"Is she in labor?" I asked.

"He's not sure, but she's definitely having some contractions," Mom said. "Let's head home and see for ourselves."

A couple of minutes later, we were on our way back to the house. I turned to Tasha and whispered, "I feel just awful that you felt like you had to lie on my behalf. About the kayaks, I mean."

"Oh, that wasn't a lie."

"You're actually in the market for a kayak?" I gave my best friend an *I'm not buying that* look.

"Well, I will be," she said. "When I open my B and B, we're going to offer lake activities too, you know. So, I wasn't lying."

Should I remind her that she didn't actually own a B and B yet? Nah. After today it would be like salt in an open wound. And if I knew anything about my best friend, it was this: she was salty enough already.

CHAPTER TWENTY

On Sunday morning, the day after the car show and our trek to Henderson House, I went to church with my family, as always.

At our church, we had Bible study at nine and service at ten fifteen. I always loved the first hour especially, because everyone in my age group studied together. Our group was led by Landon James, who had been just a few years ahead of us in school at Mabank High but was well respected in the community and the church. He and his wife, Annie, spent several weeks a year on the mission field in Nicaragua, which further endeared them to us.

When I arrived at nine, I was shocked to find Mason in the small Sunday school classroom along with a dozen or so others. They were already nibbling on donuts and sipping on coffee. And, from the looks of things, having a great conversation about antique cars. I stopped in the doorway, startled by Mason's presence.

He saw me and waved, then pointed at the box of donuts.

"They have chocolate-filled. Your favorite."

Okay, chocolate-filled donuts were my favorite, but how he remembered that after all these years confused me even more. Had he memorized everything about me?

The aroma of freshly brewed coffee, mingled with the scent of warm donuts, served as a magnet to draw me in. Who could resist chocolate-filled? And our church had really good coffee, thanks to our missionary friends in Nicaragua.

I joined him just as Tasha made an entrance wearing the cutest white blouse with puffy sleeves and high-waisted black jeans. Adorned with her cowboy boots, she looked like a million bucks, as always.

My brothers came in behind her. Well, Dallas, Gage, and Logan anyway. Jake and Carrie—if they came at all today—would be in the young married couples' class.

When Landon took his place up front to open our study in prayer, we all settled into chairs. I found myself pressed between Tasha on my right and Mason on my left.

We prayed and then shared announcements. I was happy to fill everyone in on the upcoming Easter egg hunt for the kids in the community, and Tasha spoke with passion about the need for helpers with the children's choir.

When she asked for someone to help her with that, her gaze went at once to Logan, but he shrugged and begged off. "Sorry, but that's definitely outside of my wheelhouse."

No worries. Dallas agreed to help, and so did I. Between the three of us we would get it done. Still, Tasha seemed upset, as if my brother had snubbed her deliberately.

Landon taught a great lesson on coveting, which I found ironic, considering yesterday's outing to Henderson House. Tasha squirmed in her seat when he got to the verse about not coveting your neighbor's oxen.

My family happened to have cattle, so I got the reference, of course, but Tasha argued that people no longer had oxen these days.

To which Gage argued that cattle and oxen were pretty much the same thing, and we Hadleys had our share of cattle.

Landon then explained that coveting—jealousy—showed up in all sorts of ways, whether one was talking about cattle, trucks, or people.

Tasha went quiet on us after that.

One person who didn't remain quiet was Mason. I was intrigued to see how easily he responded to questions and engaged Landon in conversation about the topic at hand. He'd always been really chatty in Sunday school;

that much I remembered. But this was a new Mason, one who spoke with confidence and authority, without coming across as a know-it-all.

After Bible study, we all headed to the sanctuary together. Even though I'd been raised in this church, I still felt a particular reverence when those back double doors swung open and I stepped inside that beautiful room.

Mom and Dot greeted us in the foyer, bulletins in hand.

"Welcome to church," Dot said with a smile. She handed Mason a bulletin, and he took it. "Happy to see you."

"Happy to be here," he said. And I could tell from the look on his face that he really was. Mason pulled me off to the side of the foyer, a serious look on his face.

"Everything okay?" I asked.

"Yeah. I know this is kind of last-minute, but I'm wondering if you want to go to Purtis Creek Lake Park this afternoon."

Ah. Was this the date he'd been referring to?

"I think my parents are expecting me to go to lunch after church with them."

"I was thinking later, like around three thirty. That would give me time to do some paperwork for a couple of hours before we head out. So, you could go with your family and I would pick you up around that time, if it works for you."

"Sure. What should I bring?"

"No worries. I'll bring everything. Just bring yourself."

"Okay."

As he smiled at me, my heart did that crazy fluttering thing it had done years ago, as a sixteen-year-old. But at twenty-six, the possibilities seemed a bit more tangible.

"Can I sit with you in church?" he asked.

"Of course."

I usually sat with Tasha, one row behind my parents, but didn't figure she would mind if he joined us.

She didn't, but for some reason she still looked out of sorts as we settled into the pew together. Her gaze kept traveling to Logan, who opted to sit with my parents and Gage. Jake and Carrie were noticeably absent, but I didn't blame them. They hadn't had much sleep lately.

Dallas took his spot on the stage to the left of the choir loft, guitar in hand. He'd only been helping with worship for a few weeks now, but I had to admit, he had a nice voice. And his guitar-playing skills were really coming along. Maybe these younger brothers of mine would make something of themselves after all.

The choir, adorned in the same robes they'd worn since before I was born, began to take their places, their voices tuning in harmony with the anticipation of the congregation.

Mason lit into a conversation with Tasha, and I sat quietly, just taking it all in. I loved these first few moments of church, when echoes of friendly greetings and the comforting sounds of "Welcome to church!" greeted me.

The air hummed with a gentle buzz of conversation as friends and families exchanged smiles and updates on their week. Our congregation was a tapestry of ages, backgrounds, and stories, and I loved every single person represented in this room.

And I loved this beautiful room. In this sacred space, the people of Mabank came together to worship and share bonds of friendship, which was exactly what made our close-knit community so, well, close. This church was a cornerstone of Mabank life, a sanctuary where the echoes of shared faith and shared lives reverberated through the ages.

We weren't the only church in town, but this was the only one I knew, so it felt like home to me.

Glancing to my right, I took in the stained glass windows and their lovely kaleidoscope of colors as the morning sunlight streamed through. Those ribbons of light sent colorful rays dancing all across the sanctuary.

I leaned back against the pew, which was worn from years of use, and smiled as the worship leader took his spot behind the podium and asked us to stand with him.

I had to smile when I saw that Dot was now seated at the piano. She must be filling in for the pastor's wife, who was in the hospital with a kidney infection. This I'd heard from Mom, who told me as soon as the news hit the prayer chain.

God bless the prayer chain.

Dot's fingers began to dance across the keys, setting the stage for what was sure to be a worship-filled morning ahead, and I had to marvel: Was there anything this woman couldn't do?

Mason stood alongside me, and I was so touched to hear his gorgeous tenor voice as we sang that opening song together. Suddenly I was sixteen again, standing next to the boy I adored, listening to him sing.

I had to quickly rouse myself from those silly memories and stay focused on the rest of the worship songs, which were particularly touching today.

My gaze traveled up to Bessie Mae, who sat next to Rena. I don't know why I'd never put it together before, that Ms. Rena Sue was actually Corina Jackson. But knowing that now—and knowing the backstory about Wyatt and my grandfather—put a lump in my throat. I couldn't help but feel sorry for her, especially after hearing she'd lost her baby all those years ago.

Pastor Burchfield took the pulpit and thanked everyone for their prayers for his wife, Melody. He cracked a joke about hospitals—probably to ease the tension—then dove right into the sermon, which echoed through the sanctuary, a beautiful message about living in community, and what that meant for the believer.

These folks were my community. They had been from the time I was born. And I was grateful for them. A palpable sense of camaraderie enveloped us all as we rose to sing the invitation hymn. This was my space. These were my folks. Hopefully nothing would ever change that.

After the service, the foyer buzzed with activity as church members visited and then said their goodbyes.

Tasha rushed my way, a panicked look on her face. "I hate to cut this short, but I'm working today."

"No way. On a Sunday?" That was unusual.

"I know." She sighed. "I never work on Sundays, but Alicia called in sick, so I'm going to be working the register."

"Oh, man. Sorry about that."

She shrugged. "Hey, it's our family business. And until I have my own B and B, a girl's gotta do what a girl's gotta do. You know?"

I did. And that's exactly how I felt about helping my parents out until I had the antique shop up and running. Just six more days and we would be open for business.

Tasha said a quick goodbye and headed off to work. I knew we would see her again shortly, as the Hadleys usually went to Fish Tales for Sunday lunch to give Bessie Mae a break from cooking.

As we made our way to the car, Logan joined us. He shoved his phone into his back pocket then turned our way, his face lighting up.

"Hey, I just wanted to let you all know that I've invited someone to join us for lunch."

"You have?" Mom's eyebrows arched. "Well, my goodness. Are we finally going to get to meet this mystery girl?"

"Yeah." His cheeks flushed pink. "If that's okay with you."

Bessie Mae was delighted. I was intrigued. And my mother was probably already planning their wedding.

Still, I had to wonder how Tasha would take the news, especially since this was all going down at her family's restaurant. This how-do-you-do was going to be a little awkward, at the very least.

Before I could say, "Oh boy, this is going to be good," we were in the car, headed to Fish Tales. Well, all but Logan, who had headed out in his truck to pick up his date. They would arrive shortly after the rest of us.

Our family's weekly tradition of eating out was one of my favorites because we usually ran into half of the church at the restaurant. I always had a blast bouncing from table to table to visit with friends and loved ones. Fish Tales felt like an extension of church, like a second service, almost.

When we arrived, I paused to take it all in. As always, the tantalizing aroma of freshly cooked seafood permeated the air. I could almost taste it all now—grilled fish, seasoned shrimp, or any number of other favorites. I could even pick up on the hint of lemon wafting through the restaurant.

I found Tasha behind the register wearing a Fish Tales T-shirt and jeans. "You changed fast," I observed.

"Yeah. It's crazy busy here today. And we just opened!"

"Sorry you have to work."

"It's okay." She shrugged. "I don't really mind."

While the hostess seated our family, I hovered near the cash register, working up the courage to share the news about Logan's incoming date.

I didn't want Tasha to be caught off guard, after all.

After a few seconds, I finally broached the conversation. "So, I thought you might want to know that my brother is bringing a woman-friend to lunch today to meet us."

"A woman-friend?" She paused. "Wait, which brother?"

"Logan."

Her smile faded. Just as quickly, she pressed on a forced smile. "Oh. Well, that's nice."

"I guess. We're finally going to get to meet this girl he's been dating. I, well, I just thought you might want to hear it from me first, before you see them together."

"Why would I care?" She grabbed a napkin and started wiping off the cash register. "It's none of my business."

"Tasha. . ."

She waved her hand as if not bothered at all by any of this. "Well, good for him. And her. Who is this girl anyway? What do we know about her. Fill me in."

"She lives in Athens. Works at the hospital as a nurse. She came into the bank where he works to make a deposit. Came out with—"

"A boyfriend?" Tasha's eyebrows elevated. "And that's all you know?"

I nodded. "Yeah, you know Logan. He's not going to give away much information, so that's about all my mom could get out of him."

"What's her name? Maybe I can find her online." Tasha reached for her phone, but I shook my head.

"He wouldn't tell us. Probably thought Mom would run a background check on her. He's been very closemouthed about it all, but I guess we'll figure it out when we meet her. You know Logan, though. He wouldn't be introducing her to the family if he wasn't serious about her."

"Right." Tasha quickly turned her attention to an elderly couple approaching to pay their bill.

I went into the restaurant—adorned with nautical-themed decor like fishing nets, seashells, and so on—and located my family at our usual table, the big one in the far corner of the room.

I joined them, and we ordered sweet teas for the whole table, then settled into an easy conversation about Logan, who had not yet arrived with this mystery woman. We were placing bets on what she would look like.

The whole family was laughter and smiles.

Until my mother clamped eyes on the young woman standing next to my brother when they suddenly appeared in front of us.

I couldn't figure out why Mom seemed to freeze up at the sight of the gorgeous brunette, who Logan introduced to us as Meghan Lowry. She was adorable, from her bright smile to her cute yellow blouse and trendy jeans.

They sat to my right, and we dove straight into a conversation that evoked more laughter. Meghan had one of those bubbly personalities that you couldn't help but be drawn to. I liked her the moment I saw her.

After we ordered our food, Meghan chatted with all of us with ease, telling us about her family in Athens, a clan that included three sisters and a single mother. Logan looked on, all smiles. I was delighted for him. This cheerful gal was his polar opposite, but I could definitely see the draw. And, based on the sweet glances she gave him, Meghan had feelings for him too.

I felt sure everything was going well, when my mom, who was seated to my left, reached under the table, grabbed hold of my fingers, and gave them a squeeze.

"What is it, Mom?" I kept my voice as low as possible as the others continued to laugh and carry on at something my dad said. "Tell me."

She made a production out of dropping her napkin to the floor beneath my chair. I took her hint. We both leaned down at the same time to pick it up.

"Mom, what in the world is going on?" I whispered as I snatched the napkin. "What's happening?"

"It's Wife Number Three," she whispered, her words hoarse and strained. "The one we don't speak of."

CHAPTER TWENTY-ONE

It took me a minute, but the reality finally sank in. My brother's new sweetheart was Harlan Reed's third ex, the biggest troublemaker of all. The one whose crime—whatever it was—was so heinous even the prayer team couldn't speak of it.

I popped back up from under the table, and Logan shot me a look that said, "You okay over there?"

I forced a smile and nodded. But everything inside of me wanted to scream, "Run!"

From what, I wasn't sure. I still had no proof to go on, and Mom sure wasn't talking. She waved her hand at the waitress, who dropped off our menus.

I peeked over the edge of mine to give my brother's date a closer look. She had clearly won over the rest of the family. Meghan carried on, chatting with my dad about her family's property on the outskirts of the nearby town, Athens. She lit into a conversation about the type of horses she loved most, and from there she told us that she had spent two years living in Papua New Guinea, fresh out of high school, doing humanitarian work before going on to nursing school here in Texas. On and on she went, one cheerful tale after another. My brother hung on her every word.

For that matter, so did my other brothers. Dallas and Gage couldn't seem to get enough of her. She was a knockout, for sure, and had that kind of demeanor that drew people in. Now, granted, she was older than Logan by a year or two. I would guess her age to be around thirty.

Which raised a few questions in my mind: Like, why had she married Harlan, who was in his forties?

Then again, if she was Wife Number Three—the one who came after Sheila but before Meredith—that was a few years back. He would've been younger.

But she would've been younger too.

I couldn't wrap my head around any of this. Neither could my mother, apparently. She sat, stone silent, pausing only to grab her water glass for a tiny sip.

Not that anyone noticed but me. They were all too engaged with the Marvelous Miss Meghan, the star of this afternoon's show.

Meghan Lowry looked as sweet and genuine as any woman my brother had ever brought to meet the family. Not that he'd brought many, of course. Logan ran on the shy side, after all. And, from what I could tell as he interacted with her, he had real feelings for Meghan.

Did he know she was...notorious? Did he realize she was so far gone even the prayer team had given up on her?

Clearly not, from the smitten look on his face.

My brother had fallen for The One We Don't Speak Of. Only, I couldn't quite figure out what she'd done, exactly, to deserve that title. The girl worked at the hospital in Athens as a nurse. In labor and delivery. She volunteered her time training up nurses to go on the mission field. All of this we learned from Logan, who shared her qualities with great gusto. I couldn't remember when I'd ever seen my brother so animated. It all felt...weird.

As the conversation unfolded, I kept a watchful eye on Meghan. The waitress returned, and we placed our orders. Meghan laughed and smiled as the waitress complimented her beautiful long hair. Her response seemed genuine and heartfelt.

By the time the food came, I was convinced this was the gal for Logan. It was clear there was genuine affection between them. I'd never seen this side of Logan before, and it made my heart happy.

My mother, on the other hand, didn't seem so happy. As my skepticism waned, it appeared hers was growing.

We found ourselves distracted with the food. The plates that arrived at our table were loaded with vibrant presentations of seafood delicacies—succulent shrimp, crispy fish fillets, and more. For sure, Fish Tales had the best seafood in town. No one could argue that point.

After just a few bites of her gumbo, Mom pushed her chair back and stood up. "Excuse me, folks. I have to go to the ladies' room."

My brothers glanced her way but only for a moment.

"Come with me, RaeLyn?" She gave me a pleading look.

I eased my chair back and stood, placing my napkin on the table.

We'd only taken a couple of steps when Meghan's voice sounded behind us. "Hold up, you two. I'm coming with."

I swung around to discover she had already pushed back her chair and was standing to join us.

Oh boy. This was going to be good.

We walked to the ladies' room, and I half expected my mom to start peppering her with questions right away. Instead, Mom plastered on a smile and mentioned something about the weather.

We headed into the ladies' room, and I had to force myself to actually make use of the facilities, then walked to the sink to wash my hands.

A couple of minutes later, Mom joined me. Neither of us could say a word, not with Meghan within hearing distance. Mom could only stare at my reflection in the mirror, and I stared at hers.

Meghan came out a few seconds later, chattering on about how good the food was.

"I'm so busy at work that I rarely make it over to Mabank anymore. I used to come this way all the time, back when I was married—" She paused and looked back and forth between us. "Did you know I was married before?"

"Oh?" My mom's eyelashes batted. "Were you?"

"Yeah." She sighed and then walked to the sink to wash and dry her hands. Afterward, she looked at both of us, tears springing to her eyes. "I know you don't know me from Adam," she said after a moment's pause.

"But you have no idea how happy I am with Logan."

"He's a good boy." Mom gave her a pensive look.

"The best. And it's been years since I've had the courage to date anyone. After my marriage ended, well. . ." She paused and dabbed at her eyes. "Let's just say that not all guys are as genuine as Logan Hadley and leave it at that. I'm so blessed God brought him my way."

"He's a great guy," I said. And I meant it. Logan was a loner, but he was a terrific human. And it made me happy to see that he'd finally found someone.

Mom didn't appear quite as happy.

"My husband definitely wasn't who he portrayed himself to be," Meghan said after a moment's pause. "Not even a year into our marriage I learned that he was cheating on me. I was so young—too young, really—and I didn't know what to do. I mean, I was only twenty-three at the time, and he was in his late thirties. I was clueless. But in the end, he didn't give me any choice. He wasn't going to give up the relationship with his girlfriend, and one of us had to go. So, I left."

"That's hard." I reached to place my hand on her arm. "I can't imagine going through that at twenty-three."

"My husband married the other woman just after our divorce was final." She released a sigh. "Don't get me started on her or we'll be here all day. She wasn't—isn't—one to be trusted."

"How so?" I asked.

"She's all show. She's not who she pretends to be. I honestly think she wanted Harlan for his money."

"Harlan?" Mom said, as if she didn't already know.

"Yes, Harlan Reed."

In that moment, I had a flashback to that time at the auction house when Meredith tried to take my check from me. And that weird incident yesterday at Henderson House, where Clayton and Meredith appeared to have some sort of private understanding.

Maybe Mom had it all wrong. Maybe Wife Number Three wasn't the one we shouldn't speak of. Maybe it was Wife Number Four.

I fought the temptation to tell Meghan that I knew Meredith. But, in truth, I didn't know her. Not really.

We made our way back to the table, but I was distracted by my mom, who still seemed very out of sorts.

About the time we ordered our desserts, Tasha made her way over to our table. It was obvious—if to no one but me—that she'd come to scope out Meghan. But the woman treated her with such kindness that even Tasha was won over.

Half an hour later, after my dad paid the check, Tasha pulled me to the side. "Well? What's she like?"

"I like her," I confessed. "She seems really genuine."

"It's kind of hard not to like someone like that. She's beautiful, sweet, and works as a nurse. Next thing you're going to tell me is that she is a missionary in her spare time."

"She's a missionary in her spare time," I said. "Well, she trains them anyway. Trains nurses to go on the mission field, I mean."

Tasha slapped herself on the forehead. "Of course she does."

Before I could say anything else, a customer approached who needed Tasha's assistance.

Not that we planned to stick around. Mom was in a hurry to get out of there. When we got into the car, the tension in the air was so thick I could've sliced through it with Papaw's pocketknife.

"Someone say something!" Mom said after a moment of painful silence.

"What are we saying?" Dad adjusted the rearview mirror. "Did something happen?"

"Did. Something. Happen?" Mom and I spoke simultaneously.

My dad stared at me in the mirror. "What?"

"That woman!" Mom countered. "Logan's girlfriend. She's Harlan Reed's ex-wife."

"Oh my." Bessie Mae buckled herself into the spot next to me. "Are you sure?"

"I'm sure," Mom said. "And of all the wives to pick, he had to pick that one."

"What's she done?" Bessie asked. "Fill us in so we can hate her too."

"I don't hate her," Mom said. "I just. . ." Her words faded off.

"Mom," I chimed in. "We definitely need more details."

"Wait, our son is dating one of Harlan's exes?" My dad seemed genuinely flabbergasted by this. "Is that what you're saying?"

Mom glared at him. "Yes, Chuck, that's exactly what I'm saying. And this is the wife that Gloria told me to watch out for, Wife Number Three."

"What are we watching out for, specifically?" I asked. "Why does everyone call her The One We Don't Speak Of? What did she do, exactly?"

"I..." Mom paused. "I honestly don't know. I just know that Gloria has always called her that because that's what Sheila called her."

"Wait." Dad tapped the brakes, then turned to face Mom in the passenger seat. "Who's Sheila?"

"Harlan's second wife. She died of cancer."

"Well, I guess we can't ask her what she meant by that, then," my dad said. "Since she's dead and all."

"Let's be logical here, Mom," I said. "If Meghan married Harlan *after* Sheila passed away, he wasn't cheating on Sheila with Meghan. So, it can't be that."

"I think it had more to do with Harlan not showing up for Sheila's funeral," my mom responded.

To which Bessie Mae hollered, "The cad!"

"Gloria feels that Wife Number Three encouraged him to keep his distance."

"But you heard her in the ladies' room, Mom," I argued.

"This is quite the conundrum," Bessie Mae chimed in. "But you know what the Duke would've said."

"What's that?" Mom asked.

"Life is just a bowl of cherries, and you happen to be in the pits."

That just about summed it up. But if I told Logan, then his life would be in the pits too. On the other hand, what if I didn't tell him and the situation was even worse?

I was in a quandary and didn't know what to do. Ordinarily I would talk this through with Tasha, but she was already upset that my brother was interested in someone besides her. And she was also still pretty bummed about not owning her own B and B.

"This story would be a lot easier if I actually knew the players." Dad slipped the car into gear. "Because right now it's just sounding like one of those serial soap operas you used to watch on TV, Flora."

"I never watched soap operas, Chuck," Mom said. "Not really."

At which point he named her favorite and even gave a play-by-play of the characters and various plot points.

"Did anyone just think of asking Harlan himself about all of this?" my dad asked after Mom went silent.

"No!" we all called out in unison.

"That would be weird," Mom said.

Still, we needed perspective right now. Perhaps Gloria was wrong about Wife Number Three. In light of my brother's attachment to her—and the fact that she seemed like a perfectly normal, genuine woman—giving her the benefit of the doubt made sense.

So, I said so. Out loud.

"I guess," Mom said. "Maybe I should talk to Gloria and try to iron this out."

"No, don't." I shook my head. "Let's don't get the gossip mill up and running up at the church. I say we let Logan have his courtship with this girl and see where it takes him."

"Without telling him what we know, you mean?" My mom didn't look convinced.

"What do we know?" I countered. "Nothing, except that she was married before. And he obviously knows that much because she was pretty forthcoming about all of that. And she said it was a huge mistake, so clearly she has regrets."

"True." Mom bit her lip. "I guess we could just leave it be for a while and see what happens."

"Agreed," I said. "Don't tell Logan a thing. He might flip out. . .and all for nothing."

"Right." She paused, but I could almost hear the wheels in her head clicking.

My dad changed the direction of the conversation, talking about how great the gumbo was at Fish Tales, and I was relieved to veer away from talking about Meghan.

Still, my thoughts tumbled all over the place as he carried on about our lunch. We needed to handle this situation with Meghan with kid gloves. This was going to be a delicate balancing act—wanting to protect my brother from potential heartache but also respecting his choices.

And giving Meghan opportunity to rebuild her life after such a trying marriage.

Before I could give it much thought, a text came through from Mason, confirming that he would pick me up at three thirty. A quick glance at the clock at the front of the car let me know that it wasn't quite two o'clock. If I played my cards right, I might be able to sneak in a little nap when I arrived home. Heaven knew I needed it.

CHAPTER TWENTY-TWO

I dozed for a short while when I got home but couldn't seem to stay asleep. If I was being honest with myself, I was too excited about spending time alone with Mason. And at Purtis Creek Lake Park, no less. We'd been to that park several times as kids, so it held a special place in my heart.

I was up and dressed in plenty of time, choosing to wear a comfortable T-shirt and jeans. I grabbed a water bottle just as I heard a rap at the back door. Only then did I realize Mason had already arrived.

I let him in, and Riley went crazy, trying to get attention from him. He knelt down and patted her on the head.

"Okay, okay." He laughed as he gave her the attention she was seeking. "You think I've come just to see you, huh?"

"Oh my." I gazed down at the dog, tickled at her response to him. "I think we're going to have a hard time shaking her."

Mason stood upright and shrugged. "Then let's take her with us."

"Seriously?"

"Yeah, why not? She'll have a great time."

And that's how we found ourselves in his Lariat with a cattle dog wedged between us. Riley was beside herself with joy over this unexpected excursion, and all the more when I put my window down. She jumped into my lap and hung her head out the window, enjoying the warm afternoon air.

After a couple of minutes of that, I shut the window, and she settled down with her chin in my lap. I stroked her head, happy to have her along for the ride.

"She loves you," Mason observed.

"That feeling is mutual. I've had a lot of dogs over the years but never one I've enjoyed more. Cattle dogs are so sweet."

"Never had one before. How old is she?"

"No way to know for sure. I got her from the shelter in Athens when I moved back after college. She came from a hoarding situation, believe it or not."

"So, she's not a purebred?"

"Nope." I shook my head. "I had her DNA done, so I have the proof."

Mason gave me a look that said, "I don't believe you."

"Really. I ordered the kit online and swabbed the inside of her cheek."

"Next you're going to tell me you found her long-lost cousins."

"I found her long-lost cousins." I smiled as I remembered the day that email had come. "And believe it or not, the test connected me to her mama too. They share very common DNA threads. Otherwise I'm not sure I would have believed she's really a cattle dog because she sure doesn't act like one."

"But she is?"

"Fifty-six percent. And she's six other breeds besides, including Staffy, husky, and basset hound."

"Surely you jest."

"Nope. For only eighty-nine dollars, you too can learn the breed of your best friend."

Mason shook his head. "I always knew you loved animals, RaeLyn, but I had no idea you would run a DNA report on your dog. Next thing you know you're going to tell me you've tested the cows and horses too."

"I stopped short of doing the goats." I quirked a brow.

"Surely you jest."

"Yes, I jest. And no, we didn't test the cows and horses. Just the dog. And only because my curiosity got the better of me. I wanted to understand why her herding tendencies were, well. . .lacking."

"A cattle dog who doesn't like to herd?"

"That's the long and short of it. Someone forgot to tell her she's mostly cattle dog. I think the basset hound part has convinced her she would be better off lounging on the back porch."

Mason reached down to scratch Riley behind the ears. "Well, whatever she is, she's a great dog. Very laid-back."

"Yeah, just what I needed after coming home from A&M. Readjusting to life on the ranch took some doing. It took a good year or so just to adapt to the routine."

"I hear you. It's not as easy as you think, coming back home again." He looked my way. "But totally worth it."

"Yeah." I had to agree.

He turned left onto 316 headed north out of Eustace, a tiny town to the southeast of Mabank. As Mason drove, my gaze shifted to the fields alongside the tiny country road.

In that moment, I was struck with a flashback. Papaw and the truck. He'd taken us kids to the fields alongside this very road when I was a little girl so that he could take pictures of us in the bluebonnets. I'd been eaten alive by ants that day.

I itched even now as I thought it through. But Papaw had lifted me up to the back of the truck and covered me in a paste that he made from a watered-down aspirin, one of his many home remedies. I'd forgotten until now. His glove box was always chock-full of quirky items to be used in a pinch.

"You okay over there?" Mason's words roused me from my daydreams.

"Oh yeah." I turned and offered a little shrug. "Just thinking about the day I got eaten alive by fire ants when our family took pictures in that field."

"My mom dropped me in an ant bed or two over the years too." He laughed. "You aren't a Texas kid unless you've been dropped in an ant pile in a bluebonnet field."

"Truth."

"Is this a hint that you want to take pictures?" he asked.

I shook my head. "Not today. But the minute Tilly is home—and I hope to have her back before all of the bluebonnets are gone—I want to come back out here and take some, for old time's sake."

He grew quiet for a moment but finally said, "We've got to be realistic." Mason turned on his signal as he tapped the brakes. "It's possible you won't find her for some time."

"Are you saying I shouldn't get my hopes up about the bluebonnets?"

"Maybe." He shrugged. "And besides, there's always next year."

"Well, you go right on and think that," I countered. "I choose to believe she's coming back sooner rather than later."

"I hope you're right." He turned on the signal to take a left into Purtis Creek State Park.

"It's just like that short story by O. Henry, if you think about it."

"What short story?" He glanced my way.

"*The Last Leaf.* Remember? The little girl was dying, but she looked out the window at the leaves on the tree in the courtyard below and decided she could stay alive as long as the last leaf hung on."

"This isn't ringing any bells, but I didn't really pay a lot of attention in my lit classes."

"I'm going to hang on, just like she did."

"So, what you're telling me is. . .she lived?" He gave me a pensive look. "Because I prefer a comedy to a tragedy."

"She lived, but there's more to the story than that. Read it, and get back with me."

"I make no promises."

Riley got more and more animated as we got closer to the picnic area by the lake. Mason pulled into a spot near a picnic table and parked the truck. He opened his door, and Riley jumped across his lap and out the door.

"So much for waiting," Mason said and then laughed.

He walked around to my side of the car and opened the door for me.

I stepped out and kept a watchful eye on Riley, who was prone to wander. Hopefully she would stick close.

The shoreline of Purtis Creek Lake was beautifully framed by towering trees and an array of bushes, which appeared to be blossoming right before our eyes, their tiny, delicate buds of wildflowers adding a lovely scene to the area.

Off in the distance, I caught a glimpse of a couple of boats on the lake, leisurely moving along under the clear spring sky. The water was calm, reflecting the late afternoon sunlight and creating a tranquil scene. Well, until Riley waded out into it, making noise and soaking herself.

Mason went to the back of the truck and got a blanket, which he spread out on the ground not far from the table. Okay then. Looked like we were having our little picnic old-school style.

Off to our right, a large family enjoyed a picnic together at their table—four kids and two parents enjoyed the afternoon with sandwiches, chips, and sodas. The kids then ran and played while the grown-ups visited and played cards.

Families and friends gathered for picnics beneath the shade of blossoming trees, their laughter and chatter echoing through the air. Hiking trails wound through the woods, offering glimpses of bluebonnets, Indian paintbrushes, and other native wildflowers carpeting the forest floor.

This was how it was in our neck of the woods. Folks knew how to take advantage of an ordinary day and make it extraordinary. This whole park was infused with splatters of joy, no matter which way you looked.

Mason grabbed a plastic Brookshire Brothers bag and set it on the blanket.

"Sorry I'm not more prepared," he said. "My picnic skills only go so far."

"It's the thought that counts. What's in the bag?"

He reached inside and came out with a couple of bottles of sweet tea, some fruit, a variety of cheeses, and some fancy crackers.

"Didn't figure you'd be too hungry after having lunch with the family, so I just brought snacks."

"Yum." I loved the idea that he'd paid attention to detail, choosing cheeses that I loved.

We settled down on the blanket, and it didn't take long for Riley to pick up the scent of the cheeses. She came bounding our way, ready for her share of the bounty. Mason humored her with a bite or two of cheese, and then she got distracted by a squirrel in the tree next to us.

We watched, amazed, as Riley tried to jump up several feet to chase that squirrel.

"You're sure she's not a cat?" Mason asked. "Maybe the DNA got it wrong?"

"Could be. She's a Heinz 57, so maybe she's got some claws in there somewhere."

The space between us fell silent as we nibbled on our snacks and watched the boats on the water. After they passed, the springtime air still carried the sounds of nature. The chirping of birds, the hum of cicada wings, the occasional high-pitched sound of a squirrel teasing Riley to climb that tree once again. . .it all drew me in.

"I poke fun at Riley, but she's been a great emotional support dog," I said after watching her chase the squirrel. "She's got a real knack for sensing my moods."

"Oh?" He looked my way. "You have moods?"

I laughed. "Well, I'd like to think we all do. But she's really good at picking up on how I'm doing when I'm down. She's too big to be an official lapdog, but don't tell her that. She seems to think she is anyway."

He glanced at Riley, then back at me. "I won't say a word."

"Thanks."

"So, bring me up to speed on your sleuthing."

I sighed. "There's not really much to tell. The police are checking out tow truck drivers to see who might have hauled Tilly off the lot. I think they suspect Meredith the most, and I guess that makes the most sense, all things considered."

"Oh? Why is that?"

"Well, she's the one with the key to the gate."

"Anyone can get in a locked gate, if they have the right tools," he countered.

"The lock wasn't broken. That's the crazy part."

"Ah." Mason paused and appeared to be thinking. "So, someone who had a key."

"Yeah. That's a pretty narrow field, though, which is what has everyone so confused."

Out of the corner of my eye, I caught a glimpse of a gorgeous butterfly, wings fluttering. Riley caught wind of it and went into a fit, trying to catch it. Thank goodness, the butterfly won.

Mason thought it was hysterical. He grabbed his phone and began to videotape my crazy dog. Afterward, he set the phone down. "You know, if she doesn't make it as a cattle dog, you can always send in videos of her to one of those funny home video shows."

"She definitely qualifies."

As if to prove it, the dog started chasing her tail, now running in circles.

Mason and I both laughed until we finally caught our breath. Winded, Riley finally plopped down on the blanket. She put her head on Mason's knee.

"Hey, you." I gave my dog a stern look. "Have you abandoned me?"

"She knows where the cheese is." Mason snuck another tiny nibble into her mouth.

I leaned back, watching the two of them. This whole thing felt so natural. So comfortable. Our laughter and easy conversation created a harmonious atmosphere, which seemed to blend in with the quiet, peaceful sounds of nature all around us.

I decided, right then and there, that I could go on feeling like this...forever.

CHAPTER TWENTY-THREE

Mason and I talked for over two hours while Riley dozed between us. Somehow, we covered every topic under the sun—from Clayton Henderson's new B and B to all I'd learned about Wyatt Jackson and his ties to my grandfather.

Mason seemed shocked at my family's connection to Wyatt. But no more than I was.

"I know what it's like to lose your parents at a young age," he said. "So, I guess I sympathize with Wyatt a little. My mom died when I was seven. Dad did his best to raise me on his own, but it wasn't easy. And now he's gone too."

"I'm so sorry, Mason." My world was filled with so many family members. They got on my nerves a lot. Well, mostly Gage and Dallas. But I couldn't imagine what it must feel like to be an only child with no remaining parents. One would feel orphaned.

Suddenly I felt quite sorry for Mason.

Only, watching him drink his sweet tea and nibble on cheese, I didn't think he seemed terribly distraught about it all. He seemed to have come to terms with what he'd been through. Perhaps God had already begun the healing process.

We sat quietly, listening to the sounds of nature. After a few moments of this, I decided to get his opinion on something.

"Hey, random question."

"Sure." He put his hand over his eyes to block out the direct sunlight. "What's that?"

"What does *checkmate* mean?"

"In chess?" He shrugged. "It just means the game's up, basically. The opponent has no more moves to save the day."

"Right, but how does a player get to that point?" I asked.

"He coordinates his pieces to limit the opponent's options, then eventually puts the king in check. Mostly, he pays attention to the board and strategizes, using pieces to create a barrier of sorts, around the king, limiting moves."

"Closes in on him?" I asked.

"Yeah. Why do you ask?"

I told him about the marble chess piece we'd found. "The word *checkmate* was written on the bottom, and Bessie Mae insists it's in Papaw's handwriting. Isn't that odd?"

"Very. He's making a point. Exploiting his opponent's weaknesses."

"Pretty sure we know who his opponent was."

"Well, the long and short of it is that the game ends right away when a player declares checkmate."

"I guess Papaw made his point, if he's the one who wrote the word on the bottom of that marble king. Only, I don't know that Wyatt ever saw that message. You know?"

"I hope not," he said.

After a little more conversation on the matter, we grew silent again. I loved these peaceful moments with Mason. At some point, the lake grew quiet and still. I knew the park would be closing soon. The wide beams of sunlight filtering through the trees narrowed as evening approached. The skies above the lake seemed to morph into a painter's canvas, one covered in pastel hues.

I watched as the serene reflections on the water mirrored the warm tones of the setting sun, causing the whole place to feel subdued.

As much as I enjoyed the interplay of light and shade, I knew it was time to pack up. But there was one thing I needed to confess to Mason first.

"So, I did something kind of crazy you should probably know about."

"Oh yeah?" He looked my way. "What's that?"

"I sent Stephanie Ingram a friend request on Facebook."

His brows arched in obvious surprise. "Um, okay. That is a little surprising. I thought you two weren't speaking."

"Well, you did say it was all water under the bridge. So, I took those words to heart."

"I see." He paused and appeared to be thinking. "So, did she accept your friend request?"

"She did. We spoke at length. Well, maybe not at length, but we did have a conversation by private message."

"And?"

I shrugged. "It went great. She seems happy in Iowa."

"Iowa?"

"Yep. Not Idaho. Oh, and her husband's a pastor of a Baptist church."

"The star quarterback is now a pastor?"

"And a really good one, if the people from his church are to be believed. I checked out their Facebook page. Everyone raves about him."

"I see."

"You couldn't have lost her to a nicer guy," I teased.

At once, Mason's expression shifted. "I didn't lose her. I'm actually the one who—" He raked his fingers through his hair. "I was honestly glad she took an interest in someone else."

"Oh?"

"Yeah." He paused and gazed at me with greater intensity than before. "Let's just say she wasn't my best fit and leave it at that."

Okay. That would do. For now.

"By the way, I looked it up," he said.

"Looked what up?"

"'Water under the bridge.' I looked it up. You can find the origin of just about any phrase online."

"Cool. So, what does it mean? Why water? Why a bridge?"

"Turns out, the phrase has nothing whatsoever to do with water or bridges," he explained.

This surprised me. "Seriously?"

"Yeah, I think those words are just symbolic. The water represents the transgression—the injury."

"Okay. . ."

"And the bridge represents the strength of your relationship with that other person, the bond you share. It's your ability to forge ahead, even if there have been some old wounds."

"I see." And I did. We had experienced a few wounds in our past, but God was giving us a fresh start, a chance to make everything right again.

"You about ready to go?" he asked after a moment of silence.

"Yeah. One second, though."

I closed my eyes for a second and took a picture in my mind, one that I would never forget. The lake. The squirrel. Riley. Our food.

And Mason.

A girl could get used to a day like today.

It didn't take long to pack up our leftovers and to fold the blanket, which he tossed into the back of the truck. Soon we were on our way to my house. When we arrived, I wasn't quite ready for the day to be over yet, so I came up with a way to stall.

"You want to see the antique shop?"

"Sure."

I led the way across the field, my gaze on the sky. By now the sun was setting on the horizon, and our family acreage took on an ethereal glow. It had transformed into a lovely canvas of pinks, purples, and oranges.

The sight took my breath away. How blessed we were, to live in such a place!

Mason must have sensed the majesty of this moment too. He reached to take hold of my hand, and I gave his fingers a little squeeze.

We remained hand in hand until we reached the barn. Then I unlocked the door and opened it. The room inside was dark, but it didn't take long to flip the switch and light up the place.

"Oh, wow." He looked around, clearly mesmerized by all we'd done. "This is great."

196

"Thank you. It's a work in progress, but I've only got a few more days. Want to take a look around?"

"Sure."

"We've got our dishes over here. Decorative items there. Old records over there." I pointed to an area that featured a vintage record player and lots of 33⅓s nearby.

I showed him the rusty signs that my brothers had collected, including the one from an old Texas station. There were also famous soda signs and a variety of road signs.

"I just love these old signs."

"Do you?" I asked.

"Are you kidding me? I collect these." He ran his finger along a rusty spot on the Texaco sign.

We've kept the things with sentimental value. They're in the house. The rest? Well…" I paused and thought it through before saying, "I mean, there are only so many teacups one should be allowed to own. You know?"

"I guess." Mason shrugged. "What's the difference between a teacup and a coffee cup?"

"I'll show you." I led him to the kitchenware department and opened a box. Then I gingerly lifted a porcelain teacup, hand painted, and showed it off.

"Whoa. Looks like something our great-grandmothers would've sipped their tea from," he observed.

"And worth a pretty penny, especially if you've still got the matching saucer." I stuck my hand back down in the box and came out with the wrapped saucer, which I showed him.

"And you have a lot of these?"

"You can't even imagine. And teapots. And silver coffee servers. And fine china dating back to the 1800s."

"Why didn't you try to sell it off online?"

I shrugged. "We did that with a few things, but making the transfer was always problematic. Mom wasn't keen on so many strangers showing up at the house. She thought it was too risky. I got fed up with meeting people halfway. It just made more sense to follow through with the plan from decades ago and open a shop."

"You've really done something incredible here, RaeLyn," he said after taking it all in.

I tried to picture it all through his eyes—all of these curated memories in one place—but could not. I was too close to the items to see them objectively.

"To me it's not just about the antiques."

"No?"

I shook my head. "It's about family legacy. The ultimate goal here is to bring in enough money from the shop to help keep the ranch afloat. One day I'll have children—at least I hope I will—and I would love for them to call this property home."

"It's a pretty idyllic place, that's for sure."

"Yeah." I released a little sigh. "So, it's worth all of the hard work to pull this shop together. It might not be the high-paying job I might've dreamed of, but I can have my cake and eat it too. I get to help my parents and keep on writing for the paper at the same time."

"I think that's nice. God arranged everything in a way that makes sense to all of you. It's hard to deny the role He's played in all of this."

"True. What's that Bible verse about how He arranges our steps?" I paused to think it through. "He's definitely arranged mine, even when it didn't look that way." And, as I gazed into Mason's eyes, I had to admit, God had even arranged bringing back the only boy—man—I'd ever truly cared about.

I took a few more steps and pointed out some of my favorite items—homing in on the beautifully restored phonograph, the vintage books, and an antique typewriter that still worked.

Mason surveyed the items with a thoughtful expression. "Wow, that record player is in mint condition. Want to turn it on?"

"Sure." I reached for an old Frank Sinatra album and set it onto the turntable. A moment later, the strains of an oldie but goodie filled the air.

Mason extended his hand, an invitation to dance.

"Seriously?" I laughed.

"Yes, seriously." He pulled me into his arms, and we moved slowly to the strains of "All I Do Is Dream of You."

My heart quickened as we moved with ease, step by gentle step. After a moment, he paused but didn't let go of me.

"Can we go back to the conversation about Stephanie?" Mason asked.

"Do we have to?"

"Kind of." He gave me a sheepish look. "I was glad we broke up because, well. . ." He paused and gave me a sobering look. "I never really got past how I felt about you."

I swallowed hard before responding, "Why didn't you say so?"

"I don't know." He kicked the floor with the toe of his boot. "By then you were off at A&M, and I saw you were dating that guy—what was his name again?"

"Joey?"

"Yeah."

"I went out with him three times," I explained. "He was a jerk."

Mason gave me a hopeful look. "Really?"

"Yeah, really. I guess I never got past, well. . ." I paused before giving away the whole game.

Mason slipped his arms around my waist and pulled me close. In that moment, that very second, the distance between us closed, an unspoken acknowledgment passing between us.

I wasn't prone to heart palpitations, but there they were, whether I had invited them or not. Memories flooded over me—memories of Mabank High football games, shared secrets, and so many other special moments besides.

"Got past. . .what?" he whispered.

"Oh, you know."

Mason placed his index finger under my chin and tipped up my face to his so that I couldn't look away. "I don't know. Tell me."

Well, shoot. Gazing into those beautiful blue eyes, noticing how perfectly they matched those beautiful bluebonnets in the field by Purtis Creek State Park. . .I couldn't.

Not that he would've let me say it anyway. Before I even had a chance, his lips got in the way.

CHAPTER TWENTY-FOUR

The days that followed my date with Mason were a blur. Nearly every minute was spent in the store, getting all our ducks in a row for the grand opening. I somehow managed to put together an article for *Mabank Happenings*, sharing my thoughts on the car show. It was great to have a firsthand account, and photos to boot. I knew my editor would be pleased.

By Wednesday I was exhausted but more motivated than ever, especially when Dot dropped by with the paperwork for the chamber of commerce. She caught me just as I wrapped up a much later than usual breakfast, which I happened to be eating by myself at the kitchen table while my aunt snoozed in a chair on the far side of the adjoining living room.

I put my finger to my lips to let Dot know that Bessie was asleep after a long morning of cooking, and she nodded as if to say, *I'll be quiet.*

We kept our voices low as we talked, but the sound of the John Wayne movie on the TV provided the usual white noise to keep Bessie from stirring.

"It's really happening," I told Dot after inviting her to join me for a cup of coffee. "I'm joining the chamber."

"A decision you will not regret," she said as she settled onto a chair at the table. "Just get those papers filled out and back to me as soon as you can."

I promised to do just that.

She passed off my copy of the directory, and I thumbed through it, surprised to see just how many chamber members we had in our local group—hundreds. And I was equally as stunned to see how many businesses Clayton owned.

"My stars," I said after looking them over. "The man really does own half the stuff in town. I had no idea he owned the laundromat."

"And the car wash. And the burger joint. And a trucking company. And that empty lot where the bookstore used to be. And more acreage than a person could ever need."

"Someone told me that he was struggling financially," I said. "How can that be when he owns so much stuff?"

"Financial struggles?" Dot looked floored by this idea. "Really? The man has more money that all the rest of us put together, so I highly doubt it."

"Yeah, that's what I thought. I just wondered if the story had legs."

"I'd be mighty surprised. And you know what a philanthropist he is, RaeLyn. He's always giving money away, and with a big splash. He gave the money for the new wing at the school. And he's even in charge of some sort of big fundraiser at the hospital in Athens right now. There's some kind of a big meeting coming up for that."

"It just seems strange to me that he stopped bidding when he did. You know? A man with a lot of money to spare would've kept going, just to come out on top."

"Maybe he just decided to bid on a different vehicle and let that one go." Dot patted my hand. "You've made him out to be a villain in your mind, but maybe he's not."

I fought the temptation to tell her what I'd seen at the B and B—that whole exchange between Clayton and Meredith. No point in spreading more rumors about him. Besides, it could have been innocent.

"I know you miss Tilly, honey." She rested her palm on my hand.

"I do. And I'm going to figure out who took her."

"I have no doubt you are. Just keep narrowing that list and looking for clues."

"I will."

Our conversation was interrupted when the back door swung open and Logan walked through. After saying hello to Dot, he glanced at all the papers on the table spread out in front of us.

"What's all this?"

"Signing up for the chamber," I said. "And later I plan to call some of these folks to see if they have items they can sell on consignment."

"Which reminds me—"Dot interrupted. "I brought a set of china that belonged to my grandmother. It's been packed up in a box in my garage for years. Finally decided to sell it. I never use it anyway."

"That's great! You'll be my first consignment customer!"

"I've created a form for that," Logan said.

"You have?" I gave my brother an admiring look. *Go, Logan.*

"It's on my computer. I'll send it to you tonight. For now, just take down the information and come up with a price you want to list the china for."

Wow.

"Hey, it's what I do." Logan glanced around the room, as if looking for something. "Have you seen Dad? I stopped by to talk to him."

"He made a run to the hardware store," I said. "Why are you home from the bank?"

"I took the day off. I had some vacation time coming. Meghan and I are going to drive up to the botanical gardens in Dallas to take pictures."

"Must be getting serious," Dot said, "if pictures are involved."

"Pictures of the *flowers*," Logan said and then laughed. "She loves that sort of thing. But I do think she'll be around awhile, so. . .yeah." His gaze shifted to the floor then back up at us with the sweetest smile on his face.

I'd never seen Logan like this before: smitten. It was nice. He turned toward the door and said his goodbyes, but I had one more piece of business to attend to.

"Hey, before you go, can I ask you a question?"

"Sure." He turned back to face me.

"I mean, I know you can't give away personal information, but does Clayton Henderson bank with Texas First?"

"Maybe he does and maybe he doesn't." My brother gave me an inquisitive look. "Why?"

"Just wondering if anything strange is going on. I overheard someone at the car show talking about Clayton. He implied there are financial struggles going on."

Logan's gaze shifted to the ground.

"Just wondering if anything odd is happening there," I queried. "Anything worth mentioning."

"RaeLyn, I really can't—"

"Sometimes folks move money around when they're struggling to stay afloat," Dot chimed in. "Maybe you've noticed something like that?"

"Well, changing investments isn't unusual," Logan said. "Happens all the time."

"Is that what he's doing?" I asked.

Logan's eyes widened, and he grabbed the back door handle, as if ready to bolt. "RaeLyn! I told you, I can't share any personal information about our clients."

"So, he *is* one of your clients." I paused.

"I have to go take pictures of flowers." And with that, he was out of there. I didn't really blame him.

Dot stayed for a few minutes, then went out to her car, returning with the box of china. We looked it up on the internet and discovered it was English ironstone. And I was shocked to see it was an eighty-four-piece set, valued at over a thousand dollars. I couldn't help but gasp when I saw a similar set online selling for much more.

"Dot, are you sure?" I asked.

"Yep. It's not doing me any good gathering dust in the garage. And let's face it, my kids aren't interested in something like this. So there's no point in passing it down to kids who don't really care about such things."

That made sense. And it was a good way for both of us to make some money. Dot would definitely benefit from the sale as well.

I jotted down some information and gave her a handwritten receipt, acknowledging that I had her items in my possession, and then I promised to be in touch after Logan helped me officially log it in.

Dot headed off on her way, which left me alone to fill out the paperwork. I pondered what Logan had told me about the form. He was a good guy.

Honestly? They all were. In spite of their arguments, Dallas and Gage had really stepped up this week. And Jake. . .well, he was the cream of the crop.

"Everything okay?" Mom asked as she entered the room through the back door.

"Oh yes. Dot came by with the papers for the chamber. I'm filling out the application. She also gave me a list of every other business in town with members so I can start networking."

"That's great."

"She brought a set of china for the shop, my first consignment item."

Mom peeked into the box and gasped. "Oh my stars. Do you realize what you've got here?"

"I do. We looked it up online. It's worth a pretty penny."

"No doubt. Well, hopefully you'll get it sold."

"I'll start by putting the expensive items in the store, but it got me to thinking we should probably open an online shop for the store as well," I said. "For higher-priced items that don't sell right away. Things collectors would be interested in."

"Talk to Logan. He's our financial guy."

I nodded. "Will do. I just have to figure out the shipping thing. I don't want to drive all over the country making deliveries again. That was awful."

"Agreed. And you'll be far too busy for that."

"Right." I nodded. "Hey, speaking of Logan, did you realize he and Meghan were going to Dallas together today to take photos of flowers?"

"He texted your father." Mom walked to the fridge and grabbed a bottle of water.

"Looks like The One We Don't Speak Of is here to stay."

"Mm-hmm." Mom opened the water bottle then changed the subject to Carrie, who was apparently having a few more contractions this morning. "Just wanted you to know, in case," she said and then headed back outside again.

I promised to be ready, if needed, and then turned my attention back to the application. It didn't take long to fill out. Then I started looking through the directory of chamber members and put together a list of people to call.

Nothing significant really jumped out at me until I read the words *Jackson Lock & Key.*

Wyatt Jackson was a member of the chamber? This surprised me. The man was completely antisocial. Why would he link arms with other businesses? My thoughts began to drift as I pondered the potential reasons.

And then they shifted in another direction altogether.

The man was a locksmith. No wonder he wanted to stay connected to the various businesses. He'd probably keyed half the shops in town. Or more. Including most of our stores and even the school.

And that's when it hit me.

Harlan said that he'd recently had the whole building rekeyed. Had he hired Wyatt, by chance?

I played out the scenario in my head, then decided to give Harlan a call. Unfortunately, I got his machine, so I left a quick message: "Mr. Reed, this is RaeLyn Hadley. The other day you mentioned having your business rekeyed recently. Would you mind letting me know who you hired? I'm working on a hunch over here."

Then I ended the call and began to pace the kitchen, talking only to the dog.

"So, Wyatt Jackson was able to get in the gate," I said aloud. "He's a locksmith. He easily could have done it."

Riley looked up from her spot on the floor, one eye open, the other shut.

"But that doesn't answer the question of how he towed the vehicle. Did he bring a tow truck, or. . ." My imagination went off in a thousand different directions. How could an eighty-something-year-old man tow a truck by himself?

"If he's got a hitch on the back of his truck, he could've done it by himself." These words came from Bessie Mae, who had obviously been awake during my ramblings. "It's a simple matter of hitching it up and driving away, girlie."

"Bessie Mae, you scared me."

"Didn't mean to do that." She stirred in her chair and then stretched before standing up. "You know what the Duke always says, right?"

I had no idea what she was about to say but had to laugh when she came back with, "Slap some bacon on a biscuit, and let's go! We're burnin' daylight!"

"What are you saying, Bessie Mae?" I asked.

"I'm saying, let's get our tails over to the Jackson place and see if there's a hitch on his truck."

"Seriously? We're just going to mosey on over to his property and ask to see his truck?"

"Nope. You're going to go over there and ask Rena Sue if she's got anything she wants to sell on consignment in the shop. And while we're there, we're going to get a look at that truck. Then we'll know. Oh, and while we're there, we might just ask Rena if her husband went missing on the morning of Tuesday, the 26th."

I gave my aunt an admiring look. She was pretty crafty, especially for a Baptist.

And just like that, we were out the door and headed to the Jackson place. We arrived in short order, and both of us gasped when we saw the property.

"Man, this place is really in bad shape." Bessie Mae clucked her tongue. "It was never like this before."

"And Rena never mentioned that he was letting things go?"

"She's not fully there. You know?" Bessie Mae's eyes filled with tears. "If I had known, we could've come out here to help."

Unfortunately, Wyatt's truck wasn't parked in the driveway, but that didn't stop Bessie Mae from wanting to park and get out of the car.

"Pull on up to the curb," she said. "Let's do a little snooping."

"I don't think that's safe," I argued.

"Well then, let's go knock on the door and see if Corina is home."

"And say what, if she answers?" I asked.

"That's up to you. I gave you my suggestion, but I'm not the brains of this operation—you are."

My aunt might not be the brains, but she was the courage. Bessie Mae led the way to the front porch then climbed the rickety wooden steps and knocked on the screen door.

A couple of minutes later, the door creaked open.

Rena's eyes widened when she saw us. "For pity's sake, Bessie Mae. Call a person first. I'm still in my house robe, and the house is a mess."

"No worries, Rena Sue," my aunt said. "We're not here to stay. RaeLyn here just wanted to ask you a few questions."

Bessie turned to face me and gestured, as if to say, "Take it away, maestro."

Only, I didn't know what to say.

And then suddenly I did.

"Ms. Rena, I don't know if you've heard, but we're opening an antique store in our barn."

"Well, of course I've heard, honey." She flashed a warm smile. "Everyone in town has heard."

"Oh, awesome. Well, here's the thing: we're short on items to sell. So, I'm visiting with the various members of the chamber of commerce to see if anyone has antique items—or really, just older items—they might want to list on consignment. It might be a way to help us fill the store while putting a little money in your pocket if you do."

Her eyes flashed with excitement. "Well now, that's an interesting proposition. This house is full top to bottom with junk we don't need—stuff going back for generations. That's half the reason we don't have folks over anymore, because the house is just too cluttered up with all the stuff we've accumulated."

"I'd be happy to take some of it off your hands. Just gather up what you want to sell and bring it by the shop anytime you like."

"Sounds wonderful." She gave me a little nod. "I wish you the best with your shop."

"Thank you." I glanced toward the roadway in front of the house as a squeal of tires sounded against the gravel. Only then did I realize Wyatt was home.

The sweet expression on Rena's face faded the moment she saw him, and I could read the concern in her eyes.

"Well, you two had better move on out, I suppose. Wyatt's not too keen on unexpected company."

Judging from the sour expression on the old man's face, he wasn't.

He glared at us as Bessie Mae and I walked back to the curb to get into the Pontiac. I eased the car away from the Jackson property, then watched as Wyatt stood glaring at us.

I could almost imagine the conversation he would have with Rena after we left.

But what really intrigued me. . .was the hitch on the back of his truck.

CHAPTER TWENTY-FIVE

On the day after we made our run to Wyatt's place, I found myself twisted up in knots over whether or not my grandfather's nemesis had stolen Tilly.

I was convinced he had. . .until I remembered that broken lock on Tilly's glove box. A locksmith wouldn't need to break open a lock, would he? This one fact alone made me think he wasn't to blame. Still, I couldn't stop my overactive imagination from running away with me.

As a form of distraction, I made several calls to local friends and business owners to see if anyone had items to place on consignment. I even reached out to Clayton and Nadine. . .just to get a reaction. If they were struggling financially, perhaps they could come up with a few items.

Nadine promised to look through her stash and get back with me. I knew the woman owned some expensive items, so maybe I would end up with something of great value. I hoped anyway.

Next, I hit up Harlan at the auction house. No doubt he had some things on hand that hadn't sold at auction. Perhaps he would be interested in selling them on consignment. Unfortunately, I got his machine once again.

By midmorning I was done making calls and ready to get back out to the shop to finish cleaning and pricing the items on the shelves. Carrie asked if she could help me, since both of my parents were in town at a church event.

"Aren't you supposed to be resting?" I asked. "I thought you were having contractions."

"It's all false labor," she said. "And I'm still a couple of weeks early, so I don't think this baby's coming anytime soon. I'm about to go stir-crazy in that house, and there's nothing left to paint."

Correction: there was nothing left to paint sage green.

"I'm pretty good at organizing," she said. "I was thinking I could help you with the smaller stuff."

That sounded good, actually. "I do need someone to help me clean up some of the little items like the salt and pepper shakers. They're pretty dusty, and we've got a lot of them. And I need help pricing them too."

"I'd be happy to do that. You have pricing stickers?" she asked.

"I do."

So she tagged along—er, waddled along—behind me to the barn, where I put her to work cleaning and pricing some of the tiniest items in the store.

But not before she went on and on about what a terrific job I'd done turning the barn into such a magnificent store. "I just can't believe the change," she said as she looked around the store, which was nearly ready to open for business.

"Hey, I had a whole team. We Hadleys work well together."

"You do." She sighed. "And I'm going to need all of you when this little one comes." She rubbed her belly.

"You've got it." I couldn't wait, in fact.

Once she settled into her work, I walked back to the inventory room, where boxes were still scattered around, to see what else I could pull up front.

Having my sister-in-law in the shop added an air of excitement I hadn't felt for a few days. Honestly? I'd been too exhausted to allow myself much celebration. But seeing all this through Carrie's eyes gave me a new perspective. I chatted at length about the china set Dot had brought over, and before long we were carefully placing the beautiful pieces onto the glass shelves of our finest china cabinet, a massive piece of furniture that had been my grandmother's.

Every now and again Carrie would pause to put her hand on her back and make a funny face. I kept a watchful eye on her, just in case.

Sometime around twelve thirty we heard a rap at the door and I opened it, surprised to discover Wife Number Three—er, Meghan—on the other side, holding a large box.

"Hey!" She offered a bright smile when she saw me. "Logan said you guys were looking for antiques for your shop, so I've brought a bunch of stuff."

"You. . .you did?" I gestured for her to come inside, and she followed behind me.

"Yep. And there's a lot more in the trunk." She set the box down, and I followed her out to her car to bring in more.

I made introductions, since Carrie and Jake hadn't been with us at Fish Tales on Sunday. The two ladies hit it off right away. Turned out, Meghan worked in labor and delivery at the hospital where Carrie was about to deliver. Go figure.

With Carrie's help, we looked through all the items, and I was beside myself when I saw the little Christmas ornaments.

"Oh, I was hoping we would find more of these! I've got a few but none that look as vintage as these."

"Well, I was once married to a man who runs an auction house," she said. "So, I kind of had my pick of things when they came in."

That made sense. And it gave me hope. Maybe she had a lot more boxes like these at home.

As if reading my mind, she said just that. Then her nose wrinkled as she mentioned her ex-husband. "I was so young when I married Harlan." She reached inside the largest box and pulled out more ornaments, then passed them my way. "I worked at his place the whole time we were married. Have you seen it?"

"The Big Red Bid." I nodded. "Yes, we're familiar."

I then shared the story of Tilly and told about how she'd gone missing.

"Oh, RaeLyn! I'm so sorry. I can't believe Logan didn't tell me that."

"Well, he's been a little preoccupied," I said and then smiled.

"Yeah." Her cheeks flushed pink. "And when we're together, it's like the hours just go by in minutes." She paused. "It's a totally different experience compared to when I met Harlan."

"How did you and Harlan meet anyway?" Carrie asked. "If you don't mind my asking."

"Don't mind at all. I met him when I brought in a vintage first aid kit from the early 1900s to place up for auction. We got to talking, and the next thing you knew, we were dating."

"I see."

"He told me his divorce was final, and I believed him." Meghan sighed. "I was young and naive. Harlan is a lot older than me. He's fifteen years my senior." She shrugged.

"Oh, wow." Carrie looked shocked by this.

"Yeah. I was young and gullible and just fell right into his trap."

"Is that what you think it was?" I asked.

She nodded. "Yeah, he knows how to woo a woman. We'll just leave it at that. And honestly? I was so naive, I just believed whatever he told me. It wasn't until after we were married that I found out he had pretty much abandoned the wife ahead of me, the one who ended up passing away right after our wedding. Her name was Sheila." Meghan looked my way. "Did you know her?"

"No." I shook my head. "But I know *of* her."

"He didn't even go to her funeral. Can you believe that?" She shook her head. "What kind of monster had I married?"

I decided it might be for the best not to respond at all and just let her keep on talking.

"I guess I was looking for a father figure. I don't know. But we married way too quickly. And that's when I figured out his real personality." She shivered. "He's not the type to settle down with just one woman. I'll leave it at that."

"I'm sorry, Meghan."

She kept working, pulling items from the boxes. "Anyway, we hadn't been married a year when he started seeing this blond. Meredith. I knew the minute he hired her to work in the office that she was trouble."

"How so?"

"She was always flirting with him. And she had expensive taste. He liked to give her little trinkets from time to time. I heard all about it from Ben, the kid who worked in the office with us."

"That's awful, Meghan."

"Before I knew it, they weren't even trying to hide it anymore. So, I just. . .left. I went back to my family in Athens and lived my life the best I could without him."

"When did all of this happen?"

She paused and appeared to be thinking it through. "Well, I left him on my twenty-third birthday. And that was seven years ago. I'm about to turn thirty."

"And Meredith?"

"From what I've heard, she and Harlan split not too long ago. Good riddance, I say." She paused to swipe on some lipstick. "I guess that's a little harsh, but I've had a hard time forgiving her. She's not the person she claims to be. We'll just leave it at that."

I quickly filled Meghan in on a few more details. I told her about Meredith trying to take the check from me, and she flinched.

"Am I right to think she might be responsible?" I asked. "She had access to the gate."

"And she had motive," Meghan said. "I heard through the grapevine that their divorce was really ugly. He was cash poor after so many divorces. It stands to reason that she felt owed. If so, she very well could have taken your truck." Meghan put her hands up. "Not that I'm accusing her, mind you. Just saying."

"Why not go through the proper channels?" Carrie asked. "She could have just sued him to get what she thought she deserved."

"Maybe she tried that." Meghan gave us a knowing look. "Courts don't always favor the wives. Ask me how I know."

"I'm guessing she felt cheated." Carrie rested her hand on her belly and winced.

"Maybe she stole the truck to try to muddy the name of the auction house," Meghan suggested. "Could be she was trying to hurt Harlan."

"Well, she hurt me too," I argued. "*If* she's the one who took Tilly. I'm still not convinced."

To my right, Carrie was taking slow, steady breaths. Meghan and I both looked her way.

"You okay over there?" Meghan asked.

Carrie blew out a long breath. "Braxton-Hicks, I think." She waved her hand and picked up a box of ornaments to move them to a nearby table. "I've had so many false alarms, I try not to overthink it when they come."

"You sure?" Meghan asked.

"Yeah." Carrie started picking through the box, oohing and aahing over the various ornaments inside. Before long, we were online, trying to price the items one by one.

"I hate to do this, but I have to get home to get changed for work," Meghan said. "I'm on the three to eleven shift this evening."

"Okay," I said. "I'll put together an inventory list with suggested prices. How would that be?"

"I trust you, RaeLyn." She reached to give me a hug.

Wrapped in her warm embrace, I couldn't help but wonder what Mom would think.

Meghan left right after that, and I got back to work alongside Carrie.

"What do you make of her?" my sister-in-law asked when we were alone again. "I think she's nice."

"Me too. I still have no idea why the prayer team was so opposed to her. The crazy thing is, Meghan has no idea we have any reservations at all."

"I think your mama is the only one with reservations."

"Right?" I paused. "I just think she's a sweet, genuine woman who's truly falling for Logan. And honestly? He's been such a loner back there in his double-wide, I'm thrilled to see that he's got a life outside of that loneliness."

"Me too. I'm happy for both of them." Carrie stretched her back and then reached into the box once more, grabbing a couple more ornaments. "Leave the past in the past. That's what I say."

"Mason would say, 'It's all water under the bridge.'"

"Would he now?" Carrie's brows elevated in playful fashion. "That's interesting."

We made quick work out of pricing everything, and I was thrilled to see that Meghan's items had a value of about seven hundred dollars total. Not bad.

Now we just needed a handful of others to come in with a similar stash.

I was engrossed in arranging vintage books on a shelf near the back of the room when I heard a scuffle. I looked up and noticed an obvious change in Carrie's demeanor. I instinctively sensed that something was amiss.

"You okay?" I asked for the hundredth time.

"I. . ." She paused, hand on stomach. "I think I just need to sit down. Feeling a lot of pressure pains."

"Sure. You've been on your feet too long. Why don't we go back up to the house?"

"I'm not sure I can. . .just yet." She released a long breath and pinched her eyes shut as she dropped into a vintage easy chair.

I kept a watchful eye on her. This time she wasn't so quick to say everything was fine. And it was obvious from the pained look on her face that something was happening.

"Do you want me to call Jake?"

"He's coaching. Big game today."

"He's got an assistant. And baseball comes second to a baby."

She paused and then flinched.

I made an executive decision to call him. Jake picked up about three rings in, sounding breathless. "RaeLyn, I'm right in the middle of—"

"I think this is it, Jakey," Carrie called out.

"What?" He paused. "Really?"

"Yeah. Pretty sure." She tried to stand, then sat right back down, a pained expression on her face.

"I've never done this before," I said, "but based on how she's acting, I think it's the real deal."

"I'll be home in five minutes."

And he was. Five minutes later he came tearing into the driveway. By now, Carrie and I were halfway across the field, headed toward the gate that would lead us to the backyard and the driveway to meet him. Somewhere along the way we paused so she could have another contraction.

Duchess came up beside us and nuzzled her as if to say, *You've got this, girl.*

Logan met us at the gate, his eyes wide in shock when he saw how red in the face Carrie was.

"Will you get my bag?" she asked. "It's on our kitchen table."

"I've got it!" I sprinted to their tiny house and bolted into that sage-green kitchen, then grabbed the bag from the table. I also snatched her purse.

By the time I got outside, they were both in his truck. I promised to gather the troops and meet them at the hospital.

And just like that, we were having a baby.

CHAPTER TWENTY-SIX

As soon as Jake and Carrie pulled away, I ran inside the house to tell Bessie Mae. She got so excited that she dropped a bowl of chocolate chip cookie dough on the floor. Thankfully the plastic bowl landed right side up.

"Are we going to meet them at the hospital?" She placed a piece of aluminum foil on top of the bowl and shoved it into the fridge, nearly dropping it again in the process.

"Yes, ma'am. I'm going to call Mom and Dad and let them know. They're at a meeting at the church, but she said to call if anything happened, and, well, something happened."

Minutes later, my aunt and I were on our way to the nearby town of Athens to UT Health. I managed to reach my mom, who was beside herself with excitement. She said they would come as soon as they could.

I didn't reach out to my brothers, figuring my mom would take care of that for me. I just put the pedal to the metal and buzzed down 175, anxious to get there. Well, I buzzed. . .until the cars in front of me began to slow.

"Why does the traffic have to be heavy today of all days?" I groaned as I approached an area of the highway that was under construction. This was normally a straightforward route, but not today.

I kept a watchful eye on my phone out of the corner of my eye, wondering if Jake or Carrie would text me.

Oh, who was I kidding? They had other things to deal with.

My mind raced with thoughts of Carrie and the imminent arrival of my new niece or nephew. This would be my first, and I didn't want to miss it.

Bessie Mae kept me engaged with chatter about past family births, including a story about the day I was born. Apparently it rained that day. Who knew. And the roads were slick, and the car almost slid off the road on the way to the hospital.

The things you learned when under stress with an eighty-two-year-old in the car with you.

Turned out there was an accident ahead, not just construction. Great. A detour sign appeared to our right. It offered a suggested alternative route to bypass the accident, but that unfamiliar detour posed the risk of further delays, so I stayed put.

Hopefully the accident happened after Jake and Carrie went by. I would hate to think they were still sitting in this mess. I asked Bessie Mae to text Mom to let her know about the construction so that she could come a different route. It turned out the accident was just a little fender bender, thank goodness. The police had it cleared just as we reached that spot.

I eventually turned off the highway onto S. Palestine and kept going until I finally arrived at the parking lot of UT Health. We went in through the front entrance and asked where we could find labor and delivery, and then I took off down the hall like a sprinter, nearly forgetting my eighty-two-year-old aunt was trying to keep up with me.

"Sorry." I paused to let her catch her breath.

"I'm not a spring chicken, RaeLyn." She put her hand to her chest and gasped. "And that baby's gonna come when it's gonna come, whether we're there or not."

"Yes, ma'am." I slowed my pace. She was right. And it wasn't like we were going to be in the room anyway. We would be hanging out in the waiting room of the labor and delivery area.

Which is exactly where I found Jake talking to Nurse Meghan, who was adorned in her scrubs.

When I walked in, she laughed and said, "Hey, long time no see."

"Right? This is crazy cool."

"I should have been more attentive when I was in your shop," she said. "I was in such a hurry to get home to change that I wasn't focused. I'm so sorry."

"We made it on time, and that's all that matters," Jake said. "And I'm glad Carrie recognized you. Funny how God works."

"Indeed." She smiled.

It was getting harder by the minute to dislike The One We Don't Speak Of.

"Why are you out here?" Bessie Mae asked Jake. "Shouldn't you be in the room with Carrie?"

I was wondering the same thing.

"Oh, they're changing her into a hospital gown and getting an IV in. And the anesthesiologist is in there talking to her about epidurals. I felt like I was in the way." He glanced at his watch. "But I guess I should probably be getting back."

"What about you, Meghan?" I asked.

"I'm on until eleven. After that, well. . ." She laughed. "Kind of depends on how far along she is, whether I stay or not. I've already texted Logan to let him know, so he should be coming by after work."

She took off on Jake's heels, which left me alone in the waiting room with Bessie Mae, who had discovered the coffee maker and a tiny refrigerator filled with snacks for family members.

"I'm a family member," she said, and then took out a container of yogurt.

She offered me a small applesauce, but I turned my nose up at it. "Maybe later."

My parents arrived about twenty minutes after Bessie finished her yogurt. Mom was carrying a door wreath, all decked out in pinks and blues.

"The baby's not even here yet," I said. "And we don't know if Carrie would want that."

"I know, but this is a gift from Dot, and I couldn't say no. Besides, everyone does this nowadays. They put wreaths on the doors of the rooms. It's a thing."

"I think it's sweet." Bessie Mae opened the fridge again and pulled out a small water bottle. "Water, anyone?"

I did too, honestly. And with Carrie's family living out of state, she probably wouldn't mind that we were playing such a pivotal role in her child's birth. I hoped.

Mom went off on a tangent about how excited she was to meet her first grandchild. "I still can't believe they haven't let us know if it's a boy or girl," she said. "That's just unheard of these days."

"I think it's kind of sweet," I said. "And I admire Jake and Carrie for being able to keep it a secret all this time."

"We'll know soon enough." Dad filled a cup with coffee then took a seat in a chair next to Bessie Mae. "Anything good on TV?"

"There's a baseball game on tonight," she said. "If we're still here, that is."

"Oh, we'll still be here," Mom said. "These things take hours, especially first babies."

Turned out, she was wrong. An hour and a half after we arrived, Jake barreled into the waiting room to let us know the baby had arrived.

"She's here!" he said, and then his eyes filled with tears.

"A girl?" Mom let out a little squeal. "Oh! Do you have pictures!"

He showed off pictures of the baby, and I erupted in tears. So did Mom, who was overcome with joy.

"When can we see her?" Mom asked.

"And how is Carrie?" I chimed in.

"Soon," he said. "And Carrie's good. The whole thing happened so fast, I think she's in a state of shock." He turned to face me. "I'm so glad you were with her today, RaeLyn. I don't know what would have happened if she'd been home alone. Annalisa might've been born at home."

"Annalisa!" Mom clasped her hands to her chest. "That's her name."

"Annalisa Mae." He turned to face Bessie Mae. "Named after you."

"Oh my." My aunt's eyes filled with tears. "That's the sweetest thing ever."

He carried on about how beautiful she was, but I was too distracted by my aunt to pay much attention. Apparently that whole "we named her after you" thing was really hitting her in the feels.

Jake returned to his wife's side shortly after that. Another half hour went by, and we stayed put in the waiting room, hoping they would call us back to see the baby. At some point along the way, Logan arrived, followed by Dallas and Gage. Tasha showed up just after that and lit into a conversation with Dallas about the upcoming children's choir event.

Bessie Mae was beside herself, telling everyone who walked in—family or not—that the baby had been named after her.

Logan seemed preoccupied, and when Meghan popped her head in the door to tell us it would be a few more minutes before we could go back because they were bathing the baby, he disappeared with her into the hallway.

When he came back, I could tell something was up.

"Just spit it out," I said at last. "You've got something on your mind."

"I do." He paused and the room went quiet.

"What's that? Logan?" Mom asked. She dropped into a chair. "Please don't tell me you've proposed to that girl."

"No." Creases formed between his eyes as he glanced toward the door to make sure Meghan hadn't overheard my mom's statement. "But I might at some point in the future, and when I do, I hope the expression on your face isn't as pained as it is now."

"I want you to be happy," she said.

"But. . . ?"

My mom shrugged. "Anyway, what did you want to tell us?"

"I've been taking some classes online at A&M."

"What?" This caught me totally off guard. "You're in college?"

"Yeah." He shrugged. "I didn't say anything, but that's one reason I moved into the trailer a couple years back, so I could focus on my studies."

"My stars," Mom said. "I had no clue." She looked back and forth between us all. "Did any of you know this?"

I was just as surprised as she was. Maybe more so. None of the others seemed to know either. Except maybe Dallas. He was quieter than the rest of us.

"How long have you been taking classes?" I asked. "And why didn't you tell us?"

"Two years, but I've been on an accelerated plan, moving a lot faster, which is why I've been distracted. Between the job and the classes, I've been swamped. And I didn't tell you, because. . ." He paused and looked down at the ground. "Well, I wasn't sure I could handle it, to be honest. Figured I'd wait until I got further along in my studies to mention it."

"Well, I'm proud of you," I said. "I don't know why you'd doubt yourself."

"Thanks." He turned his attention to our dad. "I'm working on my agribusiness degree at A&M. And having some business knowledge is also going to come in handy, now that we're opening the antique store." He turned my way. "I've been working on a business plan for the shop that's a lot more detailed than before. I'd like to run it by you."

"Sounds great," I responded.

"We're going to have to work hard, but I think we'll get there."

Our conversation was cut short by Meghan, who reappeared with a wide smile on her face. "You ready to meet the newest Hadley?"

"Are we ever!" Mom jumped up and practically sprinted out the door.

Minutes later we were ushered into Carrie's room, where we found her in bed holding the cutest little baby I'd ever seen. I couldn't help myself. The tears just flowed. Darling Annalisa was snugly swaddled in a soft pink-and-white hospital blanket. A little newborn cap adorned her head, keeping her cozy.

"Oh, Carrie!" I said. And that was about all I could get out.

Mom and Dad made up for my lack of words with nonstop chatter about how beautiful she was, about how she looked like Jake when he was born, and so on.

I found myself distracted by Annalisa's tiny hands, which were curled into balls.

At one point, she squirmed and let out the tiniest cry, like a baby kitten. We all oohed and aahed as if it was the sweetest thing we'd ever heard.

Come to think of it, it was the sweetest thing I'd ever heard. Every little sound she made was a miniature marvel to us all, a testament to the miracle of new life that God had so willingly bestowed on us.

Annalisa seemed like a contented baby, nestled in her mama's arms, surrounded by aunt, uncles, and grandparents. Oh, and great-great aunt. Bessie Mae was three generations up the line.

With that in mind, I decided I'd better take pictures of her with the baby. And that's just what I did.

The baby yawned and stretched, and I caught another shot mid-stretch. But then Carrie yawned, and I realized we'd probably overstayed our welcome.

Before parting ways, we all said our goodbyes and gushed a little more over the newest family member. I felt such overwhelming adoration from every family member as they planted tiny kisses on her forehead. And, as we left the new mom and dad alone with their baby, we left behind a sense of joy and excitement our family hadn't seen in ages.

Annalisa was just what we needed right now—hope that our family would live on another generation. Her very presence added a new layer of warmth and love to our lives.

After we left the room, Mom burst into tears. I knew she wasn't upset, just emotional. Imagine our surprise when the one who wrapped her in a big hug was none other than Wife Number Three. She held Mom closely and left us with the promise that she would keep watch over our loved ones while we were away.

Mom offered a faint smile, and we turned to leave. We made our way down the main hall of the hospital and through the emergency room exit.

Just as we passed through that door, we were met by an ambulance unloading a patient. A familiar patient.

Wyatt Jackson.

The medics lowered his stretcher from the ambulance and pushed him through the door.

Rena entered closely behind him, her brow furrowed.

I wanted to stop her, but she didn't seem to notice us. I didn't blame her. She headed straight back to where they had taken Wyatt into triage.

"I'm sorry, ma'am," the nurse at the desk said. "You'll have to wait out here for a bit. But we'll call you back when we can."

She looked lost. Completely and totally lost. And that's when the dam broke. She began to sob aloud.

Bessie Mae headed that direction and engaged the overwrought woman in conversation. I couldn't hear much but could definitely see the distress on Rena's face.

When my aunt finally returned to join us outside, we all spoke at once. "Well?" Mom asked. "What happened to him?"

"Apparently he was out working in his old shed and cut his hand. Rena said it's pretty deep."

"What did he cut it on?" I asked.

"She didn't say. She said he's got some sort of workshop out there where he does woodworking and such, and tinkers on their cars. That sort of thing."

"Tinkers on their cars?"

"Yes. She wasn't altogether sure. She said she hasn't been out there in years because he fusses at her when she disturbs him. I've told you, he's not the nicest man."

But even the grumpiest man didn't deserve to be laid up in the hospital with a busted hand.

"I told her we'd pray for him," Bessie Mae said. "Oh, and I told her about the baby, and how she was named after me and all. That cheered her up."

"Don't you think someone should stay with her?" I suggested. "I hate to leave her alone like this."

I was surprised when Tasha offered.

And even more surprised when Dallas said he would stay too.

What really shocked me, though, was what happened a few moments later as Bessie Mae and I crossed the now-dark parking lot, headed toward her car. I noticed a familiar Lexus, the one belonging to Clayton Henderson.

And inside, barely visible through the shadows of the evening, I caught him in a romantic embrace with a blond woman. . .who very clearly wasn't his wife.

CHAPTER TWENTY-SEVEN

On Thursday night, I had a hard time falling asleep. Riley must have picked up on my worries because she tossed and turned at my feet in the bed.

I couldn't stop thinking about what I'd seen at the hospital—Clayton Henderson and Meredith Reed, alone in his car. In an embrace.

Thank goodness Bessie Mae hadn't noticed. She probably would have rapped on the window and threatened to call Nadine.

Which raised an interesting question: Should I tell Nadine? Or have Mom tell Nadine? What did one do in a situation like this?

I finally dozed off and dreamed about the duo. In my dream, Meredith and Clayton were alone in a moonlit clearing at Purtis Creek State Park. I tiptoed from tree to tree, retreating into the shadows, in an attempt to hear their hushed conversation, which wove a web of secrets and deceit. As I strained to catch their words, a chilling revelation emerged. They had stolen Tilly. Together. This dastardly duo was entangled in a sinister plot that went beyond their illicit affair.

The night air was thick with tension, but I remained in place, listening as they gave away all their dirty little secrets. Meredith's lips curled up in a sly smile, and Clayton brushed a loose hair off her face, then gave a devilish laugh.

"Clayton, our little secret is safe. . .for now." These words came from Meredith, who wrapped her arms around his neck and pulled him close for a kiss.

A rustle in the bushes to my right caught their attention, and they turned to discover me hiding behind the tree. My heart and mind raced as I stepped out into the moonlit clearing. I took off running through the forest and straight into the lake, where I dove in then began to swim with every ounce of strength in me.

I woke up exhausted, my arms hurting. Had I been swimming in my sleep?

The dream ended with haunting uncertainty, which left my heart racing and my hands trembling. I rose and dressed but couldn't think clearly of what to do. The reality of what I had witnessed—in the parking lot of the hospital, not in my dream—settled heavily on my shoulders.

I couldn't help but think the two of them were engaged in some sort of sinister plot. But how could I connect the dots between their affair and something more? Just the thought of them as a couple made me nervous.

Which made things even more awkward when Meredith stopped by the shop midmorning to sell some things on consignment.

She rapped on the door, and my heart went into overtime as I saw her through the glass, holding a large box.

I had no choice but to act like everything was perfectly normal, so that's what I did. I opened the door and offered a bright—albeit somewhat fake—smile with a chipper, "Can I help you?"

"Hey, there." She grinned and held up the box. "Now, I know you don't officially open till tomorrow morning, but a little birdie told me that you're gathering things on consignment, and I've got some things I think you're really going to be interested in."

"Really? That's great." I wanted to add, "And who, exactly, was that little birdie?" But didn't.

"I've got some things here I don't need anymore." She marched over to the register counter and plopped the box down. "Figured it was about time to let them go."

I gasped when I looked down into the box and saw it was filled with beautiful items, including the most gorgeous miniature hand-painted carousel. She lifted it out and showed it off.

"What do you think of this? Pretty, right?"

"Wow, it's. . ." I hardly knew what to say. This thing had to be worth a fortune.

"It was my mama's," she said, and she wound it up and then set it on the counter. It began to go around in circles, playing the merriest little tune. The carousel horses went up and down in a magical fashion.

"And you're not keeping it?"

"No. I used to enjoy looking at these old things, but they're just a reminder of my past now, and I'm ready to move on."

I'll bet you are.

She reached down into the box to come out with more items, each more precious than the other.

"These are family heirlooms, but my parents have both passed away, and I don't have any need for these things, so. . ." Her nose wrinkled. "You know how it is. It's not really my style anyway."

"Right."

She emptied the box and set it aside, but I noticed a wallet down at the bottom. I reached down and grabbed it, and a familiar sensation settled over me.

"Did you mean to include this?" I lifted it up to show her.

Creases formed between her finely plucked brows, and for a moment I thought I saw panic in her eyes. "Oh no! I forgot that was in there. That was. . .Daddy's." She snatched it out of my hand.

Very strange.

"I hate to sell off Mama and Daddy's things," she responded with a little sigh. "But I'm in a position where I have no choice. Do you think these will sell? I could sure use the money. Things have been kind of tight since. . ." Her words trailed off.

"I guess we'll see." I started giving the items a closer look. "It might take me a while to come up with prices for them. I'll need to do some research to determine value."

"So, how does this work? Do you take them on consignment or buy them outright from me?"

"I sell them on consignment."

"Oh." Her smile faded. "I was kind of hoping it was the other way around, but I suppose that will have to do."

I talked her through the process, and she left with the promise that I would be in touch once I'd figured out the value of the items, which she left in my care after I handed her a receipt.

My whole family showed up a short while later, and we went into hyperdrive, cleaning. Mom took care of the floors. Bessie Mae dusted. Logan—who had taken a vacation day just to be with us—went over every square inch of the plan for the store's finances. And Dallas and Gage moved shelves around and helped me clean out the storeroom.

Carrie and Jake would be coming home from the hospital at some point tonight, and Bessie Mae planned to cook up a feast. So we lost her around four when she headed to the house. The rest of us kept at it, polishing and shining until every surface in the store sparkled. I could hardly believe it. Tomorrow at this time this room would be filled with customers. Our family would embark on a new adventure, one—I prayed—that would turn things around financially for us.

Just about the time we wrapped up our work, Dallas walked up to the register counter to join me. He glanced down at the floor and leaned down to pick something up. "Hey, what's this?"

He came back up with the leather wallet. The one that belonged to Meredith.

I took it from his outstretched hand, and those same familiar feelings swept over me again. The softness of the leather. The color. I felt swept back in time and wanted to look inside...for a piece of clove gum.

And in that moment, I knew. I knew this wasn't Meredith's father's wallet. It was Papaw's. I gave the wallet a sniff and in that moment was transported back to an afternoon with Papaw, one where he'd taken me to the hardware store with him. He'd pulled a piece of gum out of this wallet. It was soft and smelled of leather, but I chewed it anyway.

"What?" Dallas gave me a curious look. "You look like you've seen a ghost."

"I. . .I have." I called out for my parents to join us, then held the wallet up.

My dad gasped. "Where did you find that? I looked everywhere for it after your Papaw died."

"You're not going to believe me. I got it from Meredith Reed. She brought a bunch of stuff for me to sell. This was in the bottom of the box. She said the things in the box were from her parents, that they were heirlooms, but this clearly is not."

"But how did Meredith Reed get your papaw's—" Mom's eyes widened. "Oh my!"

Dad opened the wallet and came out with one thing—a lone stick of clove gum, tattered and worn, but still carrying a hint of that scent I knew so well.

And in that moment, I lost it. I cried tears of grief. Tears of joy. Tears of confusion. Bittersweet tears from a girl who wanted nothing more than to spend five minutes more with the grandfather who had meant the world to her.

Someone had to be the practical one, so Logan stepped up. He grabbed his phone and called the Henderson County Sheriff's office. Fifteen minutes later, Officer Warren joined us in the antique store.

He recognized me right away and entered with a bright smile and a warm Texas "Howdy, y'all."

Then we were all business. I showed him the items that Meredith had brought by earlier in the day, and we laid them out on the counter side by side.

"These don't exactly look like family heirlooms," he said.

"Hang on a second." I quickly got online and looked her up on Facebook, where I found a fairly recent photo of her. . .with her parents. Unless they had passed away in the last five months, she'd lied to me about that too.

"What are you thinking?" Mom asked.

Warren looked up from the items and reached for his phone. "I'm thinking we need to give Harlan Reed a call and ask him if he's missing anything from the auction house."

And that's what he did. Officer Warren placed the call, and Harlan answered right away. Twenty minutes later, he was standing in our store, gawking over the vast array of items and carrying on about what a thief Meredith was.

"She must've taken them a few at a time, when she knew she was leaving me," he said.

"You didn't notice?" Warren asked.

He shook his head. "Well, not at first. We've got a really large inventory of items that we've acquired through the years. But Ben noticed and started telling me a few months back. We thought these things had just been misplaced. I can't believe Meredith would. . ." His words drifted off. "That woman's a hot mess."

Before we could respond, Bessie Mae came barreling into the shop. "What is wrong with you people?" she said. "I cooked up a feast, and you folks can't even come inside to eat? What's so important that you—" Her gaze shifted to the officer. And to Harlan.

We brought her into the loop, explaining what had happened. And the moment she held that wallet in her hands, she began to weep too.

"You should warn a person!" she said. "I'm not sure my heart can take this."

I wasn't sure mine could either.

Then she turned to tell Harlan and Officer Warren that we had a new baby in the family, one that had been named after her.

A flurry of activity happened after that. Officer Warren left us his card before heading off, and Harlan gathered up the items on the counter to take back to the auction house with him. I hated to lose them from our inventory, but I couldn't keep the man's property.

Our family met in the kitchen and settled around the table just as Carrie and Jake walked through the door with Annalisa Mae. Then the tears started all over again. I was an emotional mess today, but who could blame me? My family meant the world to me—from generations long gone to those just arriving.

We took turns holding the baby, and as I gazed into her precious face, as I kissed those adorable pink cheeks, I was overcome with joy. And excitement. And anticipation. I couldn't help but wonder if this was what Papaw felt like, the first time he held me, the only baby girl in the Hadley family at that time. Did his heart swell with pride, as mine did now? Did he gaze with tenderness into my eyes—hoping, praying I would grow into a woman he would be proud of?

I was that woman now. And I would go on doing everything I could to make him proud, especially when it came to Tilly.

Tilly!

I passed the baby back to her mother and called Officer Warren, using the number on his card. He answered on the third ring.

"When you get to Meredith's place, look for Tilly!" I said, my words breathless.

"We're here now, but there's no truck. If she's stolen it, it's somewhere else."

My heart sank as he shared this news. All of this. . .and no Tilly?

CHAPTER TWENTY-EIGHT

On Saturday morning, I awoke with so much anticipation I could hardly contain it. Bessie Mae was up with the chickens, fixing a hearty breakfast for us all. The shop was set to open at nine, and many of our friends and neighbors had agreed to come. We needed to be ready to greet them.

I wrapped up breakfast by seven forty-five, dressed in my favorite blouse and jeans, and put on comfortable shoes. Then, with Riley at my side, I made my way out to the shop, ready for the adventure of a lifetime.

I stopped short of the gravel parking lot, as the realization hit me that Tilly wasn't here.

In my imagination, she would be situated in the parking lot, near the front door, a beacon of Hadley joy, welcoming all guests to step back in time. Her bright red paint would be shiny and clean, offering a trip back in time to 1952, the same year Papaw had acquired her. She would surely put folks in the mood to shop.

Only, she wasn't here. Not yet anyway.

A lump rose in my throat, but just as quickly I pushed it back. Tilly might not be here, but I was. And today, I carried something extra special with me.

I patted my back pocket to make sure Papaw's wallet was still there.

I didn't believe in good luck charms, but I did believe in legacy, so having his wallet with me seemed the appropriate thing for a day like today. And there was a zero percent chance I would ever remove that tattered piece of gum. It would live in his wallet. . .forever.

I walked in and turned on the lights, then tried to see the shop through our guests' eyes. What would they think when they poured through that door? Would this store seem real to them, or just an old barn with a few shelves and knickknacks?

I got my answer a little over an hour later when Dot arrived at eight fifteen to pick up my completed application for the chamber of commerce.

"Oh, RaeLyn!" Her purse strap slid off her shoulder as she turned to give the shop a close look. "I just can't believe it. It's perfect!"

"You think?"

"I know. And I heard that you called up a lot of the chamber members, asking for their help, so you can expect most of them to show up with bells on. Several are bringing you consignment items. I've heard from many of them myself."

"Speaking of people bringing me things. . ." I quickly shared the story of what had happened last night with Meredith.

Dot put her hands up. "Oh, honey, I know. You don't have to tell me a thing. Meredith was arrested last night."

I gasped. "She was?"

"Yep. Thanks to you. She admitted that she'd stolen all of that stuff from Harlan."

"And the wallet?"

"What wallet?" Dot looked perplexed.

I pulled Papaw's wallet from my back pocket and showed it to her. "My grandfather's wallet. She had it on her, with the rest of the stuff. She accidentally dropped it before leaving, or I wouldn't have figured any of this out."

"Oh my. Well, I heard that she admitted to breaking into the glove box of his truck, so that makes sense."

"But Officer Warren said she claims she didn't steal Tilly, so we still don't know where she is."

"Dot gave me a compassionate look. "She'll turn up, honey. I know it. If Meredith has her, she'll eventually break and let them know. You just keep your eye on the prize. Today is all about Trinkets and Treasures."

True.

I did my best not to get too depressed as I thought about Tilly. I was just so glad to hear that Meredith had been arrested, though the whole thing seemed so strange.

My parents walked in and Dad took several rushed steps my way, all business. "Now listen, RaeLyn, don't you go letting folks take advantage of you."

"What do you mean, Dad?"

"People love to haggle. You stick firm to your prices, you hear? The minute you start haggling, everyone in town will hear about it and think this is a flea market, not a store. You don't budge an inch. That's our policy. . .firm prices."

"Says the man who went crazy trying to outbid Wyatt Jackson on the truck at auction," Mom chimed in and then rolled her eyes.

She and Dot headed to the front door to hang a chamber of commerce poster and to turn the sign to OPEN.

Should I remind them that it was only eight thirty-five?

Logan arrived next with Meghan at his side. I couldn't believe she was here to work, but she made that announcement as soon as she came through the door.

"Whatever you need, RaeLyn," she said. "I'm off today and want to help out."

I made an executive decision that she should work alongside Mom and Dot, welcoming customers and guiding them around the store. My mother looked none too pleased by this announcement, but surely by day's end she would be speaking to The One We Don't Speak Of.

At five minutes till nine, the first customer pulled into the parking lot. Mason.

He ambled from his Lariat and headed my way, all smiles.

I met him at the front door with a bright, "Welcome to Trinkets and Treasures. C'mon in!"

Next thing you know, Dot was showing him around the place. As if he hadn't seen it all before. But he was a good sport. I managed to get him to the side to tell him all that had transpired with Meredith, but we got cut off halfway into that story because a majority of our church's congregation showed up en masse. They were followed by several business owners, including the manager of Brookshire Brothers, who was duly impressed with the place.

By nine thirty-five the store was filled to the brim with people who were in serious shopping mode. Turned out they all loved antiques. I took my spot at the register, completely overwhelmed. I should have come up with a better plan for ringing up and bagging their items but did the best I could. By ten the line was down the aisle, and my slow but steady process wasn't enough to keep this train rolling down the track.

"Here, let me help." Logan stepped into the spot at the register and started ringing them up. I thanked him and turned my attention to wrapping the breakables in paper and then bagging them.

A couple of minutes into this, Mason joined us behind the counter. Without even asking my opinion, he started wrapping alongside me. We worked together like a team, all of us doing our part. Off in the distance, I saw Mom, Dot, and Meghan visiting with Gloria Pappas. Man, my imagination really kicked into overdrive at that point.

Before long, Meghan and Gloria were hugging, and Gloria was in line with a handful of items to purchase. Hopefully Mom would bring me up to speed later.

The morning moved on like clockwork. I was tickled to see my editor arrive from the *Mabank Happenings*. She peppered me with questions—for an article she was writing about the store, apparently. Go figure. She even snapped a photo of me behind the counter, next to Mason.

Around noon Nadine Henderson came in. I had the strangest feeling the woman had been crying, based on her red, puffy eyes. But she smiled and made a few purchases, then promised to return later in the week with items for consignment.

"I really do wish you the best," she said as she reached to pat my hand. "You folks are good people."

After she'd gone, Mason leaned over and whispered, "You heard what happened, right?"

I gave him a curious look. "Which part?"

"Clayton bailed Meredith out of jail last night."

"W–what?" No way.

"Yeah, we got cut off earlier, so I didn't get to tell you. Late last night he went up to the jail and bailed her out. Paid the money himself to do so."

"Whoa." I paused to think this through. "How do you know all of this?"

He gestured with his head to Dot. "Oh, trust me. I know things. And I don't blame his wife for being upset."

"Me either." I'd be upset too, especially after what I'd witnessed in the parking lot at the hospital the other night. Should I tell Mason that part? No, there would be plenty of time for that later. Right now, I needed to stay focused.

As the day rolled on, I saw one familiar face after another. Many of the chamber members came through with items for consignment and promises that they would do everything they could to help me spread the word about our new business. I'd never been more grateful to live in such an amazing community.

As the crowd thinned in the afternoon, I finally allowed myself to think about Tilly. I remembered that day at the library when Bessie Mae and Dot and I had talked about what great sleuths we would become. I hadn't done a very good job, had I? I definitely suspected Meredith but couldn't stop thinking about Clayton and Wyatt as well. A true sleuth would've figured this out by now.

A shiver ran down my spine as I thought about Clayton bailing Meredith out. After what I'd seen last night, I had zero respect for the man.

Still, that didn't make him a car thief, so I shifted my thoughts to Wyatt. Was he still in the hospital? I'd have to ask Bessie Mae later on.

Only, I didn't have to. Tasha arrived just before closing time with Rena Jackson at her side. Dallas met them at the door and lifted a large box from Tasha's hands then placed it on the counter in front of me.

"What's this?" I looked back and forth between them.

"Ms. Rena has some things to put on consignment," Tasha said. "Isn't that nice?"

"It is. Very."

"Sorry I wasn't here for your big day," Tasha said. "I had to work all day at the restaurant or I would have come to help." Her gaze shifted to Meghan and Logan, who were standing nearby, talking. Then she looked back at me. "Then Ms. Rena called and asked if I would give her a ride over, so here we are."

"I'm here to sell some things," Rena said. "Like you asked me the other day when you stopped by." She rested her hand on mine. "And can I just say how nice it was to have folks come for a visit? I can't tell you how long it's been since we had people over. Used to happen all the time, but these past several years. . ." Her words drifted off and she shook her head.

"I'm so happy we did," I responded. "And I'm glad you've brought items in as well. Your timing is perfect!" I went on to explain that people had purchased so much of our inventory that I was thrilled to have more coming in.

I opened the box and gasped when I glanced down inside and saw several items, including hand-tatted lace and embroidered desk scarves.

"Oh, these are amazing!" I held one of the desk scarves up and eyed it closely. "The stitching is beautiful."

"Thank you." Her lips curled up in a smile. "It used to be a hobby of mine, back in the day. But my eyesight isn't what it used to be and. . ." She paused. "Oh dear. What were we talking about, again?"

"About how lovely your embroidery skills are, Ms. Rena," Tasha said.

"Thank you." She smiled all over again.

I pulled several more items out, finally noticing what had been hiding at the bottom of the box. No wonder it was so heavy. Beneath all the softer items, I found a beautiful chessboard, made of marble, along with a velvet pouch holding the pieces.

"Oh, Ms. Rena, are you sure about this?"

"Well, I don't play, that's for certain. I can't rightly remember ever playing, to be honest, so I don't know why we even had the silly thing. It's just been sitting around all of these years, gathering dust."

"But it's an expensive board, made of marble. And the pieces are marble too." I pulled out a couple of the pieces and gave them a closer look.

Bessie Mae took several steps in my direction, her eyes wide. "You're sure Wyatt is okay with you selling this, Rena? This set was his father's, passed down to him after his parents died. One of the few things that survived the fire."

She chewed on her lip and looked confused. "Well, I don't rightly know. I just know that I'm ready to be done with it. How much will you give me? We need grocery money as soon as possible."

Whoa.

"Well, we normally work on consignment," I explained. "You leave the items with me, and when they sell we split the proceeds."

"That won't put food in my stomach." Her hand trembled as she reached into the box and came out with a beautiful figurine. "How much for this one, then?"

We already had several Precious Moments figurines on our shelves, but if the woman needed food in her pantry, how could I say no?

She also had a few other trinkets of interest, including a beautiful beaded purse that probably dated back to the 1920s, and a hat that dated back to the '40s, which I knew I could sell, no problem.

In the end, I offered her three hundred dollars for everything in the box, cash up front. No consignment agreement. My parents would flip, but we had the money in the cash register, and right now all that seemed important was making sure Rena had what she needed for groceries. I did so with the knowledge that the chess set would be returned to Wyatt ASAP.

Tasha looped her arm through Rena's, and they headed out together. Dallas offered to go along for the ride, and before long it was just our family left to clean up the shop and shut down for the night.

Mason carried the chess set back to the house. We put it in my room so I wouldn't forget to return it. Mom invited Mason to stay for dinner, and he happily obliged. I had a feeling he'd be staying a lot more. Meghan too.

When we gathered around the table for dinner a short while later, Bessie Mae shared her thoughts with the rest of us.

"I'm telling you all right now, when Wyatt hears what she's done with his marble chess set, he's going to hit the warpath, and we'll all be in the line of fire."

"Oh, I'm definitely taking it back to him," I said. "I made up my mind to do that right away. I just didn't think I could make her understand. You know?"

"I know." Bessie Mae sighed. "Such a shame, how she's losing her memory."

"That chessboard doesn't really have a lot of market value anyway, right?" I said. "And I don't know anyone else who's looking for a set like that."

"Right. But what about the money you gave her for it?" Dad asked.

I didn't care about that, especially with the knowledge of their current financial woes. "They can use it for groceries. I don't care about that. If they're really in bad enough shape that she has to sell off items to feed the two of them, we need to let the church know. We have a food pantry, right?"

"We do." Mom nodded. "I can set something up right away."

"Well, if I know Wyatt, he won't accept charity."

"But he will take his chess set back. And I'm going to be the one to take it to him."

I rose and carried my plate to the sink, deep in thought.

And that's when it hit me.

The marble king. The one we'd found in Carrie and Jake's attic.

It was a perfect match for this set.

CHAPTER TWENTY-NINE

"Bessie Mae!" I let out a cry, nearly dropping the glass plate into the sink. "What did you do with that king we found in the attic?"

"You found a king in an attic?" My dad looked amused by this idea. "Sounds like a news headline."

"We found a marble chess piece—a king—in Jake and Carrie's attic the other day. We didn't know where it came from or where the rest of the set was. But now. . ."

I made room on the kitchen table and then went to my room and grabbed the box with the chess set in it. Then I quickly scrambled to put the pieces on the board in their proper places. Sure enough, one king was missing.

I shot a glance in Bessie Mae's direction. "What did you do with him?"

"I put him in my top dresser drawer. Let me go fetch him."

Moments later she returned with the king in hand, which she passed to me.

I put the king in place, and we all stared in silence at the board.

"Checkmate," I said, then lifted the king to read the word scribbled underneath. "But. . .why? And what does it mean?"

"I have no idea," Bessie Mae said.

"I do." These words came from Mason. "You said that Wyatt and your grandfather were jealous of one another?"

"That's the short way of saying it," Bessie Mae replied.

"Your grandfather got the truck. Wyatt got the girl. And he also got chess set that had been his parents'. But someone stole the king so the board wouldn't be complete. Maybe it was a statement on your grandfather's part, a real-life checkmate."

"Are you saying my grandfather was a thief?" I asked.

Mason shrugged. "I never knew the man. But I'm guessing that's one reason Wyatt was so interested in buying that truck, so he could have the final say in the matter."

"Well, anyway…the chessboard is now complete." Bessie Mae beamed. "That's nice, isn't it?"

"I'm still giving it back," I said. "And I'd feel better if I did so right away, so he doesn't come storming onto our property looking for it. He might even call the police on us if he thinks we have it."

"Are you saying you want to go tonight?" Dad asked. "I'm not sure that's a good idea, RaeLyn."

"Better under the cover of darkness," I argued. "Don't you think?"

"How, though?" Mom asked. "We can't just leave it on their front porch. Rena will see it and will probably try to sell it to us all over again."

"We could take it to his shed out back," Bessie Mae said. "We can set it inside, along with a note, and Rena Sue won't be any the wiser."

"And I'll leave the groceries tonight too," Mom said. "I've got plenty on hand in our pantry and Deepfreeze. And that way if we're caught in the act we'll have an excuse."

I shook my head. "We all know that Wyatt won't accept them. I say leave the chess set at the shop with Wyatt and the groceries at the front door of the house with Rena. Her memory is so far gone she might just think that she bought them herself and forgot to bring them in."

"True." Mom sighed. "Why is this all so complicated?"

"I don't know, but I can't bear the idea that Rena is going without." Bessie Mae dabbed at her eyes. "Maybe I should take her a pie or one of my cobblers. She loves my cobblers."

"We can do that next time, Bessie Mae," Mom said. "Bringing back the chess set and then loading them up with groceries is probably enough for one day, don't you think?"

I felt sure she was right.

At this point, we all flew into action. Mom went shopping in our own pantry—a room filled with enough food to keep our family going for weeks on end. She filled bag after bag with all sorts of things and even pulled several packages of beef and venison from our Deepfreeze.

"This should tide them over for a while," she said.

I offered to drive her car, and she and Bessie Mae and I headed down the road to the Jacksons' place. Dad and Mason followed behind in Mason's Lariat, in case they were needed.

I parked half a block away, and we carried the bags of groceries to the front porch and left them. Then I went back to the car and got the box with the chess set inside. I'd written a quick note to Wyatt, explaining as best I could how we had come to acquire the set. I'd also placed the missing king back inside with the rest of the pieces.

My mom and Bessie waited in the car, with Mom now in the driver's seat, in case we needed a quick getaway. I carried the box past the house to the shed behind it with Riley at my side, just in case I needed protection. I knew this shed well, since Mason and I had snuck around back here all those years ago, picking dewberries.

I reached the door of the shed just as the sun dipped below the horizon, casting long shadows across the yard. My breath caught in my throat when Wyatt emerged from the shadows, moving from the house toward the shed. My heart quickened, and I discreetly moved to the side of the shed, careful to stay in the cover of darkness and willing Riley not to bark.

She might not be a very good cattle dog, but Riley was turning out to be the best sleuth in our group. She sniffed like mad at the ground beneath us and tugged at the leash.

"Easy, girl," I whispered.

As Wyatt approached the entrance of the shed, he fumbled with a set of keys. They had a distinct jingle—a sound that was all too familiar. In that moment, I was struck with a memory of Papaw opening the passenger door for me with a set of keys that jingled just like that.

The realization hit me like a bolt of lightning. Did this shed house more than Wyatt's woodworking supplies?

I tiptoed to the door of the shed as he stepped inside. The dim light inside revealed a variety of yard tools and other items, and rows of shelves holding all sorts of old coffee cans and other canisters. Curiosity and determination fueled my steps. I peeked through the slightly ajar door and immediately saw the silhouette of a vehicle.

I couldn't tell for sure without the light and certainly didn't want to be discovered by Wyatt.

Riley let out a low growl in the back of her throat, and I quickly retreated, my mind racing. How should I handle this? I took a moment to strategize.

First things first. I set the box down. Second, I ran toward Mason's Lariat and asked him to call the sheriff's office, after telling him that Wyatt was inside with a vehicle I couldn't quite make out.

"Don't go back up there until the police arrive, RaeLyn," Mason said.

Only, I couldn't help myself. I had to go back. And I arrived just in time to see Wyatt come out of the shed and stumble over the box I'd left at the door. He reached down and opened it, muttering something under his breath as he noticed the chess set.

"What in the world?"

"It's your chess set, Mr. Jackson," I called out, doing my best to keep my voice steady. Then I stepped a little closer.

"Who is that? Come where I can see you." He turned on the flashlight on his phone and pointed it at my face, his eyes widening as he saw me. "You?"

"Yes, me. RaeLyn Hadley."

"And Mason Fredericks." Mason's strong voice sounded from beside me.

"And Chuck Hadley." My dad's voice sounded out too, not quite as strong.

"I know all of you Hadleys, every last one of you. What are you doing here? I don't need no Hadleys on my property."

"We brought back something that belongs to you." I pointed at the box he'd just tripped over.

"At this time of night?" He reached to flip a switch, and a porch light came on in front of the shed. Then he turned off the flashlight on his phone and shoved it into his pocket, hands trembling.

"Yes, sir. I thought you'd want it. Your wife brought it over to our antique shop earlier to sell on consignment, and after seeing it, I figured it must've been a mistake."

"We decided you might not want to let it go," Mason chimed in.

"What is it?" He crouched down and opened the box, his eyes widening as he took it in. "My marble chess set? What was she thinking? I would never sell this."

"I figured as much, which is why I brought it back. Ms. Rena was hoping I'd pay top dollar for it, but we're not set up for that, at least not yet."

He fished around in the box, muttering all the while, and paused when he came up with one king. . .and then another. He looked back and forth between the two, clearly perplexed.

"Look at the bottom," I said.

He turned both over, and I watched as Wyatt's face turned ashen.

"Checkmate?" He looked my way, as if to ask what it meant.

But I think he already knew. His brother got the last word.

Only this game wasn't quite over yet, was it? And we both knew it. I still didn't have Tilly in my possession, after all.

"Where did you get the missing king?" he asked. "I've been looking everywhere. For years."

"We found it in the attic of the little house," I said. "The one you lived in when you came to stay with Papaw's family after the fire."

Wyatt's gaze shifted to the ground. "I haven't seen this king since 1952 when it went missing. The last time I saw it was in the glove box of your Charles' new truck. So, I thought. . ."

"Thought it would still be there after all these years?"

He brushed the toe of his boot against the gravel driveway. "It was mine. Belonged to me. And he took it the day I lost that tournament, just to make a point. He was the king. I was. . ." Wyatt's words trailed off. "Nothing. Nobody."

"So, you thought you'd take what should have been yours all along?" I asked. Only, I wasn't talking about the king anymore. "Where's Tilly, Wyatt?"

"I don't know what you're talking about."

"Charles' truck. Where is she, Wyatt?" These words came from Bessie

Mae, who now stood just behind me next to Mom. "RaeLyn won that bid fair and square."

"And paid six thousand dollars for her to boot," I added. "She belongs to us."

His expression tightened. "Everything belongs to you Hadleys, doesn't it? You always get to have your cake and eat it too."

What that had to do with anything, I couldn't be sure. But in that moment, I felt like I understood Wyatt Jackson. He sounded like me, talking about Clayton Henderson. Or Stephanie Ingram. Only, he'd allowed his years of bitterness to build up to a breaking point.

"Where is she, Wyatt?" Bessie Mae asked again.

"Even if I knew, I wouldn't tell you," he countered.

Only, of course I did know. The vehicle in his shed was my baby.

A squeal of tires sounded at the end of the drive, and I turned to discover the Henderson County officer had arrived. Wyatt spun around and grabbed hold of the shed's door handle.

"You know what the Duke always says, Wyatt," Bessie Mae interjected.

He turned back around to face her, and I could read the curiosity in his eyes.

"'Men should be tough, fair, and courageous, never petty, never looking for a fight, but never backing down from one either.' That was you and Charles. But these are different times now, and we need to move on."

His expression shifted from anger to something I could only describe as remorse. By the time Officer Warren emerged from the patrol car, Wyatt was already opening the door to his dilapidated old shed.

And when he flipped the switch to flood the room with light, there sat Tilly. . .in all her rusty glory.

CHAPTER THIRTY

"Did you hear about Clayton and Nadine Henderson?" Mom asked as we gathered around the breakfast table the following morning.

"Saddest thing," Bessie Mae chimed in. "We never saw it coming."

"What?" My dad and I both responded in unison, stopping our forks midlift to get an answer.

"Well, it's not confirmed," Mom said, "but I had a call from Dot this morning, who heard from Gloria who heard from Melody, who just got out of the hospital last night."

"So, in other words, the prayer chain has been activated." Dad shoved a bite of the bacon into his mouth.

"It's cause for concern and prayer." Mom dabbed at her lips with her napkin. "Apparently, Nadine has made an impromptu decision to leave on an extended cruise in the Mediterranean with her sister."

Dad gave her a curious look. "And that's problematic because. . ."

"She's calling it a sabbatical from Clayton," Mom explained. "From what I gather, all is not well in paradise."

I swallowed down the bite of grits, relishing the sweet buttery goodness with hints of sugar and cinnamon. Should I tell them what I'd seen the other night outside of the hospital, or just let it go?

I'd let it go. I sure didn't need to get involved in anyone's marital disputes.

"Maybe building out the B and B was too much for them?" Dallas suggested. "It's hard to work on a project and keep your relationship afloat. You know?"

"Maybe." Mom released a sigh.

"There's more to it than that." Bessie Mae rose and walked over to the stove, where she dished up more grits into the serving bowl. "Nadine has been hiding a lot of pain all these years but does her best not to let it show."

"I don't think she likes how Clayton always puts her—and all of their belongings—on display," Mom added. "There's a perceived level of perfection that's not easy to keep up with."

"You're saying he treats her more like a possession than a wife?" Dad asked. "Is that it?"

"Partly." Mom shrugged. "I think she's weary with always having to be perfect."

"It does get old," my dad said with a wink. "But I've managed to do it all these years."

Mom slugged him with the back of her hand. "I'm being serious, Chuck. She's not happy."

"And if a wife ain't happy, ain't nobody happy." Dad laughed. Well, until Mom glared at him. Then he settled down and shoveled a big mound of grits into his mouth. "These grits are just delicious, Bessie Mae."

"I use real butter," she explained. "Makes all the difference, don't you think?"

And just like that, the Hadley family was back to normal. Well, as normal as we got anyway.

My brothers started arguing over something silly, and my parents carried on about marriage while Bessie Mae served up more sweet cinnamon grits.

Still, I couldn't stop thinking about Nadine Henderson. Was she really unhappy because she'd married a man who expected perfection? That would be a hard act, for sure.

The phone rang, and my dad took the call. It didn't take long to figure out he was talking to the police about Wyatt. Whatever the officer was saying on the other end of the line, Dad was agreeing with.

And when the call ended, he explained that Wyatt's arrest had been seamless, but there were now things that we, the Hadleys, needed to consider. Would we press charges or let this go? He went on to explain that Wyatt was in poor health and that his wife seemed lost without him.

It didn't take long to come up with our answer. Tilly was coming home, and that was really all that mattered to us.

The next hour was spent dressing for church and then making the drive. When we arrived, I found the place buzzing with activity, even more so than usual. Bible study went by at a rapid-fire pace, and before long we were all in the sanctuary, prepping for morning service.

Tasha came rushing my way, her eyes wide.

"I just heard from Dot that they let Wyatt go."

"We decided to drop the charges," I explained. "Because of his age, the prosecutor agreed that he should just pay a fine and be done with it."

"And that's okay with you?"

"It is." I shrugged. "The man is almost ninety years old. He's got major health issues, and his wife is in the beginning stages of Alzheimer's. I think it's time we put the past in the past."

"You're a better person than I am."

"No, I'm really not."

A stir at the back of the sanctuary interrupted our conversation, and I turned to see an elderly woman entering on her walker. Rena Jackson. Shuffling in behind her. . .Wyatt Jackson. The man himself.

I did my best not to gasp aloud. The sea of people parted in the center aisle as Rena and Wyatt made their way to her favorite pew together. Then, as he slid into the spot, he dropped his gaze to the hymnals. Moments later, he attempted to pick it up with trembling hand, but it slipped and hit the floor at his feet.

Before I could do or say anything, my brother Dallas was at his side, picking up the hymnal and handing it to him with a smile.

"For pity's sake, will you look at that." Bessie Mae sidled up next to me. "Thought I'd never live to see the day, but there he is, in the flesh."

"Fresh out of jail," Mom said.

Bessie Mae quirked a brow. "Well, you know what the Duke would say, right?"

I paused and attempted to think through his famous quotes, hoping I could guess it before she spoke it aloud. But Bessie Mae was too quick for me.

"Tomorrow is the most important thing. Comes in us at midnight very clean."

"It's perfect when it arrives, and it puts itself in our hands," I interjected.

"It hopes we've learned something from yesterday," she said, completing the line. Then she nodded her head in Wyatt's direction. "I say the least we can do is trust that the Duke got it right on that account. We need to learn from the past and appreciate each new day. Agreed?"

"Agreed." I gave her a hug. "And in case I haven't said it in a while, Aunt Bessie, you're a real peach."

"Oooh, peaches! It's almost peach season. I can't wait. I saw the most tempting recipe online for some peach crisp. Doesn't that sound delectable?"

It did indeed.

Dallas stepped into the spot next to me in the pew. "Everyone looks so serious."

Tasha rose and scooted over to give him space between us.

Which, I supposed, had been his intention all along, judging from the smile on his face as she lifted her purse and moved it to the other side.

My brother's face lit with a smile. "Hey, Tasha, I have some information you might be interested in."

She looked up from her phone. "What's that?"

"I was talking to a Realtor friend, and he told me there's a piece of property on the lake on the Payne Springs side. My friend's grandmother lived there, but she passed away."

"Oh?" Tasha looked intrigued. She pressed her phone into her purse.

"Yeah, nobody in the family is really interested in it, so they're about to list it. He said they're selling it for pennies on the dollar because they really just need enough to pay the back taxes on it. There's a house on it—pretty run-down, but it's got good bones."

"Really?" Her eyes lit up.

"Yeah. I mean, it would take some work to get it up and running, but you've been talking about having your own B and B for as long as I can remember. Maybe this is God's answer for you."

I wanted to throw my arms around my brother's neck and give him a big hug. But he was so focused on Tasha that he probably wouldn't have noticed.

"Want to take a ride over there after church?" he asked. "Daniel said he left the key under the mat."

"Do I ever!" She gave him an admiring smile. "Thank you so much, Dallas."

"You're welcome." He offered a quick nod then headed up to the stage to grab his guitar.

Bessie Mae turned to Tasha with a smile. "Well now."

"Such great news, about the property on the lake," Tasha said. "Can you believe it?"

"The Lord moves in mysterious ways," I said.

"Indeed. Here's what I think, honey." Bessie Mae gave her a thoughtful look. "Right address, wrong fella."

"What?" Creases formed between Tasha's brows.

"Right address, wrong fella."

"Are you talking about the address of the property on the lake?"

"Nope." Bessie Mae laughed. "I'm talking about our address, the Hadley ranch. You've been coming around with that lovesick look on your face for months now. You've had the right address all along, just the wrong fella."

Bessie Mae gestured with her head to Dallas.

Ooooh. *That's* what she meant.

My best friend's eyes widened. I was pretty sure mine did too. Was Dallas smitten with Tasha. . .who was smitten with Logan. . .who was smitten with Wife Number Three, the one we were finally able to speak of?

From the looks of things, yes. And judging from the crooked grin on Bessie Mae's face, she'd been in on it all along. She chuckled, her laughter echoing the wisdom of her years.

Bessie Mae fussed with her purse and adjusted her position in the pew. "You know, kiddos, life's a lot like a John Wayne movie."

"How so?" Tasha asked, her eyes still riveted on my younger brother, who slung his guitar strap across his shoulder.

"It's full of twists, turns, and the occasional shoot-out. But in the end, the good guys always come out on top." Bessie nodded in Dallas' direction, and he looked up from his guitar to offer Tasha and I a warm smile.

"My brother Charles once fancied himself to be in love with Rena Jackson," Bessie added. "But instead, he married the right gal, and between them they produced this beautiful family you see right here. So, don't pooh-pooh the idea just yet." Bessie Mae began to hum a little tune and turned her attention to Corina and Wyatt, who were now talking to the pastor.

"Is she kidding?" Tasha looked back and forth between Logan and Dallas.

Not that one could look at Logan for long without seeing the love in his eyes for Meghan, who hung on his every word. And I was pretty sure that feeling was mutual, based on the way he gazed at her and reached for her hand as the music began.

Tasha was going to have to get over any infatuation with my older brother, and quick.

Perhaps Bessie Mae was right. Maybe Tasha did have the right address. And, if Dallas played his cards right, she might just end up with the right fella too.

I glanced up as someone approached the end of the pew.

Mason.

"Just heard from my tow truck driver that he got Tilly, safe and sound. He's headed to your place now to drop her off."

"Thank you." I reached over to give his hand a squeeze. "I don't know what I'd do without you."

"Hopefully you won't ever have to." He gave me a look so sweet, so tender, that it made my heart race. "If you have any plans after church, please cancel them. I've got something up my sleeve."

"Oh?"

"Yep. Those bluebonnets held on long enough for Tilly to get back home where she belongs. That's why I had her towed to your place and not the shop, so you can take pictures of her in the flowers."

"You remembered."

"Oh, I remember everything, RaeLyn Hadley, like that time we picked dewberries behind the Jackson shed and you tried to steal a kiss from me."

"I did no such thing." I slugged him on the arm, and he laughed.

He took the spot next to me without asking, as if he'd belonged there all along.

Which, I supposed, he had. And even now, as I contemplated the years that lay between us and all those times I'd forced my heart to push feelings for him aside, I could really only conclude one simple fact:

It was all water under the bridge now.

Bessie Mae's Dewberry Cobbler

INGREDIENTS

For Berry Mixture:

- 1 pound dewberries (fresh or frozen)
- ¾ cup sugar
- 1 tablespoon water
- 2 tablespoons lemon juice
- 1 teaspoon lemon zest (optional)
- 3 tablespoons cornstarch
- ¼ cup water (more or less)

For Crust:

- 1 cup flour
- pinch salt
- ½ cup Crisco
- cold water
- egg (for wash)
- sugar (to sprinkle)

How to Make Bessie Mae's Dewberry Cobbler

To Make Berry Mixture:

Put berries into medium-sized saucepan. Add sugar. (The recipe calls for ¾ cup, but if you want to go sweeter, you can add a full cup of sugar.) Add 1 tablespoon water and turn on medium-low heat. Bring berries to a boil. Add lemon juice and lemon zest. Stir. Combine cornstarch and ¼ cup water in small bowl and stir until cornstarch is dissolved. Add cornstarch slurry to berry mixture. Simmer over medium-low heat until berries thicken. If it's too thick, just add a little bit of water to thin it out. Remove from heat.

To Make Crust:

Put flour and salt in medium bowl. Grate (or cut) Crisco into flour. (Note: Some people add a stick of salted butter in place of Crisco. It's your preference. If you only have unsalted butter on hand, you can certainly use that, but don't skip the pinch of salt.) Add water. Combine with fork and then turn out onto prepared (floured) surface or piece of waxed paper. Work with your fingers until flour is fully incorporated. Roll into ball and then use rolling pin to roll out crust. You can apply the crust any way you like. Many traditional cobblers have strips of dough staggered across the top. You could even form a lattice, as you might for a pie, if you like.

Time to Put Dewberry Cobbler Together:

Butter bottom of 8×8 baking dish. Pour in berry mixture. Place crust on top in any design you like. In small bowl, whip up egg with tiny bit of water. (You could use whole milk in place of water.) Use pastry brush to add tiny bit of egg mixture to crust. Sprinkle with sugar. Bake cobbler at 425 degrees for 25 to 30 minutes. (Mine took 27 minutes.) Time will vary depending on your oven. Make sure your pie crust is golden brown. The berry mixture will be bubbly and ready to go! Remove from oven and cool for about 10 minutes before serving. You can serve with the additional crust pieces or without (your preference). Some people love a scoop of vanilla ice cream with their cobbler. Whipped cream is another great option. Enjoy!

JANICE THOMPSON, who lives in the Houston area, writes novels, nonfiction, magazine articles, and musical comedies for the stage. The mother of four married daughters, she is quickly adding grandchildren to the family mix.